MURDER IN MANHATTAN

MURDER IN MANHATTAN

JULIE MULHERN

FOREVER

New York   Boston

Forever
Hachette Book Group
1290 Avenue of the Americas, New York, NY 10104
read-forever.com
@readforeverpub

First Edition: December 2025

Forever is an imprint of Grand Central Publishing. The Forever name and logo are registered trademarks of Hachette Book Group, Inc.

The publisher is not responsible for websites (or their content) that are not owned by the publisher.

Forever books may be purchased in bulk for business, educational, or promotional use. For information, please contact your local bookseller or the Hachette Book Group Special Markets Department at special.markets@hbgusa.com.

Print book interior design by Marie Mundaca

Library of Congress Cataloging-in-Publication Data

Names: Mulhern, Julie author
Title: Murder in Manhattan / Julie Mulhern.
Description: First edition. | New York : Forever, 2025.
Identifiers: LCCN 2025031025 | ISBN 9781538773567 trade paperback | ISBN 9781538773574 ebook
Subjects: LCGFT: Romance fiction | Novels | Fiction
Classification: LCC PS3613.U4353 M87 2025
LC record available at https://lccn.loc.gov/2025031025

ISBNs: 9781538773567 (trade paperback), 9781538773574 (ebook)

Printed in the United States of America

LSC-C

Printing 1, 2025

CHAPTER 1

Taken from A Touch of Rouge—June 6, 1925, issue of Gotham magazine

When I tell you the weather is hot, I'm hardly reporting news. Nor is it news when I say our fair city bears a striking resemblance to the place where my last young-man-about-town's dear mother said I would be going when I toddle off this mortal coil.

When my invitation to the North Shore for last weekend fell through, I had no choice but to embrace the rising mercury.

Embrace I did—the weight of overheated air, the cloying scent of wilting flowers pinned to pretty girls' shoulders, the sheen of sweat on orchestral brows, and butter-and-egg men thick on the ground. Imagine my surprise when Zelda and Scott Fitzgerald floated into the evening's boîte on a cloud of gin and Tabac Blond. Scott, who claimed a meeting with his publisher kept him in this sweat box masquerading as a city, suggested a change of venue and nothing would do but piling into a taxi and motoring to the Biltmore Cascades. Who was I to argue? What could be cooler than a rooftop garden? Besides, sometimes a girl needs caviar.

Roses and out-of-town visitors bloomed in profusion. Nestled in the bower, the latest favorite guest of every hostess on the Upper East Side charmed members of the fairer sex. One wonders how the much-in-demand Jake Haskell found time to dine alfresco.

Afterward, a visit to Tex Guinan's club of the moment. Tex, in her usual good humor, was unfazed by the showgirls who deemed the mercury too high for their costumes. The men, in particular, enjoyed the floor show. One man with the look of a dyspeptic county judge was so taken by a flamboyant redhead with obvious assets, he failed to notice his necktie marinating in his drink. As far as this correspondent knows, he may yet be there. Drooling still...

A Touch of Rouge

FREDDIE ARCHER ADJUSTED THE cool cloth draped across her forehead and eyes—not that the cloth was terribly cool. Nothing stayed cool in this heat. It was hardly morning—barely nine o'clock if the sounds outside her office were any indication—and already the day was stifling.

"Freddie? Are you decent?"

The gentle utterance of her name was accompanied by the sound of the door opening. Such were the dangers of sleeping on the divan in her office—someone was bound to disturb her. In this case, someone was her secretary, Annie.

"I am dying." Given the knitting needle lodged in her brain, the declaration wasn't remotely dramatic.

"Sorry to hear that." The unseasonable heat had curdled whatever milk of human kindness Annie had once possessed. The lack of genuine sympathy was positively galling.

Why hadn't she held out for a secretary with a nurturing soul?

"I brought you a bottle of aspirin and a glass of water."

Maybe Annie wasn't completely lacking in compassion.

Freddie lifted onto her elbows. That accomplished, she pushed herself to sitting and lifted the cloth hiding her eyes. The office was brighter than the gleam in a chorus girl's eyes when a rich man came calling. Why must the sun shine with such verve in the morning? She closed her eyelids, but the light burned a red halo in the darkness.

"Here." Annie pressed a glass into her left hand. "Two or three?"

"Four." Freddie held out her empty right palm.

Annie shook the tablets from the bottle, then her footsteps crossed to the window. The sound of blinds being closed was lovelier than a symphony. "You have messages."

"Do I?" Freddie tossed the pills into her mouth and washed them down with a swig of water.

"The writer of *A Touch of Rouge* has messages," Annie amended. "There's a reader who takes umbrage with your description of the Fox and Hound as a club best reserved for those chasing the dragon."

"There's an opium den in the back room."

"Also, the police are here to see you."

"The police?" Freddie opened her eyes and surveyed her now dim office. Her shoes were abandoned near the door. A single silk stocking was draped over the back of a chair facing her desk. The other stocking circled her ankle. Last night's frock was a pool of crumpled silk next to the divan. An open beaded clutch rested atop the dress. "Whatever they want, I didn't do it." She spoke with assurance she did not possess.

"Do what?"

"Anything. Drink in a speakeasy. Dance on top of a patrol car. Go for a late-night dip in the fountain outside the Plaza Hotel." She'd done that and more. Many times.

"He's a detective."

"A detective?"

"I thought you'd want to see him before Gus arrives."

Freddie rested her throbbing head against the back of the divan. While the stories of her antics earned her an enormous readership, the antics themselves shocked her boss to the bottom of his born-in-Iowa soul. Gus would frown upon a morning visit from the constabulary. "I suppose I'd better see him." She raked her fingers through her bobbed hair and kicked the stocking from her ankle. "How bad do I look?"

"Like something the cat spat up." Annie bent and picked up the stocking.

If Freddie bent like that, her brains would leak out of her ears.

"A detective, you say?" What could a detective want? Freddie scrubbed her face with the damp cloth. The white linen came away smudged with the remnants of last evening's mascara, rouge, and powder. Her lipstick had long since decamped—she'd wager it was on a young man's collar. "Do I have anything to wear?"

Annie opened the narrow wardrobe in the corner of the office, pulled out a deceptively simple crêpe de chine dress, and held its hanger aloft. "This?"

"Perfect." Freddie glanced down at her bare legs. "I don't think I can manage stockings." The mere thought of reaching for her toes made her stomach flip like a Ringling Brothers' trapeze act. But no stockings meant she wouldn't be able to leave the cover of her desk. So be it. "Do you have a comb?"

"Of course."

"A lipstick?"

"Of course."

"What's his name?" Freddie stood. Just stood. She could do no more—her stomach and head needed time to adjust to their new fully upright positions.

Annie chose not to answer her question. "Finish your water, and I'll get you some more."

Freddie drained the glass. "I need coffee."

"You need to write your column then go home for a long nap."

"The new column is written." She pointed at her desk, an oasis of calm in the disorderly room. Pad of paper. Pencils in a cup. Typewriter. A stack of letters from readers who either loved A Touch of Rouge for her breezy writing style or hated her for glamorizing nightclubs. And neatly stacked pages waiting for Annie to take them to an editor. "As for a nap, that sounds positively luxurious. Too bad there's a detective here."

"His name is Mike. Mike Sullivan." Was that a touch of pink on Annie's austere cheeks?

"Mike, you say?" Freddie ventured a step—a small one. Somewhat surprisingly, the floor did not open and swallow her whole. She took a second step. A third shuffle forward carried her to the mirror hanging on the back of the office door. There, she gasped. Even in the blessedly dim light, the woman in the mirror looked positively haggard. "I'll need some powder, too."

"What did you do last night?" Annie held out a comb.

"Nothing nearly as exciting as last week. I didn't encounter the Fitzgeralds. I didn't hop in a fountain. Nope. Last night was nothing special. Dinner at the Colony, a show in Harlem, dancing at Corona de Oro." Freddie ran the comb's teeth through her tangled hair. "It's all there in my new column."

Annie, who was a huge fan of Scott's short stories, harumphed. Freddie suspected Annie was also a secret fan of Scott and Zelda's escapades, not that she would ever admit it.

"Nick Peters was there. Apparently, he's in the city working on his new show." She tried—tried—to keep her tone casual as she tugged at a snarl.

Annie wasn't fooled. "You spoke to him?"

"We were very civilized." Had being civilized hurt him as much as it hurt her? "He was there with his leading lady." Why were all leading ladies impossibly beautiful? Last night's had been a honey blonde with rounded cheeks and bowed lips painted a brilliant cherry red. Freddie had hated her on sight. On good days, Freddie could best be described as pretty—such an anemic, little word. She didn't need a second glance in the mirror to know today was not a good day.

Annie reclaimed the comb and put the frock in Freddie's hands.

The dress whispered over her shoulders. She smoothed the fabric over her slip and patted a stray hair into place. "I believe I'll take you up on that second glass of water." She kept her voice light and airy, as if spotting Nick dancing with another woman hadn't left her breathless. And thirsty. For copious amounts of champagne.

She wasn't carrying a torch for him. She absolutely was not. But it was galling how quickly he'd moved on.

"Of course." Bless Annie for pretending not to see the cracks in the façade.

The price for all that champagne was this—a painful morning. "And coffee."

Annie collected the stocking hanging from the chair. "Of course."

"Are there any shoes in that wardrobe?" Last night's black satin pumps and today's crêpe de chine dress would be ridiculous together.

"No."

"I'll go barefoot."

Annie's brows rose.

"I'm not stepping out from behind my desk. Your Detective Sullivan will never know."

"He's not my detective." Annie's voice was a shade too sharp.

"Yet."

Annie flushed a deep pink.

"Give me a minute or two to fix the wreckage"—Freddie circled her hand in front of her face—"then bring him in."

Five minutes later, a ginger-haired man the size of a rhinoceros settled into the chair across from her.

The chair groaned.

Freddie forced a smile. "How may I help you, Detective?"

"I read your last column, Miss Archer." Detective Sullivan, with his size, open features, and maleness, did not resemble her usual reader.

"Oh?"

He held out last Saturday's magazine, carefully folded to her column. "You were at the Biltmore Cascades with the Fitzgeralds."

"Are they in trouble again?" What had they done now? Freddie rested her arms against the desk. "They mean well. They do!" Zelda had a tendency to get caught up in wild moments and forget she was an adult. And Scott egged her on. Either too drunk, too enamored, or too desperate for material for a short story to care that Zelda had flashed a wide-eyed beat cop walking Fifth Avenue.

"They're not in trouble."

Well, that was a relief. She leaned back and considered Detective Sullivan's bright blue eyes. "Who is?"

"Who is what?"

"In trouble. Someone must be, or you wouldn't be here."

"How do you know Jake Haskell?"

Jake Haskell. "Tall. Blond hair. Midwestern accent. Divot in his chin. And"—she tapped a finger on the center of her own divotless chin—"terrible taste in neckties."

"How do you know him?" Detective Sullivan fixed his gaze on her.

The intensity of that gaze made her feel like a butterfly pinned to a board. Freddie shifted in her chair. "I don't know him. Not really. I met him at a party."

"But you put him in your column?"

"Say what you will about New York, but with this heat, the city is most attractive to those who can leave. While I don't begrudge anyone a single breath of ocean-cooled breeze, half the city has gone missing. That means finding warm bodies for the column is a challenge." A bead of sweat formed between her breasts and trickled down her torso. Freddie ignored the tickle of perspiration and waved a languid hand at the closed blinds. "By the end of August, I expect I'll be writing about shoeshine boys."

"Who introduced you?"

So many questions. Freddie snuck past the ice pick lodged in her brain and searched her memories. The night blessedly cool. The stars impossibly bright. She'd danced on a veranda overlooking the ocean. "John. John Burcham introduced us."

Detective Sullivan pulled a small notepad from his jacket and made a note. "Who is John Burcham?"

"A reporter. A friend of my brother's."

"Was your brother there that night?"

"No." That was all he was getting. She didn't talk about Gray. Ever.

"When did you meet Mr. Haskell?"

"I think we met in May." The breeze had made her shiver. What she wouldn't give for a shiver now. "Definitely May. Early in the month."

"And you didn't see him again till the other night at the Cascades?"

"I might have." Haskell was a bootlegger—a bootlegger who brought bottles of scotch as hostess gifts to cocktail parties. Real scotch. From Scotland. Not the brown-tinted bathtub swill some speakeasies passed off. As such, Haskell was a sought-after guest—it was that popularity that had earned him a mention in last week's column. But Freddie wasn't about to tell a police detective about Jake Haskell's bottles of scotch. The admission would land too many friends in the soup.

"You're aware of Haskell's profession?"

When, oh when, would the aspirin kick in? "His profession?"

"You're aware Haskell was a bootlegger?"

"I might have heard something to that effect." A nice, safe response. "Did he retire?"

"Retire?"

"You said he was a bootlegger. Was."

"He didn't retire. He died."

The gasp that escaped her said almost everything—what a pity, and how awful, and he was much too young. "How?"

"He was murdered."

The air in her office stilled, and her lips struggled to form a simple word. "Murdered?" Maybe the fault was not on her lips but in her throat. The one word emerged as a strangled plea.

Detective Sullivan's eyes searched her face. Thoroughly. What was he looking for? Surely he couldn't suspect her? "He was shot."

"Shot?" Yet another strangled word. "Who shot him?"

"We're hoping you could help us with that."

"Me?" She crossed her hands over her chest and winced as the ice pick in her brain bored another inch toward the center of her gray matter. "I barely knew the man. How could I help?"

"Who was at the Cascades the night you dined with the Fitzgeralds?"

"No one."

"No one? You mean it was empty?"

"Of course not. But there was no one there to write about— a crowd of out-of-towners—"

"You can tell someone is from out of town just by looking?"

"Can't you? There you are." The last she directed to Annie, who stood in the doorway with a tray.

"I brought coffee." She'd also taken time to comb her hair and powder her nose.

"Bless you."

"And Danish."

"You're an angel." The Danish was for Detective Sullivan.

Annie never brought pastry when Freddie was alone. "Isn't she an angel, Detective?"

Sullivan flushed and pulled at his collar.

Annie stepped into the office and put the tray on the desk. "Do you take cream or sugar, Detective?"

"Sugar, please."

"One lump or two?"

"One." The detective returned his notepad to his jacket and watched Annie use tiny silver tongs (where on earth had she found those?) to plunk a sugar cube into his coffee.

"Here you are." She held out the cup.

Their fingers brushed, and the cup rattled against its saucer. The two made calves' eyes at each other for a long second.

Detective Sullivan finally accepted the coffee. In his enormous hand, the cup looked as if it belonged to a child's tea service.

Annie, whose cheeks were flushed a becoming shade of rose, abruptly turned to Freddie. "Black?"

"Please." She always drank her coffee black. If one was going to drink calories, there'd better be liquor involved.

Annie poured a cup and handed it to her.

Freddie took a grateful sip. "Where were we, Detective?"

"You were telling me who was at the Cascades."

"That's right." Freddie closed her eyes and pictured the rooftop dining room—tables covered with crisp white linen, tuxedoed waiters, the pleasant hum of genteel conversations, the less pleasant sounds of the streets rising up to them. She went often enough that one night melted into another. "Haskell was there at a table for two."

"Who was he with?"

"A woman."

"What did she look like?"

"Silk dress—sky blue with crystal beadwork—quite stylish. Ropes and ropes of pearls. Light brown hair—bobbed. Pretty in a kittenish way." Freddie opened her eyes in time to see Detective Sullivan lean toward her, an avid expression on his freckled face.

"Kittenish?" he asked. "Do you know her?"

"Never set eyes on her before."

He slumped. "Would you recognize her if you saw her again?"

She was good with faces. And names. Skills that came in handy when writing a weekly feature on the places to see and be seen in New York. "I'd definitely recognize the dress and the pearls. Why all these questions?"

"The woman might know something that can help us catch Haskell's killer."

Freddie stared at the giant across from her. He still held the cup and saucer, and they still looked like a little girl's toys in his meaty hands.

He stared back at her. "I need your help."

"My help?"

"She'd be happy to help." Annie, who'd forgotten to leave after serving the coffee, wore the slightly stunned expression of a woman who'd met the man of her dreams.

Freddie lifted her brow and stared at her secretary. "I would?"

The detective rubbed his chin. "I've talked to everyone we can find who was at the Cascades that night. You're the first person who could give me a decent description of the woman Haskell was there with."

"What could I possibly do?"

"Let me know if you see her again."

Freddie put her cup down on the corner of her desk. "You mean search her out at clubs?"

"No!" Detective Sullivan held up his hands and shook his massive head. "Absolutely not. If you see her, you let me know. Nothing more."

Freddie stared at her lap and pressed two fingers against each of her temples. God save her from this headache and from men who wanted women to be nothing more than pretty—and, in this case, talking—accessories. "If I spot her, it will likely be in the middle of the night." She raised her gaze. "Are you in your office then?"

A cloud passed over Detective Sullivan's face. She'd presented him with an unforeseen wrinkle. "I'd still like to know where you see her. Like I said, she might know something about the murder."

"This sounds too dangerous." Annie's voice fluttered like a chiffon hemline.

A second cloud passed over the detective's visage, this one darker than the first. His face cleared, and he spoke to Annie. "Miss Archer will be perfectly safe as long as she doesn't approach the woman."

Annie's forehead wrinkled. "You're sure?"

"This mystery woman is just a witness. If a female decides to kill, she doesn't do it with a gun."

The detective was dead wrong. If she ever decided to kill someone—say, someone like Nick—she'd use a gun. She even knew exactly where she'd shoot him.

"If you see her, you'll call me?" Detective Sullivan held out his card.

"Call you"—she glanced at the number on the card—"and do nothing else."

"I would never ask a lady such as yourself to do anything remotely dangerous."

Annie sighed as if she actually saw the gauntlet Detective Sullivan had thrown on Freddie's desk. "She'll call you if she sees her. She won't approach her. She won't follow her. She won't speak to her." Annie might be directing her words at the detective, but she was speaking to Freddie. "I'll see you out, Detective."

Freddie stood and extended her hand.

Detective Sullivan hauled himself from his chair and shook her hand. "Thank you for your assistance, Miss Archer. Remember, if you see the woman, call me. Do not interact with her."

Freddie ignored Annie's worried gaze. "I'll remember."

Annie closed the office door on the detective's broad back and whirled around. "Don't."

"Don't what?"

She held up a restraining finger and jabbed at the air. "I know you. You'd run into a burning building if a man told you not to. Please, don't go looking for that woman. Do not."

"This is New York. The chances of seeing her again are slim." Not exactly true. Despite more than five million people in the city, she still ran into Nick with disturbing regularity.

"If by some miracle, you do see her, call the detective. Nothing more."

"What else would I do?"

They both knew the answer to that question.

CHAPTER 2

WAS THERE A PAEAN to napping? If not, someone needed to write one. She could write one.

> *"Sleep that knits up the raveled sleeve of care." One suspects that Will Shakespeare was no stranger to afternoon naps. He called sleep a balm and a nourisher in life's feast. One can be certain that he put down his pen of an afternoon to catch forty winks.*
>
> *This writer is no bard, more a scribbler of bon mots and random witticisms, but a good nap inspires eloquence. Perhaps that was Shakespeare's secret. After all, is there anything better than a soft pillow, sweet dreams, and waking to the knowledge that one has snoozed through the afternoon heat?*

Hardly the sort of thing the magazine would publish.

Freddie stretched, and yawned, and stretched again. Mercifully, the ice pick in her brain had shrunk to a mere embroidery needle, and her stomach no longer felt like a dinghy tossed on rough seas.

She luxuriated in one last full-body stretch and then pushed herself out of bed, stumbled into the bathroom, and turned on the taps.

A long soak in the bath finished what the nap had started. She was a new woman, ready to conquer worlds—or at least Manhattan. The silver chiffon frock suited her mood and weighed no more than a whisper. The shoes she'd picked up at B. Altman's. Hair. Makeup. That darling evening bag from the clever little shop on Madison. She was ready for almost anything.

Freddie traipsed down the hall and summoned the elevator with a quick jab of her finger.

When the doors slid open, she stepped inside and trilled, "Good evening, Ernest."

"Good evening, Miss Archer." Ernest didn't approve of her. And while he was always polite, she never failed to detect censure lurking in his tone. *Young ladies should not live alone. Young ladies should not go out every evening. Young ladies should behave like ladies.*

The exact same opinions her mother expressed—out loud—on a daily basis.

At least Ernest didn't remind her of her advancing age by urging her to find a husband while she was still young.

The doors slid open, and Freddie practically skipped into the lobby. Ernest's opinions didn't matter. Nor did Marjorie Archer's. Not tonight. Tonight New York was a magical place—a mystical Eden filled with wild, soft summer darkness. An enchanted realm where the night's sins disappeared with the dawn. A modern-day Xanadu where anything might happen.

"Good evening, Miss Archer." Unlike Ernest, the doorman kept his tone censure-free.

"Good evening, Bert. I'll need a taxi, please."

"One moment, miss." Bert stepped outside, and his shrill whistle sliced through the velvet night.

A cab rolled to a stop next to the awning that covered the sidewalk.

"Where to, Miss Archer?"

"The Greenwich Village Inn, please."

Bert relayed her destination to the cabbie, saw her safely tucked into the back seat, and closed the door.

The cab pulled into traffic, whisking her downtown.

They passed through streets filled with boys hawking papers, couples walking arm in arm, and the streetlights glowing yellow in the hazy evening air. The claxon blare of horns, the hawkers' young voices, and the unexpected chirp of crickets poured through the taxi's open windows.

When Freddie arrived at the speakeasy, Dotty already sat at a small table. Dotty who was seldom on time. Dotty who was never, ever early.

Freddie sat in the chair directly across from her. "What on earth happened? The sky fell? That sure-fire stock headed south? The rain washed out your parade?"

Dotty grimaced. "Worse. Writer's block." She took a long drag from her cigarette. "It didn't help that Mr. Benchley typed like a madman while a blank page mocked me." Dotty and Robert Benchley, who shared an office, had acquired the quaint habit of calling each other Mrs. Parker and Mr. Benchley.

Freddie made a sympathetic noise in her throat and regarded her friend's ebony ensemble.

"I wish you wouldn't do that."

"Do what?"

"Raise your left brow as if you'd like to send me home to change my dress."

"You do wear a lot of black."

"I like black."

"It's summer." Freddie nodded toward the murals of bathing nymphs painted on the restaurant's walls.

"What's your point?"

"There are thousands of colors. Everything from verdant greens to sunny yellows. There are heart-pounding reds and thoughtful blues. There are lavenders and roses and irises. There's even virginal white." Although that wouldn't work for Dotty. "And you wear black."

"I look good in black."

"You do," Freddie ceded. "But you'd also look good in blue."

Dotty held up a hand. "Enough. I like black. I wear black. And all your well-meant advice won't change that." Dotty picked up her drink. "Tell me, what did you do last night?"

"Dinner at the Colony. Dancing at Corona de Oro." Was that a wince on Dotty's sharp features? "Then I shuffled back to the office and wrote my column. You?"

"Mr. Benchley and I dined at the rooftop of the Astor. How was Corona de Oro?"

"I saw Nick."

"Out with that actress?"

"You knew?"

"I saw them at the Astor. Nick mentioned they were going dancing."

And where else would Nick Peters go dancing but Corona de

Oro? "She's his leading lady." The cost of a light voice was obscenely high. Freddie shifted in her chair and looked for the waiter.

He shimmied over to the table. "Miss?"

"A tonic with lime, please."

"Of course, miss. Right away." He returned to the bar.

Meanwhile, Dotty's eyes drooped with sympathy. Or maybe it was empathy—Dotty wasn't exactly lucky in love. "Men can be such beasts."

Freddie didn't reply. Instead she smiled at the waiter, who deposited her drink on the table. When he turned his back, she pulled a silver flask from her evening bag, unscrewed the lid, poured a healthy dose of gin into the glass, and drank deeply. "Eight weeks ago, Nick was begging me to marry him."

Dotty blew a plume of smoke at the ceiling. "You did return his ring."

"Whose side are you on?"

"Yours. Always, yours." Dotty reached across the table and patted her hand. "But you sent him packing."

"I would have liked him to pine for at least a month or two. The least he could do is pretend I broke his heart."

"We're talking about Nick Peters." Dotty was ever the pragmatist. "He's moved on. You should do the same."

Dotty was absolutely right—especially about moving on.

"What happened between the two of you? You seemed so well-suited. Are you ready to talk about it yet?"

Freddie closed her eyes and saw Nick slipping a ring the size of a martini olive onto her left hand. They'd fallen into bed and awakened to tangled sheets and a soft breeze blowing through the open windows. It was then, snuggled in arms she'd come to count on, that Nick had suggested she look for a house in Connecticut.

His plan—she would move to Connecticut, bear his children, and quit her job—made perfect sense to him.

He didn't seem to understand that New York was her home, and children weren't her immediate priority. Nor did he grasp her love for her job.

"You love that job more than you love me." Nick's words still rang in her ears.

"Don't do this, Nick."

"If you loved me, you'd quit."

"If you loved me, you wouldn't ask that of me."

They'd glared at each other. Angry. Hurt. Resentful. Until she'd lowered her eyes.

He'd kissed her, told her their life together would be heaven, and then hurried off to a meeting.

She'd dressed slowly, thought furiously, and left Nick's enormous ring and the broken pieces of her heart on the bedside table.

Freddie opened her eyes and surveyed the room. Bohemian Villagers in need of shaves and shampoos claimed a certain number of tables. Bright girls wearing silk stockings, shoulder-baring frocks, and hopeful expressions gazed at brash young men. Actors and actresses peppered the room. And there—at a table in the corner—was a woman with light brown hair, ropes of pearls that went on for days, and a fabulous dress. Was she Jake Haskell's missing date? A haze of cigarette smoke softened the edges of those who sat close by. Freddie couldn't make out details without getting closer.

"What happened between you?" Dotty repeated.

Freddie returned her gaze to Dotty. "He wanted to move to Connecticut."

"There are worse fates."

"He wanted me to quit my job."

Dotty's eyes narrowed. "Why?"

"The wife of a successful producer doesn't work."

"So he planned to move to Connecticut and leave you there?" Dotty's voice held the proper amount of outrage.

"I was allowed to come to New York for opening nights, shopping, and the occasional luncheon as long as I promised not to be too clever."

Dotty crushed out her cigarette. "And you passed that up?"

"Inconceivable, isn't it?"

"Who knew Nick had rocks for brains?"

"Not me. At least not till we'd wandered a fair distance down the path."

"You need to meet someone new. Someone with some sense. A man who can take your mind off Nick."

"Pish." Freddie's gaze returned to the woman draped in pearls. Was she the woman the detective sought?

"There. To the left. He's handsome enough."

Freddie looked left. "He's a butter-and-egg man if I ever saw one."

With the smallest of shoulder shrugs, Dotty admitted the man she'd selected probably hailed from a dairy farm outside Buffalo. "What about that one?" She tilted her chin toward a likely lothario.

"Not my type."

"What type is that?"

"The type that prefers women."

Dotty wrinkled her nose. "You're sure?"

"About my type, or the man?"

"Both."

"Then I'm positive on each count."

"Well, if you're going to be picky"—Dotty rubbed her chin, and a dangerous light dawned in her eyes—"you could reform him."

"It doesn't work that way."

"Too bad. He's handsome." Again she searched the crowded club. "What about Brandt Abrams?"

"Who?"

"Brandt Abrams." Using her cigarette, Dotty pointed at someone behind Freddie's back.

Freddie glanced over her shoulder and spotted a man with the sharp-planed cheeks of an intellectual who regularly forgot meals. Lean as his cheeks were, his lower lip belonged to an aesthete. That lower lip hinted at passion. Freddie raised her gaze to the man's eyes. Those were dark, storm-tossed, dangerous.

An unwelcome breathlessness invaded her lungs. "Tell me about him."

"His name is Brandt Abrams."

"You already said that. Who is he?" Where did men who looked like that come from? Olympus? It didn't matter. "He's out of my league."

"He's pretty enough for both of you. Besides, the man is not interested in looks. The last time we spoke, he told me he wanted a woman with a brain."

"That's what they all say." And then they tried to send you to Connecticut.

"Yes, but Brandt means it."

"How do you know him?"

"I'm not really sure. I met him...somewhere."

Whoever Brandt Abrams was, he'd noticed them gawking, and he was walking toward their table.

"Dotty." He bent and brushed a kiss across Dotty's upturned cheek. "Always a pleasure."

"Brandt Abrams, meet Freddie Archer."

Eyes darker, stormier, and positively fraught with danger when seen up close took her measure. "Freddie?"

"Short for Winnifred," Dotty supplied.

"Freddie suits you better."

Words never failed her. Never. They fell like dew on a summer morning, reliable as rain in springtime or brown leaves in autumn. Words were her constant companion. Until this moment. Freddie searched for a witty reply and found not a single syllable. Her hand rose to her throat, and she managed only a sickly smile.

"Join us." Dotty nodded toward an empty chair.

Had Dotty lost her mind?

"I'm meeting someone."

"Join us till she gets here," Dotty insisted.

Brandt glanced at his wristwatch. "He. Ewan Duncan."

A rare smile touched Dotty's lips. "Sit."

"I hate to intrude."

"You're not intruding. Is he, Freddie?" The tip of Dotty's shoe connected with Freddie's shin.

Still mute, Freddie shook her head.

Brandt claimed the seat next to Dotty, and Freddie had no choice but to look at him. Beautiful men were their own subspecies. They were spoiled. They were vain. They could teach Narcissus a thing or two about self-absorption. Just when one had convinced oneself they were more trouble than they were worth, they sent one a look so smoldering it was a wonder the tablecloth didn't burst into flame.

Freddie shifted her gaze to her gin.

"Freddie is a writer."

"Oh?"

The pointed toe of Dotty's shoe met Freddie's shin a second time. Dotty expected her to say something witty or charming or coherent. Failing that, Dotty expected her to at least ask about his work.

But Freddie had no words.

"She writes for *Gotham*. Funny columns. Smart columns."

"I suppose that makes you a wise woman of Gotham?"

"You know the story?" She'd found something to say. Barely.

Brandt nodded. "I do."

"I don't." Dotty arched her brows and waited.

"Would you care to tell it?" Brandt asked.

"No, no. You go ahead." She might run out of words before the end of the first sentence.

"There was a town in England—Gotham—and the people who lived there learned the king was planning a visit. Knowing the chaos and expense his arrival would bring, the good citizens of Gotham took the advice of a wise woman. They feigned madness, which, at the time, was believed to be contagious. They tried to drown an eel. They built a fence around a bush to cage a cuckoo. Their antics worked. The king, fearing madness, visited a different town."

Dotty tilted her head. "The moral is that New Yorkers are crazy?"

"Like foxes." There. Freddie had added an additional two words to the conversation.

"Do you write about the foxes?" Brandt asked.

Freddie swallowed more gin. "I do. Foxes, their dens, and fashion."

"Their dens?"

"Clubs and speakeasies and restaurants and shows. That sort of thing."

"Ah." Brandt's gaze flickered back to Dotty. "What about you? Selling lots of poetry?"

Forty-five seconds. No more. He'd lost interest in her that quickly. Now that his attention had shifted to Dotty—call her contrary or nonsensical or even ridiculous—Freddie wanted it back. "What do you do, Brandt?"

"I'm in sales."

"Of what?"

He raised a dark brow.

Just like that, she knew. "You're a bootlegger."

"A rash guess."

"Is it?" What else could he be? He wasn't a banker or lawyer—no everyday mortal man would trust him. He wasn't a bond man—again, the trust issue. Maybe he was an ad man. Maybe.

"What if I sold hats? I'd be mortally offended."

"You don't sell hats." Of that, she was certain.

"Yes. But how do you know?"

"Because I know."

He was too handsome to be a haberdasher. And he knew it. Cats who'd swallowed canaries looked less pleased with themselves than Brandt Abrams. He cast his satisfied gaze about the room. "Is this the kind of place you write about?"

"It is."

"And what would you write?"

They were back to the foxes and their dens. "I'd write that the murals"—she nodded her chin toward the frolicking nymphs—"are worth the price of admission." She ignored the things his sudden smile did to his lower lip. "I'd write that the service is reasonably good." She would not write that there was a man there who could induce drool with a quirk of his brow. "And I'd write the band plays music to which one can dance."

"Would you like to?"

"Would I like to what?"

"Dance."

Wearing a smile she borrowed from the devil himself, Dotty waved at the dance floor. "Don't mind me. Go."

Brandt extended his hand.

The band ended its lively number and began a slow song. What could one dance hurt? Freddie rose from her chair and allowed Brandt to lead her to the dance floor. They found a spot among the sharp elbows and glowing brows of enthusiastic hoofers.

Brandt gathered her into his arms. Of course he danced like a dream. No crushed toes or missed steps or crashing into other couples. He glided and turned and spun as if he'd been born on a dance floor.

He bent his head toward her. "Tell me your story."

"My story?" Freddie looked at the other dancers. Staring at other women's dresses was a safer bet than looking up at Brandt.

"You know mine."

"I do not know your story. And I don't have one." She searched out the mystery woman, who was glancing at her watch with a pout on her lips. The woman rose from her table in a swirl of seafoam chiffon. Was she leaving? Freddie ought to get a closer look at her. She could very well be the same woman who'd dined with Jake.

"You're a writer." Brandt reclaimed her attention. "You know better than anyone that everyone has a story."

"My story's not worth telling."

"See, you do have a story." He spun her in a giddy maneuver. "Nursing a broken heart?"

"Is it that obvious?" She stole another quick glance at the woman in seafoam and pearls—or at the woman's empty table. The woman was gone.

"Tell me, Freddie Archer, why aren't you married to a stockbroker or banker?"

She looked up at Brandt. "I'm a writer."

"And you can't write when you're married?"

"Apparently not." Bitterness snuck into her voice.

"And we're back to the broken heart."

"Let's talk about you. How long have you been in New York?"

He spun her across the dance floor. "Since I got back from the war—"

Freddie tripped.

Only Brandt's arms saved her from falling.

"You lost someone." His voice was flat, as if the peaks and valleys of emotion were more than he could bear.

Her throat tightened, and she nodded.

"A husband?"

"A brother." Now came the wheres, and the hows, and the ranks, and the battles. Her spine stiffened in anticipation of his questions. Gray's story was one she couldn't bear to share.

"I'm sorry." He sounded sincere.

Freddie let her gaze rise north of his shoulders. Those dangerous eyes stared down at her with something like sympathy swimming in their depths. "Thank you."

Notes washed over them, daring them to spin or twirl or attempt intricate footwork, but Freddie simply stared into Brandt's eyes.

And he stared into hers.

She should say something. Something smart. But words had deserted her again. And lost in his eyes, she didn't miss them.

In the street, a car backfired. Twice. Loud enough to vanquish the song's last chords. Loud enough to break the spell between them.

Brandt dropped her hand and pushed toward the door.

A full second passed before Freddie realized she'd been left on the dance floor. What had happened? Some men who'd been in the war reacted badly to loud noises. Was Brandt one of them? She cut through a gap in the dancing couples and followed him, catching the fabric of his jacket.

He looked down at her as if he'd never seen her before.

"What's wrong?" she asked. "Where are you going?"

"Outside."

"But why?"

"Didn't you hear the gunshots?"

CHAPTER 3

FREDDIE TIGHTENED HER HOLD on Brandt's sleeve. Had the poor man heard artillery from the Western Front? Could a soothing voice silence the guns? "It was just a car."

He replied with a quick, decisive shake of his head. "It was gunshots." He sounded so certain, and his eyes...His eyes had narrowed to slits.

Arguing with him would accomplish nothing. She kept her tone level, cool, calm. "Even if it was gunshots, why run toward trouble?"

He looked down at her as if she were the one lost in the darkened corridors of a war-ravaged mind. "Someone might need help." He shook loose of her hold on his jacket and raced out the door.

Freddie blinked back her surprise. Brandt Abrams had struck her as a man who looked out for himself, not the sort to put himself at risk for others. Swallowing a sigh, Freddie followed him into Sheridan Square.

The sepia halos cast by the streetlights bled into the buildings' brown bricks. The air was heavy with exhaust and humidity.

Somewhere nearby, a street vendor sold sausages, and sizzling fat and fennel perfumed the air.

And on the sidewalk lay a man.

He clutched his chest and stared at the jaundiced light, where all manner of bugs, unconcerned with violence, swayed in dances of their own making.

Blood, a growing pool of crimson horror, colored the sidewalk. So much blood. Who knew there was so much blood in a single body?

The street sounds faded away, leaving only the crickets and the thud of her heart. Brandt had been right. Gunshots. And a wounded man. Freddie's knees swayed, not sure if they wanted to hold her upright.

A few feet away, a man in a tuxedo retched in the gutter.

A woman sobbed.

Brandt knelt on the pavement next to the bleeding man. His brows drew together, and his dark eyes looked too big for his face. "Ewan!" Anger and disbelief and denial turned the name into a challenge.

Ewan didn't answer. Instead he gasped for air.

Brandt lifted the man's head off the pavement and rested it on his lap. "Ewan?"

Ewan was dying. There was no way anyone could lose that much blood and live.

The crowd around the two men tightened.

"Who is he?" A girl in a dress nearly as red as Ewan's blood spoke from behind the hand she'd clasped to her mouth.

"Has anyone called the police?" asked a man who looked like a banker.

"It's too horrible," said a woman whose avid gaze remained locked on the grisly tableau.

"Did anyone see the shooter?" The girl in the red dress lifted her head and stared across the street as if the gunman would be lurking there.

The circle around Ewan and Brandt grew. A man in shirt-sleeves whose pants were dotted with paint. An ashcan artist? A couple, their hands clutched tightly together. Clubgoers in dancing shoes. A disheveled man with an iron grip on a silver flask. And the woman with the ropes of pearls.

Was she the same woman Freddie had seen at the Colony? Maybe. What was she doing here?

A rattling breath caught Freddie's attention. She looked down at the dying man. The creases etched into Ewan's face softened, and the light in his eyes faded away. He'd left them.

Freddie's throat tightened. This was death? A light fading? Was this how Gray died? She clenched her teeth against the sudden ache in her jaw, pressed her lips together, and returned her gaze to the woman.

But she was gone. She'd stepped out of the circle surrounding the dead man, and the gap she left behind had closed as if she'd never been there.

Freddie stepped out of the circle, too. Her gaze swept the sidewalk. Where had the woman gone?

There. At the corner. Crossing the street.

Freddie's satin slippers had a mind of their own. They walked to the edge of the sidewalk, paused as a taxi raced past, and then ventured onto 4th Street.

Honk!

A truck barreled past, and Freddie's heart exploded into an impossible-to-maintain gallop. Another step into the street and she'd have been flattened, lying in her own bloody pool. Despite the night's heat, her hands felt icy cold. The inside of her mouth was a desert.

What was she doing?

If she was right, if it was the same woman—she was now linked to two murders.

She was also Detective Sullivan's problem. Not Freddie's. Why run toward trouble?

What had Brandt said when he ran toward gunshots? Maybe he could help someone.

What would Gray do—if he could?

Freddie's gaze returned to the woman in seafoam. She hurried down the opposite sidewalk. Maybe her presence at another murder was a coincidence.

Maybe Freddie could buy the Brooklyn Bridge.

With a quick glance—both ways—Freddie raced across the street. The cars on the opposite curb were parked bumper to bumper. Not more than an inch of space separated a Ferris sedan from a Tin Lizzie. Less than a whisper separated a Packard Twin Six and a Moon roadster. To get to the sidewalk, she'd have to walk to the corner—but that meant losing sight of the woman.

Gathering her hem, Freddie slotted the toe of her left shoe onto the spokes of a Nash's front wheel. Her right foot found a higher spoke. From there, she climbed onto the car's hood.

Who knew hoods were so slick? Her knees slid, her stockings snagged, and her dress rode up—high up. She should have probably considered those perils before beginning her climb. If she wasn't careful, she'd reveal her pink silk slip-ins to the people across 4th Street.

A truck whizzed by, creating its own gust of wind, and the hem of Freddie's dress flew up to her neck. She yanked it back into place and glanced over her shoulder. Of course half the people on the opposite sidewalk were looking right at her. Heat warmed her cheeks, but she waggled her fingers and produced a cheeky grin.

She swung her feet around, slid off the Nash's hood, and assessed—dress, stockings, and shoes all in the appropriate places. And none were irreparably soiled. Thank heavens she'd chosen a clean car.

Better yet, the woman was still on the sidewalk. She strode with purpose.

Letting the woman walk away was tempting. So tempting. But Freddie had a chance to see where the woman was going, maybe even a chance to get her name. And if she did get the name, she could wrap it up with a bow for Detective Sullivan, a man who thought her too delicate, too womanly, to do anything more than observe. She tugged at her hem. Half of 4th Street had just seen her lace-edged underwear—the other half didn't need to see them, too—and followed.

The woman walked quickly, as if late for an important appointment.

Freddie trotted behind her and ignored the trickle of perspiration tracing a path down her back.

Whenever she sensed the woman might turn her head, she ducked—behind a couple entwined in a passionate kiss, into a doorway that reeked of grime and smoke and paint thinner, and behind a man the size and width of a Wells Fargo delivery truck.

Following the woman was exhilarating—a lark. Freddie's blood fizzed with excitement. Right up until the moment the woman disappeared into Washington Square Park.

Freddie's steps slowed.

Once upon a time, Washington Square was the best address in

New York. Those days were gone. Nowadays, the square's former residents called Riverside Drive home. Admittedly, a few of the homes facing the park still housed the well-to-do—only last week, the *Times* had rehashed the story of Mary and Albert Shattuck, who lived at 19 Washington Square North. The Shattucks had been locked in their wine cellar while thieves stole $100,000 in gems from their home.

In the thick darkness, the park seemed treacherous. Were thieves—or worse—hiding in its shadows? Was it too dangerous to follow?

The mystery woman had entered the park without pause.

She'd come this far. Freddie breathed deeply and crossed MacDougal Street.

The dark trees twisted like monsters, and the too-distant Washington Square Arch shone like a beacon. Freddie's heels sank into the grass. Where had the woman gone? And why? She scanned the night and saw no one.

The crickets' song was near deafening, drowning out everything but the noisiest trucks and the loudest shouts of laughter. She felt alone—marooned in a sea of night. Despite the cloying heat, she shivered.

That's when it started—a prickle on her neck—as if someone was watching her.

She spun around but saw no one.

Silly. She was being silly. Now if only her heart would stop beating like a kettle drum.

Freddie tiptoed forward. There it was again—that sense of being watched.

This time, she merely glanced over her shoulder.

No one was there. But she couldn't shake the sense that someone meant her harm.

Had the woman somehow turned the tables? Was Freddie now the one being followed?

Behind her, a twig snapped. In the entire history of twigs snapping, never had the simple sound held such evil portent. Someone lurked behind her. Watching. Creeping closer.

Freddie ran.

She emerged from the trees, got her bearings, and raced to the edge of the park.

She flew across the street and pounded on a blessedly familiar door.

A piece of the door slid to the left, revealing suspicious eyes. "Password?"

"White mule," she gasped.

The door swung open, and Freddie fell over her feet in her eagerness to get inside Club Gallant.

Barney Gallant, looking dashing in a tuxedo, stood next to his bouncer. "Miss Archer, what's wrong?"

"I was at the Greenwich Inn"—a place Barney knew well since he'd managed it until he opened his own club—"and there was a shooting. I was rattled." It was an easier explanation than the disappearing woman or the sense of dread and danger that pursued her through the park.

"Anyone hit?"

She nodded. "A man named Ewan."

Barney paled. "Ewan Duncan?"

"He was covered in blood." Inexplicably, her eyes filled with tears. "I watched him die."

Barney blinked. "What an idiot I am. You need a drink. Come in. I'll get you something to calm your nerves."

Club Gallant was housed in a mansion, and Barney led her to what had once been the ballroom. Now an oval bar stood in the room's center, and white-coated bartenders mixed drinks while those privileged to gain entrance to Barney's club listened to a chanteuse croon on a small stage set against the far wall.

The tension in Freddie's neck and shoulders eased. Slightly. Nothing bad could happen in this elegant room filled with ladies in silk frocks and gentlemen in evening dress.

"Thank you, Barney." Ewan's murder had filled her with sadness and horror and a sharp reminder of Gray's loss. But what she'd felt among the trees—that feeling of being watched, like a large cat was stalking her, just waiting to pounce—had left her worse than rattled. She did need a drink.

"What can I get you?"

Freddie looked down at her empty hands. "I'm afraid I left my bag at the Village Inn. I don't have any money."

"How many times have you mentioned my place in your column?"

"No idea."

"Seven. Seven times in six months. Your money is no good here."

Which was sweet, but it wouldn't get her a cab home. "Is there anyone who could run down to the Greenwich Inn for me? I was sitting with Dotty Parker. She might still be there. I'm sure she'd be happy to bring me my handbag."

"I'll take care of it," Barney promised. "You sit yourself down and relax."

Freddie settled into a chair at a small table and accepted the glass of champagne the waiter offered. She sipped and did what calmed her—she composed a column in her head.

Is there anything more delectable than well-chilled champagne? One thinks not.

No. That wouldn't do. The mere mention of golden bubbles would bring the police to Barney's door. Barney already had the dubious honor of being the first man in New York to be prosecuted for serving alcohol. She couldn't set him up for a second stint in the pokey.

Well known for its midnight entertainment, Club Gallant has added a chanteuse for the enjoyment of early arrivals. The raven-haired crooner knows her way around a song.

Better.
She scanned the ballroom looking for inspiration.

If you've not yet made your way to the Village, not yet made the owner's acquaintance, one wonders what you've been doing. Barney Gallant is a—

Barney Gallant was a small man with dark hair, a nose that could not be ignored, and a smile that welcomed all the right people. But she could hardly write that.

Barney Gallant is a hospitable man of superior vocabulary (one blames his youth spent sharing a garret with

Eugene O'Neill). So well-spoken is he that bounders asked to leave the club thank him for the honor of being ejected.

Freddie closed her eyes, drew breath deep into her lungs, and held it.

If one comes to the Village looking for Bohemia, one should skip right by Club Gallant. No self-respecting artist (unshaved and unbathed) would deign bump elbows with the debutantes spotted at Barney Gallant's latest venture. The place is simply too posh. And yet, thanks to the owner, there exists that informal gaiety so much in demand.

"What in the hell?"

Freddie's eyes flew open.

Dotty dropped the missing handbag on the table and dropped herself into the open chair. "You leave for a dance and end up at another club?"

"It's a long story."

"It always is." Dotty glanced at her watch. "I have scads of time."

"What happened at the Village Inn?"

"The police came."

Had Detective Sullivan been among them? "I guess that's not surprising. There was a dead man out front."

"Exactly! And I was wild with worry. I had no idea what had become of you."

"You should have asked Brandt." Surely he'd noticed her climbing over the hood of a car with slip-ins exposed to half of Greenwich Village.

"He disappeared, too." Dotty lit a cigarette. "For a brief instant, I considered you might have disappeared together."

"But?"

"But you left your handbag." She jabbed her cigarette at the blameless accessory. "No woman, no matter how devilishly seductive the man's smile, leaves her handbag."

"Good point."

"So, there I was. Alone. Well, alone except for a disturbing number of New York's finest. Where"—she leveled her dark gaze directly at Freddie—"were you?"

"I thought I recognized someone. I followed her."

"Here?"

"Not exactly."

"You realize I was questioned by the police? By a homicide detective?"

Freddie's heart skipped a beat. "Really?"

"His last name was Sullivan. He was most interested to learn I'd been out with you."

"Was he?" Freddie's voice was faint.

"He seemed to think you'd know him."

"Did he?" Fainter still.

Dotty nodded. "He asked me to give you a message if I saw you."

"Oh?" Barely audible.

"He'll stop by your office in the morning."

Annie would be thrilled.

"Do you want to tell me why a homicide detective is coming to your office?"

"No."

Dotty's expression was fearsome.

Freddie swallowed. "But I'll tell you anyway. I saw a woman at the Colony with Jake Haskell, and the detective wants to speak with her. The problem is, he doesn't know her name. He asked me to let him know if I saw her again."

"The same Jake Haskell who was murdered?"

"Yes."

"And you saw the woman tonight?"

"Maybe. I thought it was her. So I followed her." Up until the moment she'd felt watched, it had been the most thrilling thing she'd ever done.

"Let me get this straight." Dotty rested her cigarette on the edge of a crystal ashtray and steepled her fingers. "There's a homicide detective who wants to question this woman about a murder. You know that, you saw her at the scene of a second murder, and you followed her?"

"You make it sound reckless."

"It was reckless. Where did she go?"

"I lost her," Freddie admitted. "Then I got spooked, so I came here."

"Thank God you lost her. You do realize you might have been following a killer?"

CHAPTER 4

The blank paper in the typewriter remained resolutely white. The dratted page remained indifferent to Freddie's ire, unmoved by scowls, pleas, or being called *a waste of perfectly good pulp*.

Eloquent words about champagne bubbles, the rustle of silk, and the pursuit of the perfect evening were elusive—any words were elusive. Freddie blamed the image of Brandt Abrams holding his dying friend. Ewan's blood on the sidewalk had seeped into her psyche and refused to fade. Then there was the stalker in Washington Square Park. She shivered at the memory.

Long minutes passed before she admitted defeat and opened the office door. "Annie?"

Annie, who still wore her hat and gloves, looked up from sorting the mail, a question in her eyes.

"I'd bet a case of scotch your detective will stop by this morning."

Annie's lips pursed. "He's not *my* detective."

"Be that as it may, you might want to straighten the seams of your stockings, run a comb through your hair, and touch up your makeup."

Not that Annie's round cheeks needed additional color. As soon as a certain detective was mentioned, they'd flushed their telltale pink. She set her letter opener on her desk. "Did something happen last night?"

"Happen?" She feigned innocence.

"To make Detective Sullivan return?"

"A murder."

Annie gasped and pressed her hands to her chest. Her eyes widened to the size of dessert plates. "Why is he coming here? Are you a witness?"

"Heavens, no." Freddie blinked away inexplicable wetness. "I didn't see the murder. Just the body."

"Are you . . ." Annie's hands rose from her chest to cover her mouth, as if her thoughts were too terrible to utter.

Shocked? Scared? Stunned? All those. Plus, Freddie's stomach wasn't quite right, and her eyes itched with the grit of a restless night. "I'm fine. Is there more coffee?"

The suspicious tilt of Annie's chin said she wasn't buying the *I'm fine* line.

"Coffee?" Freddie repeated.

Annie harumphed and stood. "I'll get you a cup."

"If it's made, I can get it myself." She put off returning to her desk and the blank page that brought to mind a scarlet pool spreading across the pavement.

The shrill ring of the phone on Annie's desk made Freddie grateful she'd limited last night's liquor intake.

"Miss Archer's office." Annie listened. "I'll see if she's available." She covered the mouthpiece. "Brandt Abrams."

Freddie's heart, usually found safely affixed to the upper left portion of her chest, careened like a billiard ball. "I'll take it."

Annie nodded. Slowly. And a smile ghosted the corner of her lips as if reading Freddie was as easy as perusing the pages of a magazine. "I'll put the call through then fetch your coffee."

Freddie's mouth and throat felt bone dry. "And a glass of water, please."

Annie arched a brow, and Freddie regretted teaching her that trick.

She retreated to her office, closed the door, and waited for the phone's ring. She exhaled as she picked up the receiver. "Hello." A smile snuck into her voice. Did he hear it? She frowned.

"Good morning." It was as if he expected her to recognize him. Even though Annie screened her calls, most people identified themselves. Not Brandt.

Even if Annie hadn't told her who was on the line, she'd have known his voice. It only took two words for her to distinguish him from the other men who rang her—a simple *good morning.*

What was the etiquette for a conversation the morning after a murder? Surely Emily Post addressed such thorny tête-a-têtes in *Etiquette in Society, in Business, in Politics, and at Home.* Too bad Freddie didn't have a copy handy. "I'm glad you called. I worried about you."

His answering silence outweighed the Woolworth building and lasted longer than a Ziegfeld finale.

She shifted in her chair, nibbled on the tip of her nail, and then forced her hand to her lap. Had she said the wrong thing?

"Thank you," he replied after an interminable pause. "Last night was horrible."

"Do the police have any suspects?"

"They don't share details of their investigations with me."

Properly chastised, Freddie cast about for something else to say. "I'm sorry about your friend." The image of Brandt, the blood, and Ewan's last breath played like a motion picture.

"Thank you. Under the circumstances, this question may sound crass—"

"What question?"

"Will you have dinner with me tonight?"

"Yes." Drat. She spoke too soon, sounded too eager.

"You will?" The man was more handsome than Rudolph Valentino. Why did he sound so surprised?

"Yes." A smile stretched her lips.

Tap, tap.

"Come in."

The door opened. An enormous bouquet of pink roses hid whoever held them.

The flowers entered the office, and Annie followed behind whoever carried them with a coffee cup in one hand and a water glass in the other.

The flowers came to a rest on the edge of her desk, and Freddie breathed in their delicate scent. From Brandt?

Billy, the office boy, offered a nod and a cheeky grin and scampered off.

Annie plucked the card from among the blooms and held it out. "Eight?"

Her attention returned to the man at the end of the telephone line. "That's perfect."

"Where should I pick you up?"

She gave him her address. "What should I wear?"

"I'll make reservations at Antoine's."

She'd need an evening gown. She glanced at Annie, who waited with the unopened envelope.

Were the flowers from Brandt? If they weren't, she'd best not mention them. If they were, she could thank him later. She held out her hand, and Annie released her hold on the envelope. "See you at eight."

"Looking forward to it."

"Me too." Just the thought of seeing Brandt Abrams made her heart thump faster.

"Until tonight." He hung up.

She returned the receiver to the cradle and opened the envelope.

I miss you. Nick.

Freddie dropped the card into the wastepaper basket. "Put them on your desk."

Annie frowned. "What?"

"I don't want them. Also, if Mr. Peters calls, I'm unavailable."

Annie nodded. Slowly. With portent. "I see."

Annie claimed the ridiculous bouquet. When the door closed behind her, Freddie slumped in her chair and downed half a cup of coffee in one gulp.

The phone rang, and Freddie glared at it. Was she not allowed a single moment to mope over Nick or daydream about her dinner date? She picked up the receiver.

"Your mother is on the line."

If Freddie didn't take the call, her mother would ring at fifteen-minute intervals. And Annie, usually so sweet-tempered, would lose her patience and turn to stony silence. Tomorrow's coffee would be cold, tangled typewriter ribbons would be ignored, and pastries of the French variety would be required to restore good terms. "Put her through."

"Right away."

Freddie downed the rest of her coffee, girded her loins, and picked up the line on the first ring. "Hello."

"Freddie, I expect you for dinner tonight."

"Good morning, Mother."

"Good morning. Dinner. Tonight."

"I have plans."

"Cancel them."

"I don't believe I will."

"Bernard Allerton is coming to dinner."

Freddie didn't know Bernard Allerton and had no desire to change that. She didn't need to meet him to know him. Mother had developed the deplorable habit of bringing Yale- or Harvard-educated lawyers or stockbrokers home to dinner. The men Mother picked were invariably handsome, unbelievably stuffy, and painfully aware of her father's fortune. After a stilted dinner at the Archers' table, they'd pursue Freddie with single-minded focus until she set them straight.

"I have a date, and I'm not canceling."

"A date?" Mother's voice was sharp enough to cut diamonds. "With whom?"

"You don't know him."

"Another theater type?"

"No."

Mother breathed a relieved sigh. She'd disapproved of Nick. "Who?"

"His name is Brandt Abrams."

"Abrams?"

"Yes."

"Is he Jewish?"

"I didn't ask."

"Isn't that something you should know?"

Brandt Abrams was handsome enough to weaken a girl's knees. A lesser female might swoon when he smiled. The man ran toward trouble when he could remain safely inside sipping a gin rickey. What did it matter if he was Jewish or Christian or Hindu? "It doesn't matter to me."

"It matters to others."

"Their problem, not mine."

A noise—not a snort (Mother would never snort)—erupted from the receiver. "Don't be naïve, Freddie."

Tap, tap.

"Come in," Freddie called.

The pink of Annie's cheeks told a story, or at least the first few chapters of a romance novel.

"Mother, there's someone here to see me. We can talk later."

"Freddie—"

"Now's not a good time. Talk soon." She hung up. She'd pay for that later, but she couldn't be bothered to care. "He's here?"

Annie nodded.

"More coffee, please?" Thus far, the morning had proved difficult, and an interview with Detective Sullivan didn't promise improvement. She needed coffee the way a drunk needed his next glass of gin.

"Of course." Annie stepped into the office and collected the empty cup and saucer from the desk.

"Show him in."

A moment later, Annie led Detective Sullivan into the office.

"Good morning, Detective." Freddie waved at an empty chair. "Please, sit."

Detective Sullivan settled his substantial bulk onto a sturdy chair that suddenly looked too spindly to hold him.

"How may I help you?"

A stormy expression—one that promised thunder and lightning—settled on his face. "You were at Greenwich Village Inn last night?" More accusation than question.

"I was."

"Did you see the murder?"

"I did not."

"Witnesses say you fled the scene."

"I saw her."

"Her?"

"The woman." Freddie folded her hands and rested them on the edge of the desk. Where was Annie with the coffee? "At least I think it was the woman who had dinner with Jake."

Detective Sullivan stared at her as if she were the latest exotic exhibit at the Bronx Zoo. "Where did she go?"

"Washington Square Park. I followed her." She looked down at her hands. "But I lost her trail and felt unsafe, so I gave up."

"Unsafe how?"

"Like someone was following me."

He slumped in his chair. "I'm sorry."

"For what?"

"Getting you involved. I never meant for you to follow a suspect."

She forced a smile and held out her hands. "As you can see, I am unscathed."

"Miss Archer, please forget I ever asked for your assistance. I made a mistake."

It was easy to be brave from the sidelines. Heroes ran toward those in need, no matter the danger. Like Gray. Like Brandt.

"I'm glad you asked me. And I didn't plan on confronting her. I simply wanted to know where she went."

Detective Sullivan opened his mouth, obviously ready to point out the error in Freddie's ways, but held his tongue when Annie pushed open the door with her hip, entered the office, and deposited a coffee tray on the desk. Her presence rendered Detective Sullivan mute. She really did have impeccable timing.

"Thank you, Annie. Would you please pour the detective a cup?"

Annie blushed to her roots and splashed coffee into a cup. "One sugar, is that right?"

Detective Sullivan (also ruddy) nodded.

The coffee prepared, Annie held out the cup. Her fingers brushed against his, and the two stared deeply into each other's eyes.

"Black for me."

Annie tore her gaze from Detective Sullivan, poured a second cup, and handed it over.

"Thank you."

Annie nodded and hurried toward the door as if hungry hounds nipped at her heels.

Detective Sullivan turned in his chair and watched her go. When the door closed, he blinked. Four times. "Did you see her on the sidewalk or inside?"

They were back to the mystery woman. "Both. She left before the shooting, but I saw her in the crowd gathered around the dead man."

Detective Sullivan rubbed a hand over his face. "I told you not to put yourself in danger."

"All's well that ends well. If I see her again, I'll contact you." Freddie sipped her coffee and glanced at the enamel-faced clock on the corner of her desk. "Detective, I hate to cut short our time together, but I'm due at Bergdorf's."

He stared at her as if she'd spoken in tongues.

"I also write the fashion column."

The detective rose from his seat and smoothed the front of his uniform.

"Forget I ever mentioned that woman, Miss Archer."

What a quaint notion. Freddie wrinkled her nose and shook her head.

"If you see her, stay away."

"If I were a man, would you say that?"

He scowled at cap-toed boots the size of panettone loaves from that heavenly Italian bakery on Mulberry Street, the one with the delectable sfogliatelle (surely the angels had a hand) whose name she couldn't pronounce for money, marbles, or chalk.

Men never took her seriously. Freddie gave a tight smile. "I thought not. If I see her again, I'll let you know." She picked up her handbag, a suede hexagon the same delicate shade as Annie's cheeks. The color exactly matched the roses woven into the crêpe de chine of her dress. Her straw boater had a medium-wide brim and sported a grosgrain band of the same pink. With the hat settled atop her bob, she slipped from behind the desk. "If you'll excuse me?"

"I mean it."

"That you wouldn't warn off a man?"

"That this is too dangerous for a lady."

Freddie grinned. "I'm rotten about taking advice. Ask anyone. They'll confirm. Ask Annie!" There, she'd provided the detective with a reason to linger. "If someone tells me not to do something, I'm honor-bound to give it a go."

"So you'll ignore my warning?"

"I promise not to follow anyone into a midnight park."

"That woman is now linked to two deaths. How about you promise to stay away from her?"

"I never make promises I can't keep." Freddie breezed past Annie with a finger waggle. "I'll be back after lunch."

"The mail—"

"Can wait till later," Freddie called over her shoulder.

The office elevator moved slower than a glacier and was kept running by yet another disapproving attendant. Did elevator attendants have a club? One where they traded notes about young women who went out too often and drank too much?

Since a quick exit seemed prudent, Freddie skipped the slow ride and reproachful glare and took the stairs. The skip in her step would not be denied, and she reached the ground floor in minutes.

Outside, the last vestiges of morning wilted in the rising heat. Another scorcher.

She had a choice—walk in the fry-an-egg-on-the-sidewalk heat or hail a taxi. The choice was an easy one. She waved, and a taxi pulled to the curb. "Bergdorf's," she told the driver.

"Lady, that's four blocks." A whiny cabbie—just what she needed.

"I'll make it worth your while."

The man, who smelled of stale sweat and garlic, grunted, and Freddie slipped into the back seat.

With a sharp jerk of the wheel, the cabbie cut off a Packard and entered the stream of traffic. "Hot enough for you?"

"One dreams of a week at the shore."

"I'd settle for a cold beer, a dim bar, and a ceiling fan."

Their gazes caught in the rearview mirror, and they smiled—

two New Yorkers trapped in a concrete furnace. They understood each other.

Four blocks later, Freddie paid the fare and added a generous tip.

"I hope you get your week at the shore," he said.

"I hope you get your cold beer." His chances were far better than hers. She closed the door, and he drove away.

Freddie smoothed her skirt, entered Bergdorf's, and dawdled near the perfume counter. After the cabbie's pungent aroma, the elegant store's scented air was as welcome as a cool shower. A contented smile touched her lips. She adored New York in all its guises, but on a hot day, she could think of no better place to be than here.

"Miss Archer." Gwen Arnot, the head of the millinery department, joined Freddie at the perfume counter. "Welcome."

"Thank you." Freddie sniffed a bottle of Molinard Habanita.

Together, she and Gwen wandered to the makeup counter, and Freddie eyed a tube of lipstick. "When I was a girl, my mother assured me red lipstick and rouge were reserved for the demimonde. I'm so glad she was wrong."

Miss Arnot, who was at least a decade past the bloom of youth, nodded. "Smoke and mirrors, my dear. Smoke and mirrors."

"As you say. I believe you have hats to show me?"

"All from France. They'll be the rage this fall."

"I can't resist a good chapeau. Lead the way." Freddie followed the older woman toward the elevator, but her gaze snagged on a dark blond head. Was it the woman from last night? Or was she imagining things? She slowed her steps and craned her neck.

Gwen Arnot paused, glanced over her shoulder, and raised a single brow. (Did everyone know that trick?) "See something?"

"More like someone. Who's the woman sniffing at the Shiseido counter?"

"Haven't the slightest. Hats?"

This appointment had been on her calendar for weeks. Freddie couldn't hare after a mysterious woman, not if she wanted to maintain friendly relations with one of the magazine's biggest advertisers. With leaden feet, she followed Gwen Arnot to millinery nirvana, but her thoughts remained on the first floor with the blonde holding the powder puff.

CHAPTER 5

Death, taxes, and new hats for fall. These are the things on which a woman may depend.

A morning spent in the millinery department at Bergdorf's reveals other universal truths. To wit, ladies with round faces should choose hats with tall feathers. Ladies with generous noses may balance their visages with decoration placed in the center of their hats. A strategic cluster of grapes, a generous sprig of bittersweet, or a daring gold buckle should do nicely. Failing decoration, such ladies should opt for a fold-up brim. Blondes, both bottled and natural, look best with a down-turned brim. Dark-haired ladies should choose brimless hats. No matter the style, ladies will find a dizzying range of choices at Bergdorf's. Felt, feathers, boiled wool…

FREDDIE'S FINGERS STILLED. COULD she really write about boiled wool when the weather was hotter than blue blazes?

She could not. She pulled the offending column from her typewriter, crumpled it into a ball, and added it to an already overflowing wastepaper basket. Only then did she glance at her watch and gasp.

The column would have to wait. She collected her handbag, donned her hat (no excess decoration), and breezed through the magazine's nearly empty office. When the five o'clock bell rang, the place emptied faster than a speakeasy with Izzy Einstein at the door. The Prohibition agent, who'd earned notoriety for his disguises and the number of barkeeps he'd arrested, could clear a room in a heartbeat.

"Freddie." Gus, *Gotham*'s owner and publisher, stopped her. "Where to tonight?"

"Dinner. Dancing." She'd offered the same answer a hundred times before.

He nodded, clearly expecting her response. "We have a new advertiser. Club Monaco."

"I'll add it to the itinerary for later this week." As a relatively new magazine, *Gotham* bent over backward accommodating businesses willing to buy space on its pages.

"Don't do anything I wouldn't do."

"Gus, if I followed that advice, the column would be as interesting as yesterday's meatloaf."

"I like meatloaf."

"You're making my point for me."

Gus winced, and Freddie offered him an airy wave before she stepped into the elevator.

At home, she turned on the oscillating and ceiling fans and tuned the radio to Wendell Hall's *Eveready Hour*. The fan blades whirred loud enough to almost drown out the noises from the street below. The music hid the rest. Only the occasional blare of car horns breached the open windows.

Did she have time to bathe? She did not.

Instead she filled a basin with cool water and sponged away the day's grit. Then she changed into an evening gown, powdered her nose, refreshed the kohl around her eyes, applied lipstick, and dabbed Shalimar behind her ears and at her wrists. Her sleek bob required little—just a quick run-through with a comb.

Freddie offered her reflection a nod of approval. She wasn't stop-men-in-the-street gorgeous like her friend Tallulah, but she got by.

A knock on the door sent her heart stuttering. Dinner and dancing. Just dinner and dancing. Not a grand romance. Not an evening spent tangled in linen bedsheets. Not a crossroads. Not a turning point. Not a change in the tenor of her life. So why was she nervous? She took a restorative breath before flipping the lock and turning the handle.

Brandt Abrams stood on the other side. Even more handsome than she remembered, he held out a bouquet.

She accepted the flowers and inhaled their sweet scent. "Thank you. They're divine. Come in. Fix yourself a drink while I put these in water." Her voice was too high.

Get hold of yourself. He's just a man. The rational side of her brain had spoken.

A gorgeous man! replied the side that kept her out dancing until four in the morning, encouraged her to have one more drink, and thought climbing Nashes and chasing possible murderers was an exciting proposition.

She left him alone in the living room, where a beige velvet chesterfield and channel-back chairs upholstered in cream damask invited lounging, hardworking fans rustled the new drapes (a smart scallop pattern), and bottles of gin and scotch and two glasses waited next to a soda siphon on the brass bar cart.

In the kitchen, Freddie turned on the tap at the kitchen sink, stuck a Lalique vase into the stream of water, and slowed her breathing. Brandt Abrams was undeniably handsome, but looks alone weren't enough to make her respond this way. There was something about him that made her toes curl and her mouth water.

"May I fix you one?" he called.

"Please. Scotch with a splash of seltzer."

"Mind if I change the radio station?"

"Be my guest."

Brandt fiddled with the radio, and the romantic notes of "Clair de Lune" replaced Wendell Hall.

She leaned against the counter and forced a deep breath before carrying the vase to the living room, where she shifted the bouquet on the mirrored coffee table to a chest slotted between two floor-to-ceiling windows. She centered Brandt's flowers on the coffee table. "The flowers are gorgeous."

Brandt handed her a drink, and she pretended not to notice the tinge of electricity when their fingers touched.

"Cheers." He touched the rim of his glass to hers. "Nice place you've got here."

"It's home." The apartment was larger and more luxurious than her *Gotham* salary provided. She afforded it thanks to a trust from her grandfather.

He moved among her things, pausing to stare at a photograph in a sterling silver frame, frown at a Paul Klee painting, and then glance at his reflection in a sunburst mirror. "Not what I expected."

"What did you expect?"

"I don't know." He rubbed his chin. "Bohemia with a wild mix of colors, not Art Deco chic. Not gold and beige and cream."

"Have you been to the Paris Opera?"

"I've not had the pleasure."

"When one enters the Palais Garnier, there are no colors. Only cream and gold. It's a setting for the women who attend the opera. Their dresses and smiles lend éclat. People and fashion give the building life." She smoothed her lapis silk dress over her hips and offered a self-conscious smile. "I wanted the same in my home."

"Most women wouldn't admit that."

"Admit what?"

"That they've staged their apartment to show themselves off to the best advantage."

Men weren't usually that perceptive. She'd have to watch herself with this one. "I'm not most women."

"I'm beginning to see that." His voice was approving, and something deep inside her warmed. "Freddie is an unusual name."

"I blame my brother." She nodded toward the framed photograph. "My parents brought me home from the hospital and introduced me as Winnie. Gray told them horses whinny. He named me Freddie."

"Dotty was telling the truth? Your given name is really Winnifred? I would have guessed something more exotic."

"Like Zelda?"

His lips quirked, and he sipped his drink. "You know the Fitzgeralds?"

"I go fountain hopping with them every Tuesday."

He grinned. "Really? I race cars down Fifth Avenue with them every other Thursday at midnight."

"For your sake, I hope Zelda's driving."

"Oh?"

"She might be reckless, but at midnight, chances are Scott is lit like a Christmas tree."

"You really do know them."

It wasn't as if she and Zelda shared secrets or spent much time together, but the Fitzgeralds were good fun, especially when Scott's writing was going well. Freddie had spent many an evening with them. But if she explained that, she'd be no better than the men her mother dragged to dinner—men who dropped names like Carnegie and Rockefeller in a bid to impress her. "We share friends."

A shadow passed over Brandt's face.

Oh, dear. She swallowed. "I'm sorry about your friend."

Brandt stared at the drink in his hands. "Ewan was a good man. A good friend. He left a wife and son."

What could she say that wasn't trite? "Do the police know who killed him?"

"No." He drained his glass and stood. "Shall we? I made reservations at Antoine's." His message was clear—Ewan's death was not a topic for conversation.

Antoine's dining room had mirrored walls. Above the mirrors, oscillating fans moved humid air. Intimate tables covered in crisp white linen, silver chairs, and enormous urns filled with showy flowers sat on a burgundy carpet. Chandeliers hung at regular intervals from a ceiling painted the same silver as the chairs. The place was shiny and chic and served decent food. Freddie had written about it once and never bothered to return.

They perused the menu and ordered dinner and a bottle of champagne.

Freddie sipped the wine. "I didn't realize Antoine's served liquor." The placed had been positively arid on her last visit.

Brandt gave a subtle nod toward a man several tables away, and Freddie followed his gaze. "That's Senator Wadsworth."

The senator had a drink in his hand, and he gave Brandt a friendly nod. Then his gaze shifted to her. He smiled, stood, and approached their table. "Freddie, what a pleasure."

"Senator." She stood (one stood for a senator) and offered her cheek for a kiss.

His lips barely brushed her skin. "How is your dear mother?"

"Dear as always."

"Please, give her my regards." The senator held out his hand to Brandt, who'd also risen from the table, and the two shook. "Abrams, nice to see you."

"Thank you, sir. Likewise."

"I won't keep you from your dinner. Not when you're in such charming company." The senator offered a benevolent smile before returning to his table.

When the politician's back turned, Brandt sank to his chair. "Is there anyone you don't know?"

"Scads of people. Until this week, I didn't know you." She sat, picked up her fork, and ate a bite of steak au poivre.

"It's nice to be with a woman who eats."

"Women eat." She was blessed with an enviable metabolism.

"Women pick."

Freddie grinned. "If I get hungry, I can be difficult. You've been warned."

"Define difficult."

"Cantankerous."

"Sounds terrifying. I'll endeavor to keep you fed."

Their gazes caught, and Freddie saw a flicker of flame that

could all too easily turn into an inferno. She glanced at her lap. "Where are you from?"

"How do you know I'm not a New Yorker?"

"Your tuxedo. It's from Henry Poole."

"How can you tell? And what difference does that make?"

"I can tell because I write about fashion. I go to Paris and visit ateliers. I go to London and visit tailors. I go to Italy and visit cobblers. As for the difference, New Yorkers buy local. Not from Savile Row."

"I'm from St. Louis."

"What brought you here?"

"Four years in New Haven."

"Ah."

"You don't date Elis?"

She stared at him over the rim of her champagne flute. "We seldom want the same things."

"What is it you want?"

To be treated as an equal. "We're not talking about me. Is that how you know the senator? From Yale?"

"Senator Wadsworth graduated before I arrived on campus."

"That's not an answer. Yale is positively riddled with secret societies, and their influence reaches well beyond graduation." Skull and Bones, Scroll and Key, and Wolf's Head—they all sounded vaguely menacing. "You could meet at midnight and dance around a pentagram."

Brandt sipped his drink and didn't reply.

Aha! He was in a society. "What did you study?"

"Economics and philosophy."

"An interesting combination."

He flashed a smile that made that flicker of fire burn brighter. "I'm an interesting man."

He was a dangerous man. Too handsome for his own good—or hers. Too smart. Too articulate. Too perceptive. "That remains to be seen."

"Dessert?"

"No, thank you."

"You don't have a sweet tooth?"

"I enjoy the occasional sidecar."

"So you can't be tempted with upside-down cake or Neapolitan ice cream?"

He could tempt her, but not with sugar. "Not tonight." True for so many things.

"There's a new club I thought you might enjoy."

"I do enjoy new clubs."

"Shall we?" He stood.

Freddie waited for Brandt to pull out her chair, and then rose to her feet.

"I hope you enjoyed dinner." Brandt's breath tickled her ear, and his fingers lingered at her bare elbow. "I fear I talked more than I listened."

Men loved explaining things—the stock market, baseball, why the Eighteenth Amendment should be repealed. But Brandt hadn't been dull. The opposite. He'd been fascinating. "I enjoyed every moment," she told him.

"You heard all my secrets." An intimate smile touched his lips. "And all I learned about you was the importance of keeping you fed."

"Trust me, it's an important thing to know."

"Give me a secret." His dark eyes danced.

"I have no secrets." She placed her hands on her heart as if she were sincere. "And I doubt we scratched the surface of yours."

"I suspect you have more secrets than Mata Hari. How do you spend your days?"

"You know that. I'm a writer. And you? Sneaking barrels of beer past government agents?"

"I spend my days with ledgers, in meetings, negotiating contracts."

They stepped outside, and Brandt hailed a yellow taxi. When they'd settled in the back, he gave the cabbie an address on West 52nd Street.

"Sounds dull for a bootlegger," Freddie teased.

"My work is nothing interesting."

"Now who's keeping secrets?"

"If I remain mysterious, perhaps you'll dine with me again."

The fire flickered between them. More than flickered. It burned hot enough to incinerate the taxi's back seat. The driver, unaware of his Checker cab's impending immolation, pulled to the curb and stated the fare.

Brandt handed over a few dollars and helped Freddie to the sidewalk.

She tilted her head and studied the buildings. "Lead the way." Maybe after a drink or two or three, they'd wander next door to Tony's, where Dotty Parker and Robert Benchley often landed in the wee hours.

Brandt knocked on a nondescript door, and a man with a gimlet eye allowed them entrance.

Freddie took in the nightclub. The discovery of Tutankhamun's tomb had made the whole world mad for all things Egyptian. This club grabbed that insanity by the hand, served it a few drinks, and lifted its skirts. Golden hieroglyphs covered the walls. The furniture was gold. Light fixtures shaped like inverted pyramids hung from a lapis-and-gold-striped ceiling.

The cigarette girls wore kohl on their eyes, Egyptian robes cut acres above their knees, and headdresses fit for a pharaoh.

The club straddled the narrow line between wildly innovative and wildly tasteless and landed on the wrong side.

Freddie grinned. "Who runs this place?"

"Aswan." Brandt nodded toward a man in conversation with a waiter. Aswan had a damp brow, eyes too big for his narrow face, and an industrious air.

"I bet Aswan's real name is Eugene or Humphrey."

"His real name is Charlie."

"I presume he has backers."

Brandt shrugged.

"I presume you're one of the backers." Did Brandt know she wrote for *Gotham*? She used a pen name for her column, but plenty of people knew Touch of Rouge was Freddie Archer. Had Brandt asked her out so she'd write about his club? She hoped not. If Brandt brought her here in hopes of free publicity, he'd be disappointed. This was not her kind of club.

Aswan spotted them, abruptly abandoned the waiter, and rushed to Brandt's side. "Mr. Abrams, what a surprise. If you'll follow me, we have a table waiting for you."

Either it was a surprise or he had a table waiting. It couldn't be both.

Aswan—so much more interesting than Charlie—led them to the front edge of the dance floor. "Champagne?"

"A gin rickey." Freddie needed something stronger than champagne to fully appreciate this madness.

"I'll have the same."

They sat, and Aswan flitted to the bar and hovered like a dragonfly. Then he dashed to the door to greet another patron.

Freddie turned her attention to the band. They played lackadaisical jazz on a gilded stage. "How long has the club been open?"

"Less than a week."

Well-dressed men and women filled the room, and genteel conversations competed with the saxophone's plaintive notes.

A singer, who wore an Egyptian robe fashioned in black chiffon and cinched with a wide gold belt, joined the musicians on stage. The band riffed into their next number, and she sang. Her voice was colored with midnight hues and come-hither promises.

"She's good," said Freddie. Better than good.

A waiter delivered their drinks.

"Cheers." Brandt lifted his glass, and Freddie touched its rim with hers.

Brandt leaned back in his chair. "What do you think about the place?"

"The butter-and-egg crowd will eat it up."

He frowned, and annoyance flashed in his eyes. "Not New Yorkers?"

"It's kitschy. If the owners want New Yorkers to come more than once, they need a better band."

A frown creased Brandt's forehead.

"The singer is good. Actually, she's excellent. But there are hundreds of excellent singers in New York. She's not enough to make this place a destination. What's the name?"

"King Tut's."

"Shorten the name to Tut's. Tone down the gold—"

"I told Ephram to rein it in, but he wouldn't list…" Brandt's eyes narrowed to slits, and he rose from his chair. "Excuse me." He left her before she had a chance to reply.

She watched his back as he strode toward a group of men just inside the entrance.

"May I?" A tuxedoed man stood behind Brandt's chair. He was tall, with an optimistic air and ginger hair.

"My friend will be back in a moment." She didn't need company.

"Brandt? He was a fool to leave such a beautiful woman alone."

"You know Brandt?"

"I'm his business partner." He thrust his right hand at her. "Ephram Loeb."

Ephram, the man who wouldn't rein in the gold. Freddie allowed his fingers to close around hers. "Freddie Archer."

He lifted her hand to his lips, and his eyes sparkled with mischief.

The chanteuse began a new song, and Ephram released her. Freddie tucked her hands in her lap and looked for Brandt.

Ephram's gaze followed hers. Then he muttered a curse and hurried toward his partner.

Freddie watched him walk away, listened to the singer, and began a column.

> *Tut's on 52nd brings a touch of Egypt to Manhattan. Go for the kitsch, stay for—*

She needed the singer's name.

> *Go to ogle the owners, both of whom are sheiks—*

She refocused on the door, where Brandt and Ephram faced five men. Each stranger wore a feral smile that sent shudders down her back.

One of the men reached out and shoved Brandt's shoulder. Another reached into his jacket and pulled out a gun.

The singer's voice broke.

Somewhere in the audience, a woman screamed.

Gunfire erupted.

And Freddie dove under the table.

CHAPTER 6

REDDIE!" BRANDT'S STRONG HANDS pulled her from beneath the table. "Are you hurt?"

Her heart raced faster than Man o' War, and her hands shook. She'd always imagined that she thrived on excitement, but a gun battle wasn't exciting. It was hair-raising.

"Freddie! Talk to me." Brandt gripped her shoulders and shook her gently.

She forced herself to meet his gaze and whispered, "I'm fine."

She wasn't. She'd cowered like a . . . like a coward. The realization was worse than two-day-old coffee, worse than bathtub gin, worse than the morning after bathtub gin.

Around them, women cried, men grumbled and swore, and the scent of gunpowder overwhelmed the smell of cigarette smoke and spilled hooch.

Brandt cupped her elbow. "Let's get you out of here."

"What happened?"

"We got lucky. Let's go before the police arrive."

He was right. They should leave. But Freddie couldn't move

her feet. They'd grown icy roots and were permanently attached to King Tut's floor.

Better to blame her feet than admit her knees wobbled too much to take a single step.

"Freddie?" Brandt tugged on her arm.

She took a step—a small one—and buckled.

He swept her into his arms, as if she were a bride and they were crossing their threshold for the first time, as if he were Valentino and she were Agnes Ayres, as if they were living in a Jane Austen story. Then he strode toward the door. "I've got you."

Freddie rested her cheek against his chest and listened to his heartbeat. Its rhythm was steady, even calming. The gunshots, the panicked people—they didn't affect Brandt. He radiated unwavering strength, and the ice in her limbs melted. "Where's Ephram?"

"Dealing with this mess."

This mess? Her gaze snagged on a man on the floor surrounded by a pool of blood—the man who'd drawn his gun—and all the breath whooshed from her lungs. "Oh."

"Don't look." Brandt dropped a kiss on her head. "It's not your problem."

A man died, and it wasn't her problem. So simple. So wrong. "You and Ephram—" She squeezed her eyes shut. "What happened?"

"Someone doesn't appreciate competition." Brandt stepped outside and gently lowered Freddie's feet to the sidewalk. "Are you okay to stand?" His right arm circled her waist, offering support.

She drew warm, humid air into her lungs and tested her knees. They felt limp, as if her bones had hopped a jitney, leaving the rest of her as a spineless lump. "Who shot that man?" And why was it, every time she saw Brandt Abrams, someone died?

Brandt's face darkened. "Ephram. A clear case of self-defense."

Did Ephram regularly carry a gun, or had he expected trouble? "What kind of competition?" King Tut was a vulgar flash in the pan. No self-respecting club owner would consider the Egyptian-themed boîte competition. Whoever sent those men, it wasn't the competition. "Did Charlie—Aswan—forget a protection payment?"

Brandt scowled. "No."

She believed him. Or she believed the scowl. She pressed her fingers to her temples. A mighty headache built behind her eyes, one that would require a dark room, a cool cloth draped across her forehead, and a bottle of aspirin. But pain didn't stop her from thinking. The club wasn't competition, nor was it delinquent on protection payments. That left one option. She already knew Brandt and his partner were bootleggers. Another bootlegger had sent those men.

An hour ago, she would have found that dreadfully exciting. With the dead man not yet cold, she found it dreadful.

"I need to help Ephram. Shall I call a taxi to take you home?"

She hadn't been home before midnight in weeks. Maybe months. That long line of near sleepless nights coupled with sudden death weighed so heavily on her shoulders that she lacked the strength to shrug. "Please."

Brandt's lips thinned. "This isn't what I planned for tonight. May I take you to dinner later this week?" He stared into her eyes. "No Egyptians, no dead men. Just a meal and dancing. I'll let you pick the nightclub."

The man attracted violence. Being near him was dangerous. He was dangerous. Why did she nod? Temporary madness made her say, "Most clubs are closed for the summer, but I hear Tex is in town." Tex Guinan ran nightclubs. Fun nightclubs. Clubs that drew real New Yorkers in droves. Tex welcomed her guests with a twangy "Hello, suckers" and kept them laughing and dancing and drinking until the sun rose. "We could try her new place."

"Are you free Friday night?"

She didn't let herself think. "Yes."

Brandt hailed a cab, and when a taxi pulled to the curb, he opened the back door.

Freddie slid inside.

Brandt leaned in and brushed a quick kiss across her cheek. "I'll pick you up on Friday. Eight o'clock."

"Where to?" asked the cabbie.

Brandt gave him Freddie's address and closed her door.

Freddie rested her head on the seat, closed her eyes, and composed a column.

> *A night in the city holds untold delights—the jazz band at the Cotton Club, a perfect dinner at 21, the breeze off the Hudson at a rooftop party where one sips refreshing potions and flirts with an Eli. The darkness also holds staggering risks. If one is caught in a dangerous situation—and by dangerous situation, I mean a bootlegger's turf war—one should look for a sturdy table under which to hide . . .*

She'd made a resolution about running toward trouble, but when push came to shove, she'd dropped to the floor like a faint-hearted bird. Worse, the column in her head actually recommended such craven behavior. She moaned.

"You gonna toss your cookies?" Suspicion laced the cabbie's rough voice.

"No." She closed her eyes.

"Cause it's extra if I gotta clean the taxi."

"I won't be sick." The headache had taken a firm hold, but her stomach remained strong.

Freddie sat with Tallulah Bankhead at a rooftop restaurant and sipped gin rickeys. The view was spectacular—the city's lights sparkled on the Hudson's dark water like a chorus girl's costume. A soft breeze made the lingering heat bearable.

"What did you do last night?" asked Tallulah.

"Stayed home and read a book."

"You're a laugh riot." Tallulah didn't sound remotely amused.

"I try." She'd arrived home, swallowed three aspirin, and, unable to sleep, read until her lids grew heavy.

Tallulah narrowed her eyes. "What did you read?"

"*The Constant Nymph.* When do you leave for London?" Tallulah was set to star in a new play on the West End.

"Two and a half weeks."

"Can't you find a show on Broadway?" Freddie hated that an ocean would soon separate them.

"It's a good play," Tallulah replied. "A great role."

"A challenge?"

The actress offered her signature kitten smile. Wicked, flirtatious, and wise beyond its years, the smile attracted men like real scotch attracted serious drinkers. "I do love a challenge. Now, spill the beans. You didn't stay home and read. What happened?"

"I came home early."

"From where?" Tallulah wouldn't give up until Freddie gave her a satisfactory answer.

"I went out with a man called Brandt Abrams."

"Abrams?" Tallulah frowned. "Does your mother know?" As

the daughter of a US congressman and the granddaughter of a US senator, Tallulah understood family pressures. She'd responded to those pressures by embracing her sexuality. Openly and often. With both men and women. She wrinkled her nose, and her lips twisted in a wry smile. "I can't imagine she'll be pleased."

"I don't care if he's Jewish."

"Your mother will." In that, Tallulah was one hundred percent correct.

"She's not the one dating him."

Tallulah's dark blue eyes widened. "You're going out with him again?"

"Yes."

"If you like him well enough to go on a second date, why come home early? Wait." She rubbed her hands in wicked delight. "Did he come home with you, or did you go to his place?"

"Neither."

After what she'd gone through with Nick, did Tallulah think she'd immediately hop into another man's bed? Of course she did. Tallulah regularly slept in beds not her own. Dotty said Tallulah was as pure as the driven slush. An assessment Freddie found harsh and Tallulah found amusing. So amusing she'd claimed the description was hers. Dotty had merely shrugged and said that plagiarism was the least of Tallulah's sins.

"There was a shooting."

"How thrilling!" Tallulah rested her elbows on the table and leaned forward. "Tell me more."

The evening had not been thrilling. Not in the way Tallulah meant. "It was terrifying."

"What happened?" Tallulah insisted.

"Brandt took me to a terrible new club on 52nd."

"That dreadful Egyptian place? Everyone's going now so they can crow about how appalling it was when it closes."

"That's the one."

"A shooting? What happened?"

There was no reason not to tell Tallulah about Brandt and Ephram and the details of the shooting, but sharing Brandt's business felt wrong—almost like a betrayal. "A man died."

Rather than press for details, Tallulah's eyes narrowed, and she made a moue of distaste.

Freddie resisted turning in her chair to see who'd put the look on her friend's face. "Who?"

"If I were with anyone but you, I'd make a run for the powder room." When she was angry or worried, the elocution lessons that kept Tallulah's Alabama accent in check failed her. Right now, she sounded as Southern as grits and sweet tea.

Dread settled in Freddie's stomach. "Is it Nick?"

"Worse."

What—who—could be worse than Nick with some gorgeous actress hanging on his arm?

Before she could ask, the kitten smile returned to Tallulah's beautiful face. Her eyes glinted brighter than a knife's edge. Her honey colored hair crackled with Medusa-like energy.

"Freddie."

She looked up into John Burcham's smiling face and understood Tallulah's reaction. The two had a history. Tallulah felt about John the way she felt about Nick.

Freddie offered her cheek for a kiss.

"It's been too long." His lips brushed her skin, and then he cast a quick glance at Tallulah, whose eyes promised death by glare. "May I join you?"

Only if he wanted to die. "Tallulah and I planned on a night out together."

"Tallulah." His voice was a gentle caress.

"John." Her voice was an ice pick between the ribs.

John waved at a waiter. "We need another chair." He took in their dismayed expressions, held up his hands, and spread his fingers. "I'll only take a few minutes. We need to talk."

To Tallulah or her? Freddie shifted in her chair. John and her brother, Gray, were childhood friends. They'd been inseparable for twenty years. They'd even gone to war together. John came back alone, bearing the weight of a solemn vow to Gray. He'd pledged to take Gray's place as a big brother. It was an oath John took seriously.

That vow gave him leave to scold Freddie about the length of her skirts, the number of cigarettes she smoked, the cocktails she drank, and the men she dated. Like her mother, John wanted her safely married. Then her late nights and wild lifestyle would be her husband's problem. Not his.

He scowled at her nearly empty glass. "How many drinks tonight?"

If Gray were alive and dared suggest she drank too much, she'd have socked him in the gut. When he finished wheezing, she'd have told him to mind his own potatoes.

But Gray was gone, and John wasn't her brother. Much as she wanted to, she couldn't punch him for honoring Gray's dying wish. Freddie downed a large sip of lime-flavored gin and kept mum.

The waiter returned with a gilded Chiavari chair, and John sat.

An awkward silence settled around the table.

Freddie glanced at her friend and saw Tallulah mentally catalog the numerous ways she might murder the man now sitting with them—bullet, knife, garotte, bad hooch. This situation required more gin. She stopped the waiter with a smile and pointed to her glass. Then she ignored John's judgmental frown and asked, "How's work?" John reported for the *Daily Star*.

"Fine." John fiddled with his necktie. "Fine."

Two fines? Whatever he wanted to talk about made his collar too tight. Freddie fisted her hand in her lap. No matter what he said, no matter how offensive, she wouldn't slug him. Would not.

John somehow avoided the daggers shooting from Tallulah's eyes and focused solely on Freddie. "I heard you've been out on the town every night since you and Peters split."

The decision not to punch him had been premature. "I get paid to go out. It's what I do."

"Is that wise?"

Wise? Nope. The opposite. But liquor and music and dancing and laughter acted as a balm for her bruised soul. She didn't say that. John didn't get to see her pain. He'd use it against her. He foolishly believed that happily married women didn't get their hearts broken.

John cleared his throat and stared at his hands. "I also heard you went out with Brandt Abrams."

How on earth did he know that?

"What if she did?" Tallulah demanded.

John shifted his gaze to Tallulah. "Abrams is bad news. Dangerous."

And how.

The waiter delivered a fresh gin rickey, and Freddie murmured her thanks.

"Anything for you, sir?"

"He's not staying," Tallulah replied.

John watched the waiter's disappearing back before turning

his gaze to the two drinks now sitting in front of Freddie. "Gray wouldn't want this for you." John did guilt better than her mother. It was as if he'd taken lessons in making her feel small. "Gray would disapprove of Abrams. And not because he's Jewish."

"Why?" If John knew about the shooting, she'd never hear the end of it. He must have a different reason.

John folded his arms over his chest and did his best impression of a mule.

She studied him—dark blond hair, handsome face, piercing blue eyes, broad shoulders. "How would you react if someone questioned your every decision?"

He blinked.

"How would you react if someone monitored your scotch consumption, how many cigars you smoke, the dollars you gamble on baseball games and horse races?"

His expression hardened. "I gave Gray a promise. Besides, it's different."

"What's different?"

"You're a woman. You need a man looking out for you."

She breathed deeply. Why did men assume women were helpless? "Tallulah, what did you ever see in him?" Annoyance lent her voice a sharp edge.

Tallulah tapped her chin. "I don't remember."

John flushed. "I'm just—"

"I have a job. And I'm good at it."

"She's very good," said Tallulah.

"I have scores of friends. I have—"

"You float from party to party. You spend money faster than the government can print it." John scowled at her Carmaux frock (a deep rose embroidered with gold thread, gold lamé vents, and a rhinestone buckle at the hip) as if the silk covering her body might send her to the poorhouse. "You have a new wardrobe with each season. Who needs so many dresses?"

"John. Darling." The way Tallulah said *darling* made him wince. "Without Freddie, there is no *Gotham*. She sells that magazine. Women in Paducah and Wichita and Phoenix buy a magazine about a city they may never visit so they can read Freddie's pieces about places they'll never go." Tallulah's hand tapped the table. "Places like this one. She's sophisticated and fun and funny."

I flashed a grateful grin her way.

"They read her fashion column because they trust her to tell them what to wear. Freddie's wardrobe is a business expense." The kittenish smile sharpened. "Be warned, any woman you bamboozle into marrying you will want new clothes come winter, spring, summer, and fall. Prepare your bank account, because your wife won't get the discounts Freddie enjoys."

"I made Gray a promise." John's expression matched his tone—pure mule. He refused to change his mind.

"John, Gray was my brother, not my jailer. If he were alive, he'd be visiting clubs and speakeasies with me." Maybe. Gray could be overly protective. He would have hated Nick and forbidden her from seeing Brandt. But this was her life. She deserved the right to make her own decisions. Her own mistakes.

"Gray wouldn't approve, Freddie. Not of the liquor or the wardrobe or the men."

"Perhaps," she ceded. "But this is my life, not his." And she refused to change because a man told her to.

CHAPTER 7

Gus lifted his gaze from the paper centered on his desk and adjusted his reading glasses. "How do you do it?"

Freddie, who sat across from him with her ankles crossed, her hands folded in her lap, and an active pickax in her skull, replied, "Do what?"

"This." He tapped the page. "It's funny, arch, exciting. You and Tallulah went to six speakeasies. Six. How you can live such a chaotic life and write columns like this one is the great mystery of our time."

No one spoke to Scott Fitzgerald like this, and he drank gallons more than she did. Also, she and Tallulah had visited eight speakeasies, not six. Freddie kept those thoughts to herself.

"Life in New York is infinitely more amusing after two thirty. That's when the professionals arrive and one hopes for impromptu entertainment. Dancers, singers, comedians—they come into their own in the wee small hours." Gus looked up from reading her column aloud. "It tempts me to stay out late." He frowned at her. "Did you sleep in your office again?"

How could he tell? True, she'd finished her column at five and collapsed on the divan, but she'd taken the time for a sponge bath and wore a fresh dress. "Why do you ask?"

"You look pale."

She felt pale, like a ghost of herself. "I'm fine. Never better." Such a lie. The pickax was making headway.

Gus pursed his lips and rubbed his chin. "When did you last take a vacation?"

The pickax hit a particularly sensitive neuron, and Freddie winced.

He stared at her for long seconds and then rubbed his eyes. "Go to the beach. Take a trip to the mountains."

If Gus was urging her to take time off, she must look truly dreadful.

"I'm fine." The city was hotter than a blast furnace. Sleep eluded her. And the only thing she looked forward to was an evening with Brandt Abrams. Any sane woman would run to the beach faster than Paavo Nurmi (the Olympian wasn't called the Flying Finn because he was slow). Maybe she wasn't sane. She didn't want to leave New York. She had the oddest feeling that something was about to happen. "I have plans to go to the Hamptons for the holiday."

Gus steepled his fingers. "I'm worried about you."

"About me?"

"Your nights are wilder than ever, and there are rumors..." He flushed.

"Rumors?"

Gus rubbed the back of his neck, fiddled with his glasses, and arranged the red pens stuck in the coffee mug at his elbow. "About you and—"

Tap, tap.

"Come in!" Gus sounded relieved, as if he preferred not to answer her question.

Freddie preferred that, too. She had a horrible feeling the rumors he referenced were about Brandt, and she didn't have the patience for another lecture, not even if the lecture came from her boss.

Berta, Gus's prune pit of a secretary, opened the door and simpered into the office. Simpering usually meant to smile in a self-conscious way to impress a man. But Berta didn't just simper with her lips. Her whole body simpered. "There's a call, sir."

"Who is it?"

The glance Berta gave Freddie was spiteful. "A Detective Sullivan, sir. For Miss Archer." Venom snuck into Berta's tone. She didn't approve of Freddie, or any other woman who wore short skirts, drank gin, or frequented nightclubs. Which was rich given that Freddie avoided flirting with married men, and Berta simpered for the very-married Gus's benefit.

Bushy brows met above Gus's nose. "Freddie, are you in trouble?"

Despite the sudden appearance of lead weights in her stomach, Freddie's answering smile was light. Even airy. "Me? Never."

The silence following that whopper stretched like a lazy cat in a patch of sunshine.

"He says it's important." Berta's eyes glittered. Excitement? Curiosity? Malicious joy that Freddie's nightly wanderings had landed her in the soup?

Freddie stood. Slowly. Any sudden move might topple her head from her neck. That, or the pickax might finally hit her brain stem. "I'd better talk to him."

"What's this about?" Gus demanded.

"The murder at the Village Inn."

"That was days ago."

If she could have shrugged, she would have. Instead, she grimaced and walked to the door.

"Wait." Gus's voice stopped her, and she turned and clasped the door frame.

He cleared his throat, and Freddie tightened her grip. If Gus lectured her about Brandt, she'd demand to know what gave him the right to question her choices, a response that might bode ill for her future employment.

"Ellis and Ring Lardner are having a party tonight. Virginia and I are going. You should come with us."

Relief flooded her veins—he'd decided not to meddle. "That sounds delightful." Ellis and Ring threw fabulous parties, and Gus's wife was great fun.

"We'll pick you up at seven."

Freddie hurried to her office and picked up the phone. "Detective Sullivan? I apologize for keeping you waiting."

"Good morning, Miss Archer."

Was it her imagination or did he sound annoyed? She sank into her chair, reached for the glass of water on the corner of her desk (God bless Annie), and drained it dry. "I haven't seen her."

He answered with silence.

What did he expect? New York was a big city. The chances she'd spot the woman a third time were slim. Freddie glanced at her watch. Nearly noon. No wonder she felt peckish. If she asked nicely, Annie might run to the deli on—

"Were you or were you not at King Tut's during a shooting?"

The water she'd just drunk swirled in her stomach, but when

she swallowed, her mouth was dry. This was a conversation best had when she could hit on all six. Not now. Not when she'd spent last night zozzled. Not when her head hurt worse than fifteen rounds with Jack Dempsey. "I was there."

"You didn't think to tell me?"

She could imagine Detective Sullivan at his desk in a room filled with suspicious men—men like him. "I didn't see anything of interest."

"Oh?"

"I hid under a table."

"What did you see before you hid?"

"Five men came in. They looked dangerous."

"So dangerous you decided to hide?"

Her stomach revolted, and she used her foot to edge the wastepaper basket closer. Just in case. "One pulled a gun. Taking cover seemed a wise idea."

Detective Sullivan's mistrust traveled the phone line and poked her in the chest.

"You'd have preferred I stand in the corner and take notes?"

He grunted. "Five men, you say? What did they look like?"

"Thugs."

"I need more detail."

Fair enough. "Dark hair and olive skin. Two were tall. One was short. Three wore suits. Rough looking. I never saw any of them before."

"Italian?"

"Maybe. I didn't hear them speak."

"But you noticed them walk in."

"Yes."

"Why?" His *why* sounded more like *aha!*

"What do you mean?" Freddie rubbed a gentle circle at her temple. This conversation would be much easier without a pounding headache.

"Did you notice everyone who entered?"

"No," she admitted.

"So why did you notice them?"

Because Brandt strode toward them. And Brandt had a habit of striding toward trouble. "I don't know why I noticed them, Detective. I just did." She took a breath and closed her eyes. "It was a couples sort of nightclub. Five men without women was unusual."

"Who accompanied you to the club?"

She'd practically invited the question, but a discussion with a police detective about Brandt Abrams ranked low on her list of things to do today. "A friend."

She heard his scowl. It sounded like boulders crashing against each other beneath a storm-tossed sky. "What friend?"

"Oh dear. Someone just stepped into my office." The lie came easily (she'd used it often). "I need to hang up, Detective. If I see the woman again, I'll ring you."

"Miss Archer—"

"Goodbye, Detective." She hung up, leaned back in her chair, and exhaled. Her head ached worse than ever. It threatened to split like Zeus's when Athena sprung from his forehead. There weren't any goddesses lurking in her skull. Just abused gray matter. And the dratted pickax. She groaned her pain.

Maybe Gus had a point. Maybe she should lay off gin for a few days.

Maybe.

Maybe after Ellis and Ring's party.

She crossed her arms on the desk and rested her cheek against them.

"More aspirin?" Annie's voice was so loud that Freddie was certain if she opened her eyes she'd see a bullhorn pressed to her secretary's lips. "Do you want more water?" The woman made elephants seem quiet.

"Please," Freddie mumbled.

"Aspirin or water?"

"Both."

"You shouldn't drink so much."

"Did my mother tell you to say that?"

"No."

"John Burcham? Gus?"

"I'm quite capable of telling you what to do without input."

"Please, tell me tomorrow. Today, be an angel of mercy. I need water, aspirin, and a bacon and egg sandwich."

"You should slow down. Stay in from time to time."

"Maybe," Freddie allowed. Maybe if she drank less gin, she wouldn't have to slow down. Because she couldn't slow down. Not when the next column was due.

They left late enough that the snarl of automobiles headed out of the city wasn't horrendous, merely awful. Gus planted his foot on the gas pedal and wove through traffic as if he were still in the war, evading enemy artillery shells. The good news? He focused on his driving to the exclusion of all else (even asking why a police detective called his favorite columnist). The bad news? One poorly judged turn of the wheel and that columnist would be pushing daisies.

"Gus." Virginia, his wife, kept a vise-like grip on the dash. "Ring won't run out of gin. Must you drive like you're on that track in Indianapolis?"

Her husband grumbled.

"You're scaring Freddie."

Another grumble, but Gus slowed the Cadillac V-63 Phaeton to a reasonable speed. They still arrived at Ellis and Ring's Great Neck home in record time.

Freddie had visited countless beach houses. They tended to be too elegant (as if the owners dreamed of Newport) or too beachy with lobster-themed upholstery and fishing rods used as decor. Ellis and Ring's home was neither. They'd filled their ramshackle house with comfortable shabby furniture, dogs with lolling tongues and metronome tails, and books. Evidence of their four sons was everywhere. There were footballs and golf clubs and baseballs. There were tennis rackets and hockey sticks and catcher's mitts. There were boxing gloves and basketballs and ice skates. There were swim fins, folded beach towels, and enough sand to start a new beach.

Tonight, a chattering crowd gathered on the patio overlooking the bay. The breeze off the water was delicious, and Freddie drew salt-tinged air deep into her lungs and watched a young Lardner (John? James?) slink through the crowd to the buffet table, where he cadged a brownie.

"Freddie!" Ellis Lardner gave her a quick hug. "We're thrilled you came. What are you drinking?"

Her head needed a night without gin. Her abstention had nothing—absolutely nothing—to do with everyone she knew scolding her about her drinking. "Seltzer."

If she'd surprised Ellis, the woman was too good a hostess to show it. "This way." Together, they walked to a table littered with bottles and glasses waiting to be filled.

"You're sure you don't want something stronger?"

"Positive." Freddie accepted a glass of fizzy water. "Thank you."

"You know most everyone. Dotty brought a friend, I can introduce—" A crash cut Ellis's words short, and she scanned the crowd. "Those boys. I hope no one lost a limb. Excuse me." She hurried toward the house.

Left alone, Freddie descended a short flight of stairs and walked onto Ring's dock, where a dinghy and a small sailboat were moored. The temperature so close to the bay was actually pleasant. She stared at the fading sun and sighed her approval.

"Lovely night, isn't it?" A woman dressed in black lounged in the dinghy. "I grew up near the water. Now I live on an island and go for days without seeing anything wetter than the pond in Central Park."

Freddie, whose apartment had a view, clucked her sympathy. "I'm sorry. I didn't notice you there."

The woman lit a cigarette. "I'm Eloise."

"Freddie."

Eloise climbed out of the dinghy and held out a pack of Lucky Strikes.

"No, thank you."

The woman tucked the cigarettes in her purse. "You're a friend of the hosts?"

"I am. You?"

"No. I met them tonight. I came with Dotty and Robert."

"Parker and Benchley."

"The very ones."

"They're dear friends."

"Are you also a writer?"

"I am."

"Poems? Short stories? Books?"

"Columns. For *Gotham*." A quiet pride swelled in her chest. She'd worked hard to get where she was. In a city filled with talented writers, it wasn't enough to be good. She'd had to be great. As a woman, she'd had to work harder, sacrifice more, and fight for every iota of success. She'd earned her job.

"The fashion column?"

"Yes."

"You're a genius! You can make stockings funny."

"Thank you."

"What's new for fall?" Eloise blew a plume of smoke into the night air. "Will hemlines drop?"

"Look for shift dresses in every store on Fifth Avenue. Don't be seduced by a natural waistline. They're as passé as a merry widow." Her mother still held on to several of the outrageous hats, convinced they'd make a return. Perhaps at a costumed event, but never again for everyday wear. "As for hemlines, they'll hover at the knee."

"I should take notes."

"What do you do, Eloise?"

"Entertainment."

"Singer? dancer? Actress?"

"I'm more of a hostess."

"Like Tex?" Tex Guinan had enjoyed a middling career as a film actress. She'd played cowgirls until discovering her true talent lay in running nightclubs.

"You know Tex?"

"She's among my favorite people."

"Mine, too." Eloise was older, on the wrong side of forty, and her dress was too elegant for a party at the Lardners', but she had one of those faces that invited people to like her.

"Freddie?" A too-familiar voice came carried in the dark. She stiffened.

"Problem?" Eloise asked in a whisper.

"My past catches up with me far too often."

"You should run faster."

"In these shoes?"

They both looked down at her delicate pumps. With their slender Spanish heels, running posed a danger.

"Freddie."

Eloise leaned toward her. "We're not staying late. If you need an escape, there's room in the car."

"Freddie!"

She turned. "Hello, Nick." In an ideal world, Nick would have acquired warts, a triple chin, and severe halitosis. The world was not ideal, because Nick Peters was as handsome as ever.

"The offer stands." Eloise offered her a sympathetic grimace and then climbed the stairs to the party.

"What are you doing here?" she demanded. The Lardners were her friends. Nick claimed their theater friends in the split. Except for Tallulah. She and Tallulah had been friends since Tallulah landed in New York. Freddie kept the friends with a literary bent. The Lardners were definitely literary.

"I thought I might see you."

"An excellent reason for you not to come."

"You won't take my calls."

"We have nothing to say."

"Wrong." He glowered at her. "I have plenty to say."

Nick always had plenty to say, but she refused to hear it. "Whisper whatever it is into one of your actress's ears. She'll be ensorcelled."

"Ensorcelled?"

"It's a word." She sounded defensive.

"You're jealous!" His smug grin begged for a punch in the nose.

She took a calming breath. "Of course I'm jealous. Feelings don't disappear at the finish line. They linger." Like barbed wire embedded beneath her skin. She lifted her chin. "Feelings also fade. This time, a year from now, if I see you with half the girls from Ziegfeld Follies, I won't care." She held tight to that vision of the future.

Nick grunted. "I don't believe you."

She shrugged. She didn't care what he believed. By next year, she'd be over him.

"You still care."

"I just said that. Caring doesn't change anything."

"I could make you happy."

"I am not giving up my career."

A scowl darkened his face. "Marry me, and you won't need to work."

"I don't need to work now. I want to work. It gives me a sense of purpose."

He crossed his arms, curled his lip, and looked down his nose. "Your purpose is going to speakeasies?" He'd never taken her job seriously. He considered it a diversion until she married.

"My purpose..." She folded her hand into a fist, the better to punch his perfect patrician nose. "My purpose is writing about music and dancing and gaiety and lightness. After what the world went through, people should remember those things."

"Someone else can do that."

Not with her voice or opinions or viewpoint. "Someone else can produce plays."

"Don't be ridiculous."

"So I make sacrifices, and you don't?"

"It wouldn't be a sacrifice to marry me."

"Your ego is unpardonable."

Nick's eyes flashed with evil intent. That was her only warning. His hands closed around her upper arms, and he pulled her so close that her breasts grazed his chest.

"Let me go."

"You don't mean it. I miss you." His lips crashed against hers. The kiss was a battle of dominance, and she refused to submit.

When she struggled, he held her tighter. She felt the first flutter of fear.

"I know you want me." His erection pressed against her belly.

"Stop."

His lips grazed her jawline. His teeth nibbled at her ear. "You don't have to play hard to get."

Her blood ran cold enough to freeze her toes.

A hundred feet away, a crowd of people danced and drank. Would anyone hear her if she screamed? "Please, Nick. Let me go."

"I don't want to." His voice was husky with moonlight and crashing waves and desire.

She lifted her hands to his chest and pushed. Adrenaline gave her surprising strength. Or maybe she timed her shove just right. Nick loosened his hold and stepped backward. Too bad his step reached beyond the dock. He crashed into the bay.

Suddenly, unexpectedly free, Freddie waited until Nick's head emerged above the water.

His scowl was ferocious. "Dammit, Freddie!"

She had seconds until he dragged himself from the drink. Obviously he blamed her for his current sodden circumstances. Obviously he was furious. And angry Nick was not a nice man. She did the only sensible thing. Despite her Spanish heels, she ran.

CHAPTER 8

COMPARED TO THE WHITE-KNUCKLE trip to Great Neck, the ride back to Manhattan was restful. Robert's Packard Six floated over the road with cloud-like smoothness.

Freddie sat in the back seat with Dotty, who smoked cigarette after cigarette and stared moodily out the open window. The moodiness was not a surprise; the silence was.

"Everything okay?" Freddie asked.

"Positively copacetic." Dotty's dark gaze cut toward the front seat, where Eloise sat next to Robert. "You know what Eloise does, right?"

"Entertainment."

Dotty choked so hard she dropped her cigarette in her lap.

The resulting squeals, patting of black silk, and blue language drew Robert's attention. "What's going on back there?"

"Just a small conflagration," Freddie explained.

"If it were your lap, you wouldn't call it small."

"Hold on to your cigs, Mrs. Parker." Robert's gaze returned to the road.

Freddie refrained from further comment.

Dotty examined the new hole in her dress. She pursed her lips in displeasure and then pulled a flask from her handbag and swigged before offering the liquor to Freddie.

"No, thank you."

Dotty raised her brows. "You're dry now?"

"My liver needs a vacation." They'd all been to that place where the party became painful. Dotty spent every January as dry as a teetotaler. And Robert usually joined her. Apparently, Freddie had arrived at the place where liquor actually hurt seven months early.

Dotty offered a sympathetic grimace. "I couldn't touch a drop for three days last week."

In the front seat, Robert and Eloise chatted loudly, but the wind rushing through the open windows stole four out of every five words. She heard something about a party at Eloise's apartment, but nothing more.

Freddie crossed her fingers and leaned closer to Dotty. "Where does Eloise live?" Midtown or uptown would be a blessing. The very thought of climbing in a cab in SoHo tempted her to ask Robert to drop her home.

"On 75th Street, just off Broadway."

Not awful. A taxi could cut through the park to get her home. Freddie tipped her head toward the front seat. "She's having a party but went to Great Neck?" In Freddie's experience, hostesses usually attended their own parties, but Eloise had abandoned hers to spend a few hours with the Lardners and their guests.

"She hosts parties most every night." Dotty lit a fresh cigarette and studied Freddie with glittering eyes. "Why the hurry to leave Ring's soirée?"

Heat warmed Freddie's cheeks. The satisfaction that came from shoving Nick into the water had faded. Upon reflection, it was not her finest moment. Why couldn't she be like Dotty, who emasculated her former beaux in sinfully funny poems? "I pushed Nick into the bay."

Dotty cocked a brow. "His cuffs got wet?"

Freddie winced. "We were at the end of the dock. A full-body dunk."

Dotty's answering smile transformed her from a pretty woman to a beautiful one. "I'm sure he deserved it."

"And how."

"Was he angry? What did he say?"

Freddie rubbed a hand down her face. "I didn't hang around to find out."

"Smart. You'll come upstairs with us—no, no. Don't argue. You need a bit of fun after the scene at Ring's."

Freddie didn't have it in her to argue.

Robert pulled to the curb in front of a building so new it still looked clean.

A valet stepped forward and opened Eloise's door. "Good evening, Miss Silver."

"Good evening, Gene. Thank you." She approached the gilt and glass front door and waited for her guests.

Gene opened the back passenger door, and Freddie slid across the seat and exited to the sidewalk with Dotty.

Robert got out of the automobile and handed Gene the keys.

They swept into the lobby and followed Eloise to the elevator. The attendant pushed the button for the top floor. "I have the top three floors," Eloise explained.

Freddie eyed Eloise's dress (pretty, but not couture), jewels (so large they had to be paste), and makeup (overplucked brows and green and purple shadow applied so heavily her eyes looked bruised). Her hostess didn't have the air of a fabulously wealthy woman. "How long have you lived here?"

Eloise responded with a sly smile. "I moved in as soon as the building opened."

Dotty and Robert smirked, and Freddie wondered if she'd missed a joke.

The doors slid open, and they stepped into a wide hallway.

Eloise pushed open a pair of double doors and stepped into an enormous apartment. They passed a salon done up in red silk and Chinese lanterns, where people played mahjong. Freddie slowed and gaped at the room. Eloise, Dotty, and Robert continued without her. When she entered the living room, she was alone. The windows were open and the overhead fans whirred, but the stench of cigars permeated the room. She wrinkled her nose at the smell and looked around. The furniture was new and expensive and told a story her hostess might not appreciate. Her money was recently acquired, and she'd wrongly equated costly furnishings with good taste.

Eloise appeared at her side. "What may I offer you to drink, Freddie?"

Freddie pulled her gaze from an obscene tapestry, remembered Eloise's kindness on the dock, and smiled. "Your apartment is stunning. Like a movie set."

"Thank you. I like it. To drink?"

"Seltzer."

"Nothing stronger?"

Her liver twinged at the thought. "Just seltzer, please."

The room was noisy with lively chatter and a jazz record

playing on the Victrola. There were more women than men. While the men tended toward middle-aged with comfortable paunches and thinning hair, the women were young and gorgeous. Her eyes scanned the crowded room and caught on an older gentleman, a friend of her father's.

He noticed her gaze and paled. Perhaps because a young blond woman, definitely not his wife, was plastered to his side.

As Freddie watched, he shook the blonde off and trotted toward a hallway leading away from the living room. Was he avoiding her?

"Your seltzer." Eloise pressed a drink into Freddie's hand.

"Thank you. Was that John Billingsworth?"

Eloise scanned the room. "I don't see him."

"But you know him?"

"Heavens, yes. He stops by most Thursdays."

John Billingsworth was a stick-in-the-mud. Freddie couldn't comprehend a world in which he attended a party every Thursday. Unless—she covered her lips with her palm and closed her eyes. She'd made a mistake, a fresh-faced-ingenue-just-arrived-from-the-sticks mistake. She'd assumed "entertainment" meant a speakeasy or nightclub. "You're a madam?"

"You didn't know?"

"No." And her so-called friends hadn't told her. Freddie plotted Dotty's and Robert's murders. They'd brought her to a brothel! She glanced toward the hallway where Billingsworth had disappeared and spotted another man she knew. Her stomach plummeted to her ankles. She squeezed her eyes shut. But when she opened them, he was still there. It couldn't be. But it was. Her father was staring at her, every bit as appalled as she was.

Eloise, whose gaze scanned the room, focused on someone in the corner. "Excuse me," she murmured.

When Freddie's gaze returned to the hallway, her father was gone. Her feet carried her forward as if her brain had no say in the decision. She slipped past women who listened closely to every pearl of wisdom generously dropped from male lips. In her short trip across the room, she heard a banker pontificate, a lawyer retry his latest winning case, and a doctor describe a malady that needed no description. Not one young woman showed an ounce of boredom or rolled her eyes. These girls should be on Broadway.

When Freddie reached the hallway, it stood empty.

Had he disappeared into a bedroom? She ventured a few steps.

"You're new here." The sudden gust of scotch made her eyes water.

She looked into the florid face of a man who'd followed her from the living room. "No. Just a guest for the evening."

He grabbed her bare upper arm with an enormous, clammy hand. "You look different from Eloise's other girls."

"I don't work for Eloise."

His scotch-sodden brain did not comprehend her reply. Full, wet lips assaulted her face. His touch made her flinch. That, he understood. His eyes narrowed to mean slits.

"Let me go." She struggled against his hold. Really? Another man accosting her? Would anyone in the living room hear if she screamed? There was chattering and fans and a pianist in the corner. She tried—a long, banshee-like wail.

"No one's coming." His mouth was so close that the reek of liquor on his breath made her gag. "Struggle harder. I like 'em feisty."

She folded the fingers of her free hand into a fist. "Let me go."

"You don't make the rules, girl." His tongue tasted her cheek.

Freddie shuddered, drew back her hand, and socked him on the side of the head. Gray had taught her how to throw a punch, and she put everything she had into the swing.

The man grunted but kept his hold on her arm. "That's not nice." Violence flashed in his bleary eyes, and he grabbed her other arm and leaned in. "You like it rough? We're gonna have a real good time." He pressed his lips against her cheek and licked his way to her ear.

Freddie's breath came in short pants, and her fingers chilled to icicles. She was trapped, the hallway was deserted, and she was certain she wouldn't like whatever he did next. She swallowed her fear. "This is your last chance. Let me go."

"We're just getting started." His meaty lips continued their assault on her face.

She turned her head and visualized her knee rising in a sharp thrust, his gasp of pain, and the release of his hands from her arms. She could do this; she—

"You heard the lady." Nick, still damp from his impromptu dip in the bay, clapped a hand onto the man's shoulder.

"This is a private party," said the man.

"You've made a mistake. She's with me."

"No mistake. I paid top dollar, and she's the prettiest woman here tonight."

Nick scowled at her. "Ring told me you left with Eloise. What were you thinking?" Then he turned to the man who reeked. "She's not for sale."

"They all are." Again the man leaned toward Freddie, and the sour smells of too much scotch and sweat accosted her nose.

Her revulsion must have shown on her face because menace danced across his.

"I cannot believe you came here." Nick spoke through gritted teeth.

He acted as if this situation were her fault. "Blame Dotty and Robert. They didn't tell me Eloise ran a brothel."

"You weren't born yesterday." Nick made an excellent point. She hated it when he was right. She hated more that he was her rescuer.

The man gripped her arms hard enough to leave bruises. "This is your favorite girl? I'll treat her extra-special." Again he licked her cheek. "Now scram."

"Enough." The man had fifty pounds on Nick, but her former fiancé tightened his grip on the man's shoulder and jerked him away from her.

Freddie stumbled backward into the wall.

The man made a fist...a small ham...and swung at Nick.

Nick ducked, and his answering punch landed in the man's gut.

Seemingly unaware that Nick had landed a blow, the man swung again.

This time, the ham at the end of his arm connected with Nick's chin, and Nick staggered backward.

The man advanced.

Nick had tried to save her. She couldn't let this man beat him to a pulp. Freddie launched herself at the man's back, and her arms tightened around his throat. If she squeezed hard enough, she might cut off his oxygen. Her feet dangled, and the man tried to shake her off.

"Freddie, what in blazes are you doing?"

How dare Nick sound annoyed? She was saving him! But they had better things to do than argue. "Get help!"

The man backed up and slammed Freddie into the wall.

"Freddie!"

Why was Nick still here? She closed her eyes on the constellations circling her head and repeated, "Get help!"

Nick turned on his heel and raced toward the living room.

"Your white knight left you."

"He'll be back."

"For a whore? I don't think so."

"I keep telling you. I don't work here."

He slammed her against the wall again.

Somehow, she held on. Perhaps adrenaline had granted her extra strength. Perhaps she was afraid of what he might do if she let go.

"What the hell?" Eloise stood at the end of the hallway with her hands on her hips. Dotty and Robert, who wore matching horrified expressions, stood next to her. Nick leaned against Robert as if he lacked the ability to stand straight on his own.

"Walter, what are you doing?" Eloise's voice was a warning.

Walter grunted. "This one needs to be taught a lesson."

"He's under the impression I work for you," Freddie explained over Walter's shoulder.

"Bear!" Eloise's voice cut through Walter's alcohol-induced delusions, and he held up his hands in surrender.

A grizzly bear masquerading as a man in a shiny suit appeared behind Eloise.

Freddie let her grip slip and landed in a heap on the floor.

Walter turned and kicked at her. His foot was the size of an anvil, and a shriek escaped Freddie's lips. The anvil hit the wall, not her ribs. Given the cracked plaster, Freddie counted herself lucky.

"Bear, go."

The human grizzly lumbered past Eloise, fisted his hand, and felled the previously impervious Walter with a single punch.

He crashed to the floor, and Freddie scooted away from his fallen body. She wanted to stand but worried that her legs might not hold her.

"What happened?" Eloise demanded.

"As I said, he thought I worked for you."

"What were you doing in the hallway? You shouldn't be here."

"I apologize. I recognized someone."

"Billingsworth?"

"No."

"Who?"

Freddie scooted farther away from Walter. "Gerald Archer."

Eloise's lips thinned.

Dotty and Robert exchanged a guilt-laden glance.

Bear offered her an enormous paw. "Help you up, miss?"

"Please."

He pulled her to her feet as if she weighed less than a feather. She took a few seconds to straighten her dress before forcing a smile. It wasn't her fault the smile shook like beaded fringe on a flapper's evening gown. "Would someone please call me a taxi?"

"Where are you going?" Nick demanded.

"Home."

Eloise waved at the man collapsed on the floor. "Bear, see to that."

The giant stooped, grabbed Walter's ankle, and dragged him away.

"Freddie, I'm dreadfully sorry," said Eloise.

Dotty and Robert exchanged another glance. "Us, too."

"We'll call you a taxi." Eloise clasped her hands together. "And, again, I am so sorry. Nothing like this has ever happened before."

Freddie didn't believe her, but she didn't argue. Instead, she whispered, "I just want to go home." Tonight had been an unmitigated disaster. She felt soiled. She needed an hour in a steaming hot shower. And even then, she might not feel clean. Just the memory of Walter's tongue on her cheek and tears threatened, but Freddie refused to let them fall.

"I'll see you home," said Nick.

"No!" Her voice was so loud it echoed in the hallway.

He blinked.

"I appreciate your attempted rescue, but I want to be alone." She didn't need Nick exploiting her fragility.

"You can't go home by yourself," he replied.

"I'll take her," said Dotty.

Freddie had plans for Dotty (Robert, too)—cyanide or a sharp knife. Maybe even cement galoshes. But tonight, she'd put those schemes aside. "Thank you."

Nick shot Dotty a death glare.

"I have a Stutz," said Eloise. "Bear can drive you."

"Thank you for the offer, but a taxi will suit me fine."

Robert, who still half-supported Nick, said, "We should get some ice on that."

Nick shifted his death glare from Dotty to Freddie, gave a brief nod, and then let himself be led away.

Eloise cleared her throat. "We've only just met, and far be it from me to offer unsolicited advice..."

"But?" Dotty's mouth twisted into a wry grin.

"There are men in this world who do nothing but take. The more powerful they are, the more they see the world and everything in it as theirs."

"Walter's powerful?" Dotty's voice was redolent with doubt. "Or did you mean Nick?"

A giggle rose in Freddie's chest and refused to be quelled.

Eloise shook her head in disapproval. "There was once a time when the circumstances of your birth protected you. A bubble of safety, if you will." She directed a telling glance at Freddie. "You chose to live outside the bubble."

"What are you saying?"

"You live in the real world. The next time a man grabs you, don't hesitate to kick him in the balls."

Freddie leaned against Eloise's wall. She hadn't run. She hadn't cowered. She'd joined the fight. But according to Eloise, she'd held back. She tilted her head toward the ceiling and closed her eyes.

"Shall we get you drunk?" asked Dotty.

"Home," Freddie replied.

"You need a drink."

"Maybe," Freddie allowed. "But it's nearly midnight, and I'm due at B. Altman in the morning."

"They won't recognize you without a hangover."

"That's a risk I'll gladly take."

"I'm worried about you." Dotty's face creased with concern.

"I'll be fine. After a shower and a decent night's sleep, I'll be dancing on a table at Tex's." Freddie glanced at Eloise, who still lingered in the hallway. "Eloise, thank you for . . ." Truly, there was nothing for which to be grateful.

"I'm sorry—"

Freddie waved away her apology. "And thank you for the excellent advice. If a man attempts liberties, I know just what to do."

Bear appeared at Eloise's side and offered a sweet smile. "There's a taxi waiting, miss."

Dotty claimed Freddie's elbow. "You're sure about that drink?"

"Positive."

"Then let's get you home."

"Wait." She couldn't leave without knowing.

"What?" Dotty demanded.

Freddie focused on Eloise. "Was it him? Was he here?"

"Who?" The madam fiddled with the sparkling bracelet that circled her wrist.

Freddie waited until Eloise's gaze met hers. "Gerald Archer."

Their gazes held for long seconds.

"My father."

Eloise gave one brief nod, and Freddie turned and walked away.

CHAPTER 9

REDDIE OFFERED A SMILE—ONE she hoped didn't look as tired as she felt. "Elizabeth, the morning has been an absolute delight." She'd hoped a preview of fall dresses (as predicted, not a natural waistline in sight) was what she'd needed to erase the lingering bitterness of last night. Exquisite clothes might brighten her mood, but they couldn't erase the bone-deep fatigue that threatened to crush her.

She and Elizabeth Cahill sat in plush velvet chairs in a private salon where model after model paraded the latest fashions. Whenever Freddie liked a dress, she said so, and Elizabeth instructed the model to remain with them.

"I'm so glad you came." The women's manager waved at the fifteen models who posed in Freddie's selections. Autumn-hued frocks of such beauty that it was impossible to look away. "Which one is your favorite?"

Freddie lifted a Limoges cup with a gold rim to her lips, sipped, and considered each gorgeous frock. "They're all stunning." She returned the cup to a small table nestled between them and pointed at a blond model wearing a copper dress with a deeply scooped neckline. Panels of copper beads darkened as they reached for the model's knees. The hem (or hems, since each panel ended at a different height) was a stormy gray. "The ombré. I've never seen the like. Who is the designer?"

"Madeleine Vionnet."

A French designer who cut her clothes on the bias. Freddie tapped her pencil against the notepad she held on her lap. "Did I select any American designers?"

Elizabeth scanned the gorgeous frocks. "No."

When would an American step to the forefront of fashion? "Do you carry any?"

Elizabeth wrinkled her nose. "A few."

A young woman slipped into the salon, tiptoed toward them, and whispered in Elizabeth's ear.

Elizabeth stiffened and gave the woman a brief nod. "Freddie, do you have everything you need?"

"I do."

"There's a problem that requires my attention. Would you mind seeing yourself out?"

"Mind?" B. Altman was among her favorite stores—a grand, glorious city block of fashion, makeup, and scent. "Not in the slightest. It gives me a chance to linger."

"Stay as long as you like. The models will be delighted to answer your questions." Elizabeth thought Freddie meant to linger here? She'd rather wander the store, where her fingers could explore creamy silk, where she might spritz her wrist with Shalimar or Habanita or No. 5 or ask a clever salesclerk to teach her the trick of tying a turban. She watched Elizabeth exit and made quick notes on her pad.

The dresses for daytime are entirely satisfactory, but evening? Gone is the tired adage that less is more. For evening, more is more. Beads have multiplied faster than a ticker tape on a bullish day. There's fringe, embroidery, paillettes. Lord, the paillettes! Despite the cooler temperatures, chiffon and tulle play a starring role...

The column practically wrote itself. Freddie didn't have a single question for the lovely young women wearing the beautiful clothes. She slipped her pad and pencil into her handbag, stood, and smiled. "You were simply marvelous. Thank you."

On the sales floor, she wandered toward the silk scarves as if they were magnets and she were steel. Perhaps a whole column about turbans?

Can Louise Brooks, Clara Bow, and Norma Talmadge be wrong? When it comes to silk turbans, one thinks not.

"Freddie?"

On hearing her name, she turned. Eloise Silver stood behind her.

Freddie barely kept her jaw from dropping, and she clutched her handbag a bit tighter. If she'd worn pearls, she'd have clutched those, too. Eloise belonged to last night—an evening Freddie hoped to erase from memory. Seeing her at B. Altman's was a decidedly unpleasant shock. "Eloise, what a nice surprise."

"I heard you and Dotty talking. I knew you'd be here."

Eloise had searched her out? Freddie waited for more.

"I wanted to apologize. Again."

"Please, don't give it another thought." Walter's execrable behavior wasn't Eloise's fault. Freddie hadn't wasted more than ten minutes thinking about the horrid man. No, what kept her staring at the ceiling until three in the morning wasn't Walter, but her father. At three, she'd given up on sleep and paced until dawn reflected pink and gold on the reservoir in Central Park.

"I hope you'll forgive me."

That Gerald Archer visited a brothel was something Freddie couldn't forgive. Perhaps it wasn't fair to blame the madam for her father's sins—okay, definitely not fair—but surely Eloise's chic shoulders should bear part of the fault. As such, Freddie wanted nothing to do with her. "As I said, don't give it another thought."

"Let me buy you lunch upstairs."

As if she'd dine with the madam half responsible for her father's sins. "I couldn't eat."

"They have wonderful desserts."

"My waistline."

"Then coffee?" Desperation flickered in Eloise's eyes. She looked almost frightened. "Please?"

That flicker gave Freddie pause. Why was Eloise afraid? Freddie nodded her reluctant agreement to Eloise's plan. "Fine. Let me complete my purchase." She passed two skinny scarves (one a lavender chiffon polka dot, the other silk with a geometric design) to the sales associate. "On my account, please."

"You have excellent taste," said Eloise.

"I have a weakness for scarves. I can hardly darken a shop's doors without buying."

"Shall I have them sent, Miss Archer?"

"Please." Her business concluded, Freddie turned to Eloise. "Coffee?"

Together, they rode the elevator to the eighth floor and entered Charleston Gardens.

A hostess led them to a table, and Eloise eyed the two-story, white-columned façade of an elegant Southern home that dominated the restaurant. Wisteria wrapped its wrought-iron balcony, and forest-green shutters flanked its sparkling windows. Eloise said, "It's unbelievable to me that they built an actual plantation house in the store. Or the front of one. Have you been to South Carolina?"

"Once," Freddie replied.

"Charleston?"

"Yes."

Eloise waved at the impressive façade. "Do the houses look like this?"

"There are deep porches made for lazy afternoons, hurricane shutters made to shut out storms, and gentility so pervasive it perfumes the air. The house I visited was every bit as grand, perhaps a bit bigger." Thinking about that trip with her parents and Gray, when they'd been happy, made the walls close in on her. "Does my father often attend your parties?"

Eloise smoothed the napkin in her lap. "I wouldn't say often."

"What would you say?"

"That it's your father's concern, not yours."

"I disagree."

Eloise folded her hands on the table's edge. "Would you rather he develop an emotional entanglement?"

"I'd rather he remain faithful to my mother."

"The world works differently for men."

"Oh?"

"Women aren't encouraged to succeed at anything but being wives and mothers."

Freddie didn't agree. Things were changing. Twenty years ago, if she'd been able to get a writing job, she'd have been pigeonholed at a women's magazine. Rather than argue, she held her tongue and waited for Eloise to make her point.

"Men succeed in business, at sports, at politics. Their lives are bigger, and so are their appetites."

"So you provide a service?" Last night's bitterness returned. With interest.

"Unquestionably. Perhaps your mother prefers that your father sate his appetites elsewhere."

That was less likely than a woman president. "If a man stands before God and family and swears to forsake all others, that should mean something."

A waitress pushing a cart laden with tea sandwiches stopped next to their table.

"Just coffee." Freddie's voice was so harsh that the poor woman flinched.

"Iced tea, please." Eloise waited until the waitress moved on. "My girls don't make men break their vows. They aren't Jezebels. They don't lead men to their doom."

"They don't read Bible passages to them, either."

Eloise grinned. "I hear you spend too much time in speakeasies to study the Bible."

"Certain parts have stuck with me."

"Such as?"

"The Ten Commandments. There's one about adultery. Also, do unto others—"

"What about forgiveness?" asked Eloise. "Turning the other cheek?"

"You mean I should forgive my father? Forget I saw him at a brothel?" Freddie's ability to forgive died with Gray, and her memory was long.

"To err is human, to forgive divine."

Freddie leaned heavily toward the human side of that equation. "No one's perfect."

"Not even your father?"

"Touché."

A cup of coffee appeared on the table, and Freddie thanked the waitress. The interruption gave her a chance to rein in her temper. She sipped gratefully.

"What your father does is his business—"

"And yours."

Eloise grimaced. "It would be better if your mother didn't know."

"You suggested, not two minutes ago, that my mother might be grateful my father's attentions had shifted." Such poppycock. Her father might be a powerful man, but her mother was a formidable woman. If Marjorie Archer learned about her husband's visits to Eloise's, Gerald Archer would be sleeping with the fishes. "Did my father send you to talk to me?" If so, had he been blind drunk when he made the request?

"Not in so many words."

"How many?"

"Pardon?"

"How many words?"

Eloise flushed. "He wasn't pleased that I invited you."

"I imagine not." For multiple reasons. Besides having a witness to his broken vows, no man wanted to see his daughter in a brothel.

"Your father is a powerful man with powerful friends."

"And he could make things difficult for you?"

"Especially if your mother learns where he spends his Thursday nights."

She'd hoped that her father's presence at Eloise's brothel was an unfortunate fluke. But Eloise had just admitted that her father was a repeat customer. Had she let that slip on purpose? On accident? Either way, Gerald Archer was a repeat offender. Freddie clasped her hands so tightly that the knuckles whitened, and she drew a slow, painful breath.

"Please, Freddie"—Eloise pressed her fingers together, as if in prayer—"don't tell her."

"I'll take it up with my father." It wasn't a concession. Not really. The only certainty from hours of nighttime pacing was the need to talk to her father. And what a horrid conversation that would be.

Brandt's knock came at precisely eight o'clock. Freddie opened the door and smiled a welcome. "How clever you are to be on time."

Brandt held out a bouquet of phlox and lavender and speedwell.

"Flowers again? You're spoiling me." She buried her nose in the scented blooms, sighed, and led him to the living room. "Help yourself to a drink. I'll put these in water."

When she returned, she found Brandt with a glass of scotch in his hand. He stood at the window. Below him, the reservoir looked cool and inviting.

He turned. "You look lovely."

She'd spent the afternoon napping with cucumber slices over her eyes. The hours spent sleeping had returned a bit of rose to her complexion and improved her mood. She smoothed the silk of her Carmaux frock. "Thank you."

"I hope you like French food."

"I adore it." She crossed to the drinks cart and poured herself a glass of wine. "How's Ephram?"

A cloud crossed his face. "Fine."

"I know it was self-defense, but pulling the trigger and—"

"Exactly. Killing another person is never easy."

He'd killed people? Her mouth gaped open, and she snapped it shut. Slack-jawed surprise was never attractive.

"The war," he explained. "I killed people during the war."

"Of course."

"What did you think I meant?" He grinned as if he enjoyed teasing her.

"I didn't mean to suggest..."

"That I killed people on a daily basis?"

"I wouldn't go out with you if I thought you killed people every day."

His eyes sparkled. "Just Tuesdays."

"Since it's Friday, I have nothing to worry about."

"You'd be safe with me on a Tuesday." The warmth in his eyes said he meant it. "You'd be safe with me any day."

She believed him. Except every time she saw him, someone died. The thought dried her mouth and chilled her fingers.

"You're thinking about Ewan."

She hadn't been, but she nodded.

"I didn't kill him."

She nodded a second time. She'd been with Brandt when someone shot Ewan. And Ephram had killed the man at King Tut's. But death kept pace with the man in her living room. She sank onto the nearest chair.

Brandt claimed the chair closest to hers. "I want to know you better, Freddie." Sincerity laced his voice and pierced her heart.

Was she ready to care about another man? And even if she was, shouldn't Brant Abrams's frequent brushes with death exclude him from the running? She took a large swallow.

"I'm not asking for a commitment. Just give me a chance." Brandt's dark gaze fixed on her face and held, as if he could see past the rouge and mascara, past the smiles she wore when she longed to scream, past her mask. It was as if he saw her—the real her. And he still wanted a chance.

Dotty would tell her the best way to get over one man was to get under another. But Brandt Abrams deserved better. She wouldn't use him. "I recently ended an engagement."

He sat back in his chair. "Why?"

"We didn't—don't—want the same things."

"But you still love him?"

She glanced at her lap where her fingers clutched the wineglass so tightly that the stem threatened to shatter. She forced her muscles to relax and murmured, "I don't know."

"What do you want?"

That, she knew. She swirled the wine in her glass and then sipped before saying, "Work. Independence. A voice."

"What does he want?"

"A house in Connecticut and a woman who waits up for him." Nick also wanted two perfect children, a boy and a girl, a beach house, a chic pied-à-terre in the city, and a wife who never questioned his decisions. It was a perfect, charmed life. For him. For her? She wasn't sure she wanted children, wouldn't say no to a beach house, preferred a home in the city, and questioned everything.

Brandt's gaze was steady. It was as if he was studying her, learning her, preparing for a test. "He doesn't understand you at all. You belong in the city. Its energy runs in your veins. Anyone can see that."

The lump in her throat made replying impossible. She forced a sip of wine. A large one.

"The man's a fool. And I'm glad."

"Glad?" she half whispered.

"If he had half a brain, he'd be here tonight instead of me." He smiled at her. His smile was blinding in its whiteness and devastating in its directness. Brandt Abrams knew what he wanted, and he was confident enough to declare his intentions. He reached for her hand. "I'm a lucky man."

Freddie looked away from the tantalizing promises she saw written on his face. Her gaze landed on his hands. "A lucky man with an empty glass. May I pour you another?"

"I'll get it." He stood and crossed to the bar cart. "More wine?"

"I'd better not." Her glass was still half full.

He splashed more scotch into his old-fashioned. "How was your week? Anything interesting?"

Did a trip to a brothel count? "Not particularly. You?"

"Dull as dishwater."

Somehow, she doubted that. "We've never talked about our jobs. You once mentioned ledgers, meetings, and contracts."

"And you mentioned a pen."

"I write for *Gotham*."

"I work for the family business."

She waited for more.

Brandt stared into his scotch.

He might see her, but she saw him, too. "You can tell me."

"My father started an import/export company."

"What did he import?"

"Most anything. Cloth, perfume, leather goods, British cars. He exported cotton, tobacco, and American cars."

"And now?"

He stared at her for long seconds, and again she had the sense he was seeing her. Finally, when she was certain he'd found her lacking, he said, "He has contacts in Scotland." It was as good as saying he and his father were bootleggers.

Freddie glanced at the glass of Glenromach scotch in Brandt's hands. "I hope he'd approve."

"Unquestionably. It's ours."

Now the long seconds of silence belonged to her. "Yours?"

"My uncle married a woman from Scotland. Speyside." He said Speyside as if the word should mean something to her.

She gave a bemused shake of her head.

"There are more distilleries in Speyside than the rest of Scotland combined." Brandt grinned. "My uncle did a good business before Prohibition. Now he can't age the stuff fast enough."

"You import scotch." A statement, not a question.

Brandt rubbed the back of his neck and took a sip of his uncle's product. Then he shrugged his disdain for the Eighteenth Amendment and the Volstead Act. "One day a business is legal, the next day it's not? And why? Because a bunch of privileged women decided that immigrants drink too much? The law makes no sense."

Freddie was no fan of Prohibition. The opposite. But there was a difference between perching at the bar at a charming boîte on 52nd Street and sipping a scotch and importing it. "Ewan was a bootlegger as well?"

Brandt's expression was hard, flinty, slightly dangerous. "Yes."

"And Ephram?"

"Yes."

"The men at King Tut...the ones with guns—"

"Want exclusive rights to sell Glenromach." His jaw firmed to granite. "They won't get it."

She finished her wine with one enormous gulp. "Who killed Ewan?"

Brandt's broad shoulders tightened, and the expression in his eyes was so fierce that Freddie had to force herself to remain quiet in her chair.

"I'm sorry..." she began.

"I don't know who killed Ewan. But I intend to find out." He shook his head. "This is hardly pleasant conversation. Tell me more about your column."

"Fashion," Freddie replied. Not a lie, but not the whole truth. "I spent the morning at B. Altman's viewing the dresses for fall." A man was dead. Surely, they should discuss that and not hemlines. "About Ewan. There was a woman at the Village Inn the night he died..."

He raised a brow. "You think she killed him?"

"I don't know."

"Who is she?"

"No idea."

His lips thinned. "So there's a woman you don't know who might have killed Ewan?"

Freddie nodded.

"Why?"

"No idea." She sounded like an utter fool.

"Why do you suspect her?"

"She was with someone else who died."

"At the Village Inn?"

"No. A man named Jake Hask—"

Brandt jerked to his feet, and the expression on his face chilled her blood.

Jake Haskell had specialized in scotch. Like Brandt. "You knew him," she whispered.

"He was a partner."

She should have guessed. "I saw him at the Cascades with the woman."

"What did she look like?"

"She wore a sky-blue silk dress and ropes of pearls." Freddie touched her head. "Light brown hair. Bobbed. Pretty."

"Tall? Short?"

"I'm not sure. But I saw her again the night Ewan died. I even followed her."

Brandt frowned as if he didn't like the idea of Freddie tailing a potential killer. "Where did she go?"

"I lost her in Washington Square Park." Freddie looked up from her empty glass and stared at Brandt. "She might have killed two of your friends. Are you in danger?"

"Me? No." He sounded so certain. How did he know?

CHAPTER 10

FREDDIE BREEZED INTO THE dining room of the Algonquin Hotel and found Dotty, clad in her usual black, alone at a large, round table.

Freddie claimed a chair. "Am I early?" The table was usually packed on Mondays.

Dotty fiddled with a teaspoon. "Do you ever tire of fun?"

Oh, dear. Dotty was in a mood. Freddie smoothed a linen napkin across her lap. "Pardon me?"

"You heard me." Dotty's mouth twisted into a sour expression, and her hands playing with the spoon looked cold and bone white. It was obviously one of her morose days.

"I hear you, but I don't understand." Undoubtedly, her friend would explain. At length. It was such a shame the Algonquin was dry. Freddie suspected she might need a martini and wished she'd had the foresight to bring a flask.

"I get tired." Dotty shifted her scowl from the blameless spoon to Freddie (not blameless, because she was contemplating copious quantities of gin). "Don't ever let anyone tag you as having a quick wit." She tapped the spoon's silver bowl against the white linen tablecloth. "You'll be expected to drop bon mots on a moment's notice."

"There's little chance of me being mistaken for a wit."

"You're witty."

"On paper. What brought this on?"

"Mr. Parker." Dotty's elusive husband kept himself occupied by drinking more than any human should. "I mean it, Freddie. Doesn't living up to men's expectations wear on you?"

"So in this scenario of yours, I'm fun, and you're witty?"

"Sounds about right." Dotty put down the spoon and picked up her coffee. "Now, answer the question. Do you get tired of fun?"

"Not so much having fun as being fun."

"What if one day you wore glasses, donned a black frock, and said sarcastic things about all and sundry?"

Freddie cocked her head. "What if I pretended to be you?" Had Dotty spiked her coffee? She wasn't usually so glum when sober.

"Why not? I do it all the time."

"Dotty." The sympathy in Freddie's tone made her friend flinch.

"What if one day I pretended that I held the moon on a string, had men fall at my feet, and laughed as if there were no tomorrow?"

Freddie closed her eyes, hopefully hiding the wound Dotty had inflicted. "That's how you see me?"

"It's what people expect from you."

"If so, I'm an utter failure."

Dotty looked up from her coffee with a surprised frown on her clever face.

"I disappoint my parents by being too wild and gay and fun. I've disappointed countless boyfriends by not being wild and gay and fun enough."

"Is that a euphemism for keeping your knees locked together?"

"It is."

"At least you're pretty."

"Being valued for my face isn't the blessing you assume. Anything I accomplish is secondary to the curve of my cheek."

"You shouldn't complain. There are thousands of girls, tens of thousands, who want to be you."

"They want to be A Touch of Rouge. They want to attend clubs and speakeasies and drink champagne."

"Who wouldn't want that?" Dotty narrowed her eyes. "You broke things off with Nick because he asked you to give it up."

"Wrong. Nick liked that I was wild and gay and fun." Thanks to this conversation, the word *fun* was becoming a curse. "What he didn't like was how much I care about my job."

Dotty grunted.

"As for being pretty, if I were prettier, a true beauty like Tallulah, would he compromise with an apartment in the city and a wife who kept her job?" The question niggled at her. If she were more desirable, would Nick have changed his tune?

"No." Dotty sounded so certain.

"No?"

"Nick sees himself as a successful producer. Successful producers have families in Connecticut. Ergo..."

"Ergo?"

"You'd become the bewitching former writer who gave up her dreams for the love of her talented husband."

"So getting married and buying a house in Greenwich or

Darien isn't about me? It's about Nick and how he wants the world to see him?" That smarted. "He says he still loves me."

"And he believes it. It's why you're better off without him. The man's deluded."

"And you're a terrible cynic."

"I've done love. I've done marriage. They don't last."

"Your experience isn't universal."

"Lift those rose-colored glasses from your nose."

"Nope. Firmly affixed to my nose is exactly where I like them." The alternative was bleak.

"Oh, life is a glorious cycle of song, a medley of extemporanea. And love is a thing that can never go wrong"—Dotty tilted her head toward the ceiling and pressed the back of her hand to her forehead—"and I am Marie of Romania."

Freddie swallowed a laugh. "Cynic."

"Pollyanna."

"Nothing wrong with the glad game."

"Not if you're an ostrich."

"What did Mr. Parker do?"

"Do you ever feel empty?" Dotty cut her gaze toward the entrance, where Aleck Woollcott chatted with Frank Case, the hotel manager. "Never mind. Forget I asked."

She understood Dotty's sudden reticence. Aleck Woollcott's wit was rapier sharp, and he was seldom kind. If Dotty gave him an opening, he might run her through. Freddie shifted her gaze from Aleck and scanned the dining room. "Is that Walter Ames?"

Dotty adjusted her glasses. "Where?"

"Three tables to your right."

Dotty turned her head. "That's him. Who's he with?"

The woman's back faced them.

"No idea. He's such a pleasant fellow. I gave Nick hell for sacking him."

"Remind me."

"Walter told the star of Nick's last play that she was a no-talent hack."

"Was he right?"

"It was a comedy, and Carol Hart had the lead. The loathsome woman is as funny as a heart attack."

"Ah." Dotty said so much with so little.

Aleck Woollcott cut across the dining room, bent, and kissed her cheek. "Freddie, how kind of you to join us." He claimed a nearby chair.

"No kiss for me?" asked Dotty.

"I don't know where your cheek's been."

"I feel the same way about your mustache."

"Now"—Aleck rubbed his palms together—"who are you two whispering about?"

"Walter Ames."

"A fine young actor." Aleck was a theater critic. "Nick made a mistake with that one. Is he here?"

"Behind you."

Aleck turned and craned his neck over his shoulder. "Who's that with him?"

"We can't see her face," said Dotty in a timbre that suggested Aleck was a simpleton.

He ignored Dotty's ill-concealed foul mood and returned his focus to Freddie. "What brings you here today?"

"Lunch."

"Much as I adore the Algonquin, no one comes for the food."

"I came for the charming company."

Dotty lit a cigarette. "For God's sake, don't tell him he's charming. His head is big enough."

"I also came to apologize to Ring. I disrupted his party."

Aleck chuckled. "I thoroughly enjoyed watching a sodden Nick Peters drag himself from the drink."

Freddie winced. "Not my finest hour."

"I don't know." Aleck rubbed his chin. "Could be he had it coming."

Ring's arrival with George Kaufman saved her from replying. She stood and held out her hands. "I'm so dreadfully sorry. Can you and Ellis forgive me?"

"Forgive you? There's not a man"—Ring nodded at Dotty, who blew a long plume of smoke—"or woman who frequents this table who wouldn't love to push Nick into the bay."

"For once," said Aleck, "his outsides matched his insides. All wet."

Dotty groaned. "How long have you been saving that one?"

Aleck smirked beneath the shadow of his mustache.

Freddie nodded a greeting at George Kaufman and settled into her chair.

George claimed the chair next to hers. "Aleck's not wrong. Nick has been insufferable of late."

"Let's not talk about Nick," Freddie replied. "Tell me about your current project."

"I'm writing the book for *The Cocoanuts*." The book, or script, for a musical gave the production form. Without the book to hang on to, a musical was just a random collection of songs.

"For the Marx Brothers?"

He nodded. "Irving wrote the music. The show opens this fall, and we're still revising."

"I'm sure it will be marvelous."

"We'll see. You should come to opening night in case."

"In case?"

"I'm not a librettist. The whole thing may fold like a house of cards."

The Marx Brothers were funny, and Irving Berlin was a genius. George's fears were unfounded. Freddie manufactured an encouraging smile. "I doubt that." Movement in the corner of her eye caught her attention, and she watched Walter Ames rise from the table and pull out his companion's chair.

The woman turned, and Freddie gasped.

"Freddie?" Concern laced George's voice, and he followed her gaze. "Who's that with Ames? I've never seen her before."

Freddie had. It was the woman who'd dined with Jake Haskell. The woman who'd stood over Ewan Duncan's dying body. Freddie rose.

Dotty grasped her wrist. "What's wrong? You look as if you just witnessed the Wall Street bombing."

In the time it took Dotty to ask her question and comment on Freddie's pallor, Walter and his luncheon companion disappeared into the lobby.

Freddie yanked her wrist free and ran after them, but Walter and his lunch date were gone. She'd lost the woman. Again.

Scowling at her typewriter didn't help. Not even a bit. The paper wrapped around the carriage remained resolutely blank. Freddie leaned back in her chair and shifted her scowl to the ceiling. It was as unconcerned by her scowl as the typewriter. "Annie!"

Her assistant stuck her head through the open door. "Yes?"

"Would you please get Detective Sullivan on the phone?" Annie's cheeks flushed.

Freddie had called the detective the moment she returned from lunch and had expected to hear back from him by now. "Is that a problem?"

The color on Annie's cheeks deepened. "No problem."

Freddie stood and crossed to the window. The street below was crowded with automobiles and delivery trucks. The sidewalk teemed with people in desperate hurries.

The oscillating fan ruffled her hem, and she smoothed her skirt.

"Freddie?" The voice did not belong to Annie.

She turned. "Gus."

"Got a minute?" His long face settled into a deep frown, and he tugged at his collar. "I haven't seen you since Ring's party."

"Ugh. I'm sorry I left without saying goodbye. Ellis promised she'd let you know I drove home with Dotty and Robert."

"She did. You're okay?"

She sat behind her desk. "I'm fine."

"I swear"—he gave his collar another sharp tug—"I didn't know Peters would be there."

"It's not your fault, Gus. And it wasn't a problem." A blatant lie.

Gus had made his apology, but rather than leave, he settled into one of the chairs facing her desk and nodded at the typewriter. "What are you working on?"

"Today? I have a wee case of writer's block." She spread her thumb and pointer finger as wide as they would go.

He grunted his sympathy, crossed his left ankle over his right knee, and leaned back in the chair. The man never came to her office unless he wanted something. She'd assumed it was to apologize for taking her to a party where Nick was a problem, but Gus looked ready to linger.

"Is there something else?" she asked.

"That new club I mentioned. Can you swing by there tonight? They'd appreciate the coverage."

"Sure."

"Freddie." Annie's head appeared inside the office, and the pink on her cheeks hinted at her next words. "Detective Sullivan is on the line."

Gus's brows rose, but rather than offer her a modicum of privacy, he sank deeper into the chair.

She frowned at him and picked up the receiver. "Detective Sullivan."

"Miss Archer."

She cast a quick glance at Gus, who pretended not to listen. "Did you find her?"

"It's only been four hours," the detective replied.

"That's not an answer."

"We tracked down Walter Ames. He says that lunch was a first date. He barely knows the woman."

"What's her name?"

"Anne Smith."

Freddie snorted. There had to be hundreds of Anne Smiths in New York. Maybe thousands. "Do you believe him?"

"I have no reason to disbelieve him." Freddie heard doubt in Detective Sullivan's voice.

"But you don't. Believe him, I mean."

"It seems odd that a young man takes a pretty girl to lunch and doesn't get her phone number."

Again, she glanced at Gus. He was making a great show of inspecting his cuticles. "So they ate an early lunch and went their separate ways?"

"That's Ames's story."

She pursed her lips. "Where did they meet?"

"The lobby of the Algonquin."

She blinked her disbelief. "Today?"

"That's what he told me."

"Did he tell you why he was at the hotel?"

"He didn't say." Which meant Sullivan hadn't asked.

Freddie had her suspicions. "So he's loitering in the hotel lobby and meets a girl." Such a fishy tale. "Then they decide to dine together?"

"That's what he claims."

"Hmph."

"You have another theory?"

"Walter Ames is an actor. In addition to being good, he's smart." Some might call him conniving. "Worming his way into the circle could open doors for him."

"The circle?"

"The writers and producers and creative types who eat lunch at the Algonquin every day." Heck, Dotty Parker even lived there, in a suite on the eleventh floor.

"That explains his presence, but not Miss Smith's. Are you sure it's the same woman?"

"Positive."

Across from her, Gus had given up the pretense of giving her privacy. He stared at her with avid curiosity.

"Detective, there's someone in my office. If you learn anything new, will you let me know? Please?"

"It was a mistake to involve you."

"Yes, yes. I'm a delicate flower who'll be trampled in an investigation." They'd already covered this ground. "Be that as it may, will you please keep me informed?"

He grunted. "Goodbye, Miss Archer."

Freddie placed the receiver in its cradle and steeled herself for Gus's interrogation.

"Who was that?"

She smiled. "Annie's beau. He's also a police detective."

"I gathered the latter part." Gus's voice was as dry as the Algonquin claimed to be. "Why are you talking to him?" Her boss wore a determined expression. He wouldn't drop this until she told him something.

"Two weeks ago, I mentioned Jake Haskell in a column."

"Who?"

"Jake Haskell. Man about town. Popular for bringing real scotch to private parties."

"Go on."

"Haskell was murdered. Detective Sullivan read the column and came to see me. He asked if I remembered anything from the night I saw Jake."

"Did you?"

"Haskell had a date. I described her, and the detective and I parted ways." She opted not to tell Gus that the detective had enlisted her aid. "Then I saw her again."

"Where?"

"In a speakeasy in Greenwich Village."

"And you informed the detective."

"I did."

"And you saw this woman again today?"

"Exactly." This was going better than she could have hoped.

"So why is he keeping you informed?"

"I'm a journalist. If I'm instrumental in catching a killer, I get the scoop."

"You're not a journalist. You're a columnist. And I don't want you involved in dangerous affairs." Gus glowered at her, and she hid a smile. For all his bluster, Gus was about as menacing as a cocker spaniel puppy.

"I'll be fine."

"I mean it, Freddie. A girl like you should steer clear of danger."

A *girl*? "Why is it that a twenty-six-year-old female who supports herself, pays her taxes, and excels at her job is still a girl, but a twenty-year-old male who pushes the mail cart is a man?"

"That's your argument? Not the danger?"

"Would you say this to Tom Pedersen?" Tom was the magazine's sports columnist. He was large and muscled and had an annoying habit of swaggering through the office as if he were personally responsible for Babe Ruth's home runs.

"It's different."

"Because I'm a woman?"

Gus closed his eyes and exhaled. "You're a woman without a man to take care of you."

"I don't need one."

Gus gave a brief, bitter chuckle. "You went to a brothel when you left the Lardners', and Nick Peters saved you from an overzealous customer. You needed a man then."

Freddie pressed her lips together, the better to keep a career-ending reply locked behind her teeth. Who'd blabbed to Gus? Dotty? Robert?

He tilted his head. "You're not arguing."

Winning this argument with Gus would be like teaching a pig to fly. Annoying and impossible. Also, much as she loathed to admit it, Nick had come to her rescue. "Let's not discuss Nick Peters. And you're right. I am a writer, not a detective."

She wasn't a detective, but she could be. She'd bet the value of Babe Ruth's contract she could get more information from Walter Ames than Detective Sullivan had.

"I'm glad you see reason." Gus had no call to sound so surprised. It was as if he expected her to argue, and she'd disappointed him.

She thought of flying pigs and kept her lips sealed. The silence stretched between them.

Did he recognize the pabulum she'd spooned him?

When he stood, the gaze he cast upon her was narrow and suspicious—almost as if he doubted her easy capitulation (that was a no on the pabulum). "So we're agreed? You avoid danger. And you should probably steer clear of Eloise Silver's place."

They were not agreed. And how did Gus, who was married to a lovely woman, know about Eloise Silver's brothel?

He walked to the doorway and paused. "Don't forget Club Monaco."

"I won't." That much was true.

Gus left, and she dropped her head into her hands. Did her publisher have it right? Should she let Detective Sullivan bumble along?

Freddie closed her eyes and remembered the way Walter had leaned toward Anne Smith. That action had seemed intimate, comfortable—not what she'd expect from a couple who'd just met. The actor had lied. She was sure of it.

She lifted her head and straightened her shoulders.

True, men had died. Also true, she'd been warned off the investigation. Also also true, bullets, Detective Sullivan's ire, and her boss's directives gave her pause. But she wasn't a complete coward. She could track down Walter, ask him questions, and somehow convince him to tell her the truth.

CHAPTER 11

THE SUN'S SETTING HADN'T done a bit to ease the day's heat. Freddie wore the coolest dress she owned—a lightly beaded chiffon shift—and studied her reflection in her vanity mirror.

What did women with heavy, long hair do when the temperature flirted with frying an egg on the sidewalk? Freddie's bob clung to her neck, and she lifted damp strands from her skin.

Her nose was shiny, but she didn't dare powder it, not beneath the fan. She'd learned the hard way that loose powder and electric fans made poor companions. Instead, she glanced at the diamond watch on her wrist, reached for the telephone, and dialed.

"Hello." George Kaufman's voice boomed down the line.

"George, darling, it's Freddie." She positively purred into the receiver.

"What do you want, Freddie?" His voice was flat, which meant her purr had failed.

She crossed her fingers. "Is your new show fully cast?"

"How would I know? I'm the librettist, not the director or producer."

"But if you asked Groucho for a favor..."

"Why in blazes would I do that?"

"I hear Beatrice is interested in the Paris shows." Attending was quite a carrot. The preview of couture fashion would make most women salivate. The chance to wear a must-have dress first would make any woman drool. Especially Beatrice Kaufman. George's wife was smart and funny and chic, and he bent over backward to keep her happy. Freddie was counting on that to win the day. "I may have an extra ticket." She could get one.

Long seconds passed, and she held her breath.

"What precisely do you want?" he asked.

She exhaled. "I may need to promise Walter Ames a job."

"The actor?"

No, the plumber. She kept the sharp reply to herself. "Yes. He's very good."

"Hmph. What does he have that you want?"

"Information." A name he'd withheld from the police. She needed leverage. "Please, George. I'd be forever in your debt."

"And you'll take Beatrice to Chanel?" Did George realize how much his clotheshorse wife could spend in an afternoon?

"And Lanvin, too."

"What about Patou?"

"Yes."

George was looking at an astronomical bill. He and Beatrice had an open marriage, and whenever he took a new lover, he softened the blow to Beatrice's feelings with new clothes. Freddie didn't know what happened if Beatrice diddled with a lover. The whole arrangement was terribly progressive, and Freddie tried (really, she did) not to pass judgment. What other people did or didn't do behind closed doors was not her business, but she couldn't fathom staying with a man who regularly slept with other women.

She winced. Thus far, she'd ducked her father's phone calls, but at some point (Thanksgiving sounded good), she'd have to face him.

"I have no problem with Ames, if he can play a straight man."

Could he? She had no idea. "He'll be the perfect foil for the Marx Brothers."

"I'll check with Groucho and call you back. Does this have something to do with Ames's luncheon companion at the Algonquin?"

That was the problem with brilliant friends. They figured things out.

"It might. I am working on a piece."

"Sure you are."

"Suspicion doesn't suit you."

George barked a laugh. "And intrigue is not your strong suit."

"What's that supposed to mean?"

"You're a fun girl and a good writer, but leave the cloak-and-dagger stuff to Dashiell Hammett. At least he was a Pinkerton detective before he took up a pen."

She was sick to death of being called a girl, but she bit back a sharp retort. "It's not cloak-and-dagger. I appreciate your help, George. Thank you."

"My pleasure. Where are you off to tonight?"

Freddie glanced at her reflection. "Club Monaco with Tallulah."

"Never heard of it."

"New place. New advertiser."

"So Gus decreed that A Touch of Rouge must visit. Have fun."

"I always do." She hung up the phone, rose, stood directly beneath the ceiling fan, and smiled. Her plan might just work.

At a quarter past eight, she took a taxi to Tallulah's hotel, paid the driver, and approached the front desk. "Would you please call up to Miss Bankhead's room? You may tell her Mary Pickford is here."

The man behind the desk gaped. "Of course, Miss Pickford."

That Mary Pickford was a brunette and Freddie a blonde didn't seem to register. Nor that Mary had soft pliable features, and Freddie's chin was too obstinate.

"I'll wait for her in the lobby."

She chose a wingback chair and perused the evening paper.

Clarence Darrow, who had a trial coming up, believed Christ would not bar teaching evolution in schools. Nearly a quarter million dollars of choice liquor was seized in Rhode Island. The police were to have courses in the ethics of football.

"Mary Pickford, I presume?"

Freddie looked up from the article about liquor and grinned.

Tallulah sank onto the couch. "The poor man believed you. He could hardly speak for excitement."

"Not my fault you chose a hotel with gullible staff. Also, you're an actress. Why does he care about Mary Pickford?"

"I'm merely on Broadway and the West End. Mary is on the screen."

Tallulah wore a dress as light and airy as Freddie's. Her honey hair spilled around her shoulders, and mascara made her blue eyes huge.

Men stopped and stared at her. One unfortunate fellow, who failed to stop while he stared, walked into a pillar.

"Where are we going tonight?"

"Club Monaco."

"Sounds exotic."

"I made promises to Gus. If it's dull, we'll go to Tony's."

"Tony's? What if Nick is there? You won't have a bay handy."

"Has everyone in town heard that story?"

"That and your evening at Eloise Silver's."

Freddie groaned.

"Oh, please. It's Saturday night. Zelda's sure to ride down Fifth Avenue on top of a taxi, or Edna Ferber will get drunk, and your paltry shenanigans will be as forgotten as yesterday's news. Shall we?"

Together, they left the hotel and allowed the doorman to call them a cab.

Tallulah pulled a small silk fan from her handbag. "Did you hear Tex is moving her club to the boondocks for the rest of the summer? She can't take the heat."

Well, that did it. Why stay in the city? Simply everyone was leaving. "I might as well go to Montauk."

"Montauk?"

"My grandmother and her beach house."

Tallulah fanned as if the air might cool from her efforts. "You've been holding out on me."

"As if you have the patience for that drive." The distance from New York to Montauk was more than a hundred miles. Tallulah got bored driving through the park.

"What's gotten into you?"

Freddie didn't have an answer, so she offered a Sphynx-like smile.

"You're not usually so sharp and prickly, Miss Pickford. Have you been spending too much time with Dotty?"

Prickly? Her? She gave up on the mysterious smile. "It's been a long summer, and it's only June." She waved her own fan, but it did little to move the stifling air. "Say, do you know Walter Ames?"

"A bit."

"Who's his agent?"

"Brooks Hawley. Why?"

"I'm curious."

"Why are you curious?"

Hawley could arrange a meeting with Walter. "No reason."

"You're a terrible liar."

The taxi carried them past packed sidewalks. New Yorkers had escaped their overheated apartments en masse in the vain hope of a cool breeze. Voices and horns and the rumble of engines filled the car. As did smells—hot dogs from the vendor parked near the curb, the driver's stale sweat, and Tallulah's cloyingly sweet perfume.

Tallulah leaned closer. "Tell me, have you seen Brandt Abrams again?"

Freddie squeezed her eyes shut and tried to remember if she'd told Tallulah about Brandt. "Why do you ask?"

Tallulah patted her knee. "Darling, never play poker. Your every thought plays across your face like reels at the picture show."

"I don't know what you mean."

"Yes, you do. And your face tells me you like him."

"When do you leave for London?"

Tallulah pouted. "Don't be mean."

"Just asking."

"Ha."

"Ha?"

"Ha. I'm an actress, not an Algonquin wit."

They arrived in front of the club, Freddie paid the fare, and they walked up a half flight of stairs to a pair of double doors.

"What now?" asked Tallulah.

"We knock." Freddie demonstrated.

The doors opened, and a man in a tuxedo took their measure, deemed them acceptable, and stepped aside.

They passed through a short hallway and a second set of doors before entering the actual club.

"Not the worst place I've been." Since Tallulah regularly visited holes in the walls in the Village, that wasn't saying much.

Club Monaco was dark and smoky and filled with well-dressed people. The far wall featured a stage (currently empty). Seating came in tiers. A half-moon of tables, all with a view.

They followed the maître d' to the first tier and settled at a table covered with white linen.

"A waiter will be with you shortly."

"It's stuffy," said Freddie. In a city where people longed for informality and gaiety, stuffy was as deadly as a vampire's kiss.

Tallulah nodded. "I hope they paid Gus's advertising fees up front."

Before Freddie could reply, the curtain rose, and a spotlight illuminated a woman in a silver dress.

She sang.

After four notes, the club fell silent. The singer, whose voice carried hints of smoke and velvet and sex, was that good.

A waiter appeared and whispered, "What may I serve you?"

"Two gin rickeys," Freddie whispered in reply.

He left them.

"She's good," Tallulah murmured.

"She's great." Without benefit of back-up instruments, the woman on the stage held the whole club in the palm of her hand.

Behind her, a band joined for the second verse.

The waiter quietly delivered their drinks, and they sipped and listened.

"I take it back," said Tallulah. "As long as they have her, they'll have a line around the block. Look"—she held out her arm—"I have goose bumps."

When the song ended, the lights rose enough to reveal the band. They played a jazzy number, and couples spilled down the stairs to the dance floor in front of the stage.

"Freddie?"

Tallulah's eyes widened, and Freddie turned. "Ephram."

He glanced at the two empty chairs at their table. "May I join you?"

"Of course. Please meet Tallulah Bankhead. Tallulah, this is Brandt's friend, Ephram Loeb."

Tallulah offered her hand, and Ephram brushed his lips across her knuckles. They stared at each other for long seconds.

"Dance with me?"

Tallulah shifted her gaze to Freddie. "Do you mind?"

"Not in the slightest."

As Tallulah and Ephram disappeared onto the crowded dance floor, Freddie withdrew a small pad and a tiny pencil from her handbag.

One is so seldom surprised that, when the extraordinary comes along, one feels like a child on Christmas morning. And while this child is sorely tempted not to share her new toy, those seeking brightness and fun should visit Club Monaco...

She sipped her gin, scanned the room and resumed.

At first glance, one wrinkles one's nose. Surely this place is a caricature of what butter-and-egg men expect from a club in Manhattan, but the excellence of the drinks and greatness (a word one does not use lightly) of the singer—

She waved over a waiter. "What's the singer's name?"
"Kismet Lane."
"Thank you."

—of the singer, Kismet Lane, make Club Monaco the latest "it" spot.

The song bled into a new tune, and Tallulah and Ephram remained on the dance floor.

Poor Ephram. The man wore a besotted expression.

Tallulah was set to leave for London and had plenty of men yet to kiss before she boarded the boat. Ephram was but one among many.

Except—Freddie rested her elbows on the table, leaned forward, and stared—Tallulah's expression was equally besotted.

A besotted Tallulah was rarer than Halley's Comet, a once-in-a-lifetime occurrence.

The song ended, and they returned to the table awash in the healthy glow associated with vigorous dancing. They both smiled like lunatics.

Ephram took Tallulah's hand. "I need to make a call. I'll be back before you can miss me."

"Don't be too sure about that."

Ephram departed, and Freddie lifted her brows. "Well."

Tallulah collapsed into a chair. "You sound like your mother."

"What a horrible thing to say. I most certainly do not."

"Then you sound like my grandmother, which is far worse."

"You just met him."

"Chemistry is about instantaneous reactions."

Freddie knew little about science, but she was fairly certain chemistry involved elements and test tubes. "That's lust, not chemistry."

"Don't be so starchy. I like lust. Besides, it's not as if you're looking for a picket fence."

She couldn't argue with that. "What about Ephram?"

"What about him?"

"He looks like a man who's been hit upside the head with a bag of moonbeams."

Tallulah leaned back and sighed. "He is a handsome devil."

"What if he has feelings?"

"He's a man."

"Men have feelings."

"Not after two dances they don't."

Again, Freddie couldn't argue.

"I'm back." Ephram pulled out a chair and sat next to Tallulah.

She fluttered her eyelashes. "Ephram, what do you do when you're not sweeping women off their feet?"

"International trade."

"What does that mean?"

A new song began. A slow one. And Ephram grabbed Tallulah's

hand. "What kind of fool bores a beautiful woman with business. Dance with me." He pulled her from her chair.

On the dance floor, they melted together.

"Another drink?" asked the waiter.

"Not right now, thank you." Freddie gripped her pencil and wrote.

> *The romance of dim lighting, good liquor, a saxophone whose plaintive notes can jimmy the locks to the hidden doorways in one's soul, and a singer whose voice could be mistaken for tangled sheets and languid kisses—*

She tapped the pencil. Gus would never print that last line.

"Freddie? Freddie Archer?"

She looked up and stifled a groan. "Constance." Freddie would have dearly loved to find fault with her former classmate. Too bad the dratted woman wore her hair in a shiny bob and her dress was perfection. "What a lovely gown."

"Thank you. It's Carmaux." She eyed the table as if just noticing the empty chairs. Her mouth curled in a triumphant smirk. "You poor dear. You're not here alone?"

"My friend is dancing."

"Your friend?" Her gaze scanned the dancers. There was a reason Constance Jessop's classmates at school renamed her Constant Gossip. "Who is that?"

"Tallulah Bankhead."

Now Constance stared at her with avid interest. "The actress whose grandfather is a senator?"

"We don't discuss politics."

"I heard she and Zelda Fitzgerald are childhood friends. Do you know Zelda?"

Freddie ignored the question. "What brings you here?"

"Everyone says this is the new place to go. I don't agree."

"Oh?"

"Some of the guests"—Constance's gaze slid to a nearby table—"they're not our kind."

Freddie followed Constance's gaze to two middle-aged couples. They looked a bit rough around the edges, but good cheer wreathed their faces. "What kind is that?"

Constance's eyes narrowed, and she stared down the length of her long nose. "What are you writing?"

"Just a few notes."

"For a book?"

"A column."

"I heard you left *Vogue* for a start-up." A superior smile touched her cupid's-bow lips. "I suppose the pressure of writing for a national magazine isn't for everyone."

That was Constance's sharpest arrow? Freddie almost laughed. "How are you keeping busy, Constance?"

The woman towering above her thrust her ring-heavy left hand in Freddie's face. "Planning a wedding is a full-time job."

"That's right. I heard you're engaged. You're marrying Bill Rottinghurst?"

Constance's face froze, and something akin to shame rose in Freddie's breast. Just because Constance slung arrows didn't mean Freddie should return fire. It wasn't kind to remind Constance of the man she'd pursued with dogged determination. Especially since Bill Rottinghurst was now engaged to Constance's former best friend.

"I'm marrying Tom Littleton."

"Tom. I believe I met him at a party last month." She hadn't. "He's a delightful man. I wish you every happiness."

"Is there anyone special in your life? You're not getting any younger."

Freddie regretted her kindness. "I suppose you'll be moving to Connecticut?"

"Greenwich."

Constance was welcome to it.

"Such a treat to see you, Freddie. You'll have to come visit after we're settled. If you can get the time off work, I mean."

When hell froze over.

The song ended, and Freddie hoped Tallulah and Ephram would linger for another dance. She'd prefer not to introduce Constance to Tallulah. Constance adored famous people, and if she made Tallulah's acquaintance, there was a strong possibility she'd abandon her friends or fiancé and claim the fourth chair at the table. "For you, I'll try."

It was a brush-off, but Constance didn't move. Instead, she gaped at Tallulah and Ephram as they walked toward the table. "That's Tallulah Bankhead."

"I told you I was here with her."

"I assumed you made it up."

Tallulah and Ephram reached the table, and Tallulah asked, "Who's this?" She used a tone more commonly employed for wondering aloud about a strange substance on the bottom of her shoe.

Freddie swallowed a smile. "Meet Constance Jessop. Constance, this is Tallulah Bankhead and Ephram Loeb."

Tallulah tapped her chin. "Freddie told me about you."

"She did?" Constance sounded like a new dawn, hopeful and bright.

"Constant Gossip, right?"

Constance's cheeks turned an unflattering shade of red, and she flounced off.

Tallulah's eyes sparkled, and she pressed a hand to her chest. "Did I offend?"

"Undoubtedly." Freddie couldn't find so much as an ounce of sympathy in her heart. "I'll never be invited to Greenwich."

"You may thank me with another gin rickey."

Ephram shook his head. "And I thought men were vicious."

Tallulah patted his arm. "No, darling. It's the women you need to watch out for."

CHAPTER 12

FREDDIE." EPHRAM SMILED AT her. "Would you care to dance?"

Young, gay couples crowded the dance floor, and the music was marvelous, but—Freddie cut her gaze toward Tallulah.

"Go." Tallulah waved them toward the dance floor and picked up her gin rickey. "I need to rehydrate."

Freddie allowed Ephram to lead her. As they reached the floor, the band transitioned to a slow song.

Leaving enough distance between them to satisfy the strictest chaperone, Ephram placed his hand on the small of her back.

She was willing to bet his first question would be about Tallulah. Two could play that game. "Where's Brandt tonight?"

"He'll be sorry he missed you."

"That's not an answer."

"No," he agreed. "It isn't. Tell me about your friend."

"The singer is marvelous."

Ephram cut his gaze to the stage. "I suppose."

"I go out quite often, and she's the best I've ever heard."

"Brandt hired her." He frowned, as if he hated to admit it.

"What?" Freddie felt a matching frown wrinkle her forehead and forced her face into a more pleasant expression. "This is his club?"

"Our club."

"I thought King Tut..."

"Also ours. My idea. This place is all Brandt. Now"—he put another inch distance between them—"tell me about Tallulah."

"Anything specific?"

"Is she seeing someone?"

"What do you mean 'our club'?"

"Our club. We own it. About Tallulah?"

"She sees lots of someones."

Ephram nodded, as if Tallulah buzzing from lover to lover like a nectar-starved bee was a good thing.

"How many clubs do you own?"

"Four. What's her favorite flower?"

"Gardenias. Four?"

He nodded. "Four. Favorite color?"

"Blue. How many secrets are you keeping?"

"Too many. What else should I know?"

"She's moving to London."

He tripped over his feet but recovered quickly. "She said something about that. When?"

"Two weeks."

"So soon?"

"She has a play opening. She says it's an interesting role. Nothing short of the apocalypse will keep her here." If Ephram understood that Tallulah was available for only two weeks, he might survive her.

"We'll have to make the most of the time we have."

More likely, Tallulah would break his heart in two. Freddie hoped Ephram was one of those stoic men who hid his pain. She couldn't abide anyone who wore their heart (broken or not) on their sleeve. It seemed too public, too needy. "Where are they?" she asked. "The clubs?"

"The Upper East Side and Midtown." He glanced toward the table, where Tallulah waited for them. "She's fascinating."

People found automobile accidents, gang violence, and burning buildings fascinating. They slowed down and gawked at mangled metal, gobbled newspaper articles featuring Al Capone, and gathered on the sidewalk to watch infernos. *Fascinating* wasn't always good. *Fascinating* could be devastating.

"Be careful, Ephram."

He grinned. "You're sweet to care."

Freddie blinked. No one had called her sweet since she graduated from pigtails. "I think you might be a nice man."

Ephram's grin widened.

"Tallulah eats nice men for breakfast."

The grin turned wolfish. "Can't wait."

He'd been warned. She had nothing more to say on the subject.

The song ended, and their feet slowed.

"Another dance?" Ephram was being polite. Everything from the tilt of his body to the direction of his gaze said he wanted to return to Tallulah.

"No, thank you."

At the table, Tallulah had finished her gin rickey and ordered another round. Two glasses sat at Freddie's place, her unfinished drink and a full one.

Freddie handed the fresh glass to Ephram. "To new friends."

He clinked her glass, but his adoring, *fascinated* gaze locked on Tallulah. And Tallulah's blue eyes saw nothing and no one but Ephram.

Freddie took her seat and watched electricity arc in their gazes. The two of them were more entertaining than half the plays on Broadway. They touched each other lightly—Tallulah's cheek, Ephram's shoulder. They whispered in each other's ears. They forgot Freddie shared their table.

This was more romantic than a picture starring Rudolph Valentino and Clara Bow (someone needed to make a picture like that). All Freddie needed was popcorn.

"Tallulah, will you dance with me?" Ephram asked. It was an obvious excuse to touch more of her.

Uncharacteristically mute, Tallulah nodded and let him lead her to the dance floor.

This might be Tallulah's most successful relationship. Two weeks of fun and passion and sex.

Freddie sipped her gin and studied the club with fresh eyes. Club Monaco belonged to Brandt? The tables were full. The floor was packed. The man had a hit, and he hadn't told her. Why not?

She searched for Tallulah and Ephram, but the crush of swinging, swaying bodies kept them hidden.

No matter.

She picked up her pencil.

A woman's scream pierced the air.

Freddie's own lungs seized until the rasp for air was almost painful.

The scream? It lasted. It beat the crowd into submission. It bounced off the walls. It battled the saxophone and won. Only a woman with an impressive diaphragm could scream like that, one accustomed to projecting to the back of the Martin Beck Theatre.

Freddie rose from her chair.

The band fell silent. Despite the tangle of dread in her stomach, Freddie searched for the scream's source. The patrons seated at nearby tables were doing the same, craning their necks, looking for the woman in distress.

Dancers fled the floor, tripping over themselves in their rush to escape.

Freddie raced to the stairs, but the throng of fleeing dancers kept her from descending.

The scream ended, but its ghost echoed through the rapidly emptying club.

With the dance floor nearly empty, Freddie spotted a man on the parquet.

Tallulah knelt next to him.

Freddie clutched the stair rail. Again? Not another death. Did the fleeing dancers have it right? Should she run? The gin in her stomach soured, and she clapped a hand to her mouth. A visceral need to join the people who were running away had her turning toward the exit. No! She wouldn't run. She was better than that. Freddie threw an elbow and shoved her way down the stairs.

Too bad her feet refused to work properly. They tripped and stubbed and stumbled, and only her desperate hold on the rail kept her from somersaulting downward. When her soles finally— blessedly—found the parquet, she rushed to Tallulah's side.

"He says I can't take it out." Tallulah held her arms over her stomach and rocked.

"Take what out?"

"The knife. Ephram said if I pulled it out, he'd bleed to death."

To Freddie's untrained eye, he was doing that anyway. Crimson pooled around him, coated Tallulah's hands, and soaked her hem. Never had Freddie felt more helpless. She lifted her head and caught the singer's eye. "Call for help."

The woman nodded as if waking from a trance and disappeared.

"Tallulah, what happened?"

"We were dancing…" Tallulah stared at Ephram, as if the force of her gaze might make him draw another breath.

Yes, they'd danced. Freddie had seen them. But dancing didn't explain the knife in Ephram's side or the blood pooling beneath him.

"Who stabbed him?"

"A woman."

The sudden rush in Freddie's ears rendered her deaf, and it was long seconds before she asked, "What did she look like?"

"Light brown hair, gorgeous dress." Tallulah looked down at her own frock as if the gore darkening the hem was a surprise. "How did this happen?"

Freddie had no answer to that. "Help will be here soon." At least she hoped so. "Ephram, can you hear me?"

Ephram didn't respond.

"What the hell happened?" Brandt knelt on the floor next to his friend.

Brandt was here. He'd fix this. The acid in Freddie's stomach eased its efforts to climb her throat.

Brandt squeezed Ephram's shoulder. "Don't go anywhere. Stay with me. We'll get you to a hospital. They'll sew you up, and you'll be good as new."

Tallulah sobbed.

Brandt turned and yelled, "Bring up the house lights."

The club went from dim to a lavender half light, and Freddie's breath caught.

Ephram's skin was gray. That couldn't be good.

"Where's the damned ambulance?" Brandt bellowed.

Two men with a stretcher appeared as if Brandt's rage had conjured them. They gently shifted Ephram onto the pallet and raced him toward the exit.

Brandt stood. "You can get your friend home?"

Tallulah's makeup had run. Her face was puffy. Her eyes were red. And she rocked from side to side.

"I'll get her home. Please, would you call me? Let me know how he is?"

He replied with a grim nod.

They watched Brandt follow his friend. When he disappeared, Freddie asked gently, "Did you see the woman's face?"

Tallulah wiped eyes smeared with mascara. "No. I only noticed her dress. It was a Carmaux."

"You're sure?"

A tear ran unchecked down Tallulah's cheek. "I almost bought it when I stopped by the store yesterday."

It had to be the same woman who'd killed Ewan. It had to be. And she had to be stopped. Freddie didn't care if she had to promise Walter Ames the lead in Eugene O'Neill's next play. She needed the woman's name.

Freddie woke with a sense of determination and hopped out of bed faster than a jackrabbit pursued by foxes, that or a woman hounded by last night's regrets.

She bathed, powdered, and did her hair in record time, drank a quick cup of coffee, and boarded the elevator.

"Good morning, Ernest."

Ernest barely concealed a glower. "Miss."

"Looks like another hot one."

"It's not the heat. It's the humidity."

Such a nonsensical phrase. It would still be beastly hot without the moisture in the air. Did he think deserts were pleasant? But a meteorological debate with the elevator operator did not fit into her schedule. "And how."

"The lobby, miss."

"Thank you."

The doorman greeted her with a warm smile. "Taxi, Miss Archer?"

"Please."

He stepped into the street and waved down a Checker.

Freddie climbed in and gave the cabbie the address.

"You're an actress?" asked the driver.

"No."

"That's the theater district. You sure you're not someone famous? The missus loves when I get famous people."

"Sorry to disappoint." She might have famous friends, but she valued anonymity. Dotty, who was ridiculously famous, had just this week complained about the expectation to be clever. Always. It didn't matter if the rams (her term for a cruel hangover) pulverized her brain, the public demanded wit.

The Marx Brothers enjoyed their fame, but only because it brought them a seemingly endless supply of willing women.

Of course, Aleck Woollcott adored fame. Much like he adored

the silly cape he wore to the theater. The man thrived on being the center of attention.

"I had Clara Bow in the cab. Sitting in the same spot as you."

The cabbie's interruption of her musings allowed her nerves to sneak past the wall she'd built as she watched Ephram bleed. She clasped her hands in her lap and breathed deeply in hopes of easing the tension gathering in her shoulders.

"Rudolph Valentino, too."

"Did you?" she murmured.

"He's a hit with ladies." The cabbie pulled to the curb.

Freddie studied her destination. This was it. The place she might find a name. According to simply everyone, Brooks Hawley, Walter Ames's agent, used this deli as his second office, the one where he spent the majority of his time.

She paid the fare and pushed through the door. The heavenly scent of coffee mixed with other smells—potatoes and onions frying in oil, cigar smoke, and greasepaint. This was a Broadway hangout.

A quick scan told her Brooks Hawley wasn't there.

"Freddie!"

She turned and spotted Groucho Marx. George had spoken with him and then sent Freddie a note. *Beatrice looks forward to Paris.* She slapped on a smile and walked toward the comedian.

"Sit." Nothing funny about his tone. He sounded like a misanthrope.

She sat.

"What's this about Walter Ames?"

"He has something I need."

Groucho knocked his cigar ash into a saucer. "You get what you need, and Beatrice Kaufman gets a trip to Paris. I get saddled with Ames for the run."

"He's a good actor."

He ceded her point with a brief nod. "He's also a horse's ass."

"But a good actor."

"There are good actors who are decent human beings."

"What do you want, Groucho?"

He leaned back in his chair. "Word is you wrote a play."

"How? Nick." She answered her own question. He was the only person who'd read *God Created Woman*.

"Peters says it's good. Maybe even great."

"It's not suited to you." The play was light and airy and arch, not the slapstick Groucho and his brothers favored.

"Nick says it would be perfect for Mimi." Mimi Sherman (née Shultz) was Groucho's current sheba.

"Groucho..."

"Let me read it. That's all I'm asking."

What would Groucho's wife think? Freddie liked Ruth. Letting Groucho produce the play she'd sweated over for his chorus-girl mistress felt like a betrayal of all her hard work. And Ruth. Freddie closed her eyes and considered her options. Ruth wasn't blind. She knew Groucho wandered. Casting Mimi would not come as a surprise. As for her own secret dream that Tallulah might play the lead? Some dreams weren't meant to come true. "Fine."

"Shake on it."

Freddie extended her hand.

Grouch grinned as he pumped their clasped fingers. "You didn't come here to see me."

"No."

"Brooks Hawley just walked in."

Freddie resisted the urge to turn her head. "This only happens— the play, I mean—if Walter Ames gives me a name and address."

"A girl who goes after what she wants." Groucho waggled the two enormous caterpillars that passed for his eyebrows, and his thumb stroked the back of her hand. "I like that."

The man was incorrigible. "Save it for someone who's buying."

"You wound me." He pressed his free hand to his heart while his gaze fixed on her décolleté.

Freddie extricated her fingers. "You're looking for a play for Mimi."

"Doesn't mean I ignore pretty girls."

He'd cheat on Ruth *and* Mimi? "Perhaps it should."

He wrinkled his nose and shook his head as if she'd disappointed him. "Peters's side piece did a number on you."

The world tilted, and Freddie grabbed the table's edge. Nick had cheated on her? Unbidden, her mind produced images of eager young actresses.

Groucho paled. "Hell. You didn't know? I thought you knew. You returned his ring."

Freddie couldn't speak around the lump in her throat.

"You pushed him into the bay."

She swallowed. Hard. "Nope." The *p* popped. "I had no idea."

He rubbed his palm down his chin. "I'm sorry, Freddie."

An enormous rabbit hole opened in her mind. Who? Where? Why? Did everyone know? Had they pitied her as they said nothing? Freddie crossed her arms over her belly, as if the pressure might keep the toast and coffee in her stomach. "It doesn't matter." She forced a smile. "Please don't give it another thought."

"You're a class act, kid."

She was a woman—not a girl, not a kid. But this was not the moment to make that point. Instead, she breathed deeply. She'd deal with Nick's betrayal later. Alone. When there was no one to see her tears.

Groucho nodded at someone over her shoulder. "You want me to talk to Hawley for you?"

Groucho Marx in a murder investigation? That had the makings of a vaudeville sketch. "No. I'll do it. There is one thing..."

"What?"

"Please don't tell anyone you let the cat out of the bag." She gritted her teeth so her chin wouldn't wobble. "About Nick, I mean."

For a brief second, Groucho's expression softened, and he nodded. "You have my word." He puffed on his cigar. "Now, get out of here. I have work to do."

Freddie walked to Brooks Hawley's table and waited until he looked up from his perusal of the sports section.

"You're a bit old for an ingenue."

"I'm not an actress."

"Then what is it you're after?"

"I need to speak with one of your clients."

He held up his hands. "I don't involve myself in my clients' personal business."

"This isn't personal."

"You look like a nice girl. My advice is to forget him. Go find yourself a rich banker or lawyer, marry him, and enjoy a comfortable life. Actors make bad husbands."

"Walter Ames has some information I want."

"Walter?" Hawley's eyes narrowed. "What's this information you want from him?"

"He had lunch with a woman at the Algonquin. I want her name and address."

"What's in it for him?"

"If the information is good, a part in *The Cocoanuts*."

Hawley's gaze slid to Groucho. "Is that so?"

"It is. Groucho and I discussed it. But only if Ames gives me her name and address. Her telephone number if he has it."

"Groucho," Hawley yelled, "is this dame aboveboard?"

"Part for Ames?" Groucho yelled back.

Hawley nodded. "Yeah."

"She's on the level."

Hawley studied her with cynical eyes. "What's your name?"

"Freddie Archer."

"Why do you care about Ames's lunch date?"

"She had on a gorgeous dress. I want to know who made it and where she bought it." The lies came easily.

"I'll ask Ames."

"I want to talk to him myself."

He crossed his arms. "Something is hinky."

Freddie shrugged. "*I'll Say She Is* was a big hit." Last year's Marx Brothers show had broken records. "Irving Berlin is writing the music and lyrics for *The Cocoanuts*, but if you're not interested . . ." She turned away and forced a step.

"Wait."

She hid a smile and paused.

"I'll get you what you want. Come by my office later this afternoon."

Freddie looked over her shoulder. "Where's your office, Mr. Hawley?"

He frowned and tapped the table. "Here. Four o'clock. Don't be late."

"Fine." It was getting harder to hide her smile. By four o'clock that afternoon, she'd have a name.

CHAPTER 13

REDDIE SAT AT HER desk and grimaced at the blank sheet in the typewriter. She barked at poor Annie. She glowered at the telephone and resisted calling the no-good, lying son-of-a-bitch who'd claimed to love her. She double-checked the lock on the drawer that held her play. She glared at the ceiling and wondered why she hadn't heard from Brandt. She paced. Then she ran through the whole sequence. For the eighth time.

"What's eating you?" Annie stood just inside the door with her hands on her hips and an intractable expression on her usually sunny face.

"Nothing." So many things.

"Baloney. What is it?"

Freddie wouldn't admit that Nick had played her for a fool. Her pride wouldn't allow it. She wasn't ready to talk about the play or why she'd agreed to let Groucho read it. And she didn't know if Annie, who seemed entirely too taken with a certain detective, would tell said detective about her efforts to get the mysterious woman's name. "Writer's block."

"Go." Annie made shooing gestures with her fingers.

"Go where?"

"Anywhere but here. You're not writing, and a black storm cloud followed you into the office. The whole staff is tiptoeing lest lightning strike them dead."

Freddie checked her watch. She still had an hour until she was due at the deli. "I need to make a phone call first."

Annie lifted a brow that promised retribution if Freddie didn't soon depart.

"I'll go. I promise." A fine state of affairs when she was kicked out of her own office. "The call won't take long."

When the door closed behind Annie, Freddie dialed.

"What fresh hell is this?" asked Dotty.

"It's Freddie. Do you have a minute?"

"For you?" Seconds passed as Dotty considered her answer. "Yes."

Freddie splayed her fingers across her desk, closed her eyes, and said, "I wrote a play."

"When?" Dotty's voice was a freshly sharpened pencil. Pointed. Ready to gouge.

"Pardon?"

"When did you write a play?"

Freddie pinched the bridge of her nose. What did that matter? "Over the past year."

"And I'm just now hearing about it?" Dotty was upset Freddie hadn't shared the hell (not fresh) of writing multiple columns plus a play? What would she say if Freddie had written a novel?

"I wanted to make sure it was good."

"Is it?"

"It might be." She gathered her courage. Nick had told her it was great. But Nick was an irredeemable liar. "Would you read it? Please?"

"What's it called?"

"God Created Woman."

"What's it about?"

"You know how Eve is blamed for taking a bite of the apple?"

"Yes."

"And Pandora is blamed for opening the box?"

"Yes."

"I explored that in modern times."

"Please tell me the heroine is rewarded, not punished."

"Read the play."

"Freddie—" Dotty's voice carried a threat.

"Of course, she's rewarded."

"Then I'll read it."

Relief flooded Freddie's veins. Dotty would level with her. And if Freddie had misjudged, if the play was dreadful, Dotty would tell her quietly, not razz her in front of their friends like Groucho might. "Thank you."

"When can I look at it?"

Freddie glanced first at the drawer and then her watch. "I'll drop it off at the hotel. But, Dotty, this is for your eyes only. If Aleck quotes my lines at me, I'll—" She wasn't sure what she'd do. "I'll never forgive you."

"Mum's the word. Last I checked, you keep several of my secrets. Are you coming now?"

"On my way."

"Swell."

Freddie ignored the communal sigh of relief as she jabbed the elevator button. When she reached the sidewalk, she decided to walk to the Algonquin. Only a few blocks separated the office from the hotel.

She slipped into the hotel's dim lobby, handed the sealed envelope to Frank Case, and asked him to deliver it to Dotty.

Then, keeping to the shaded sides of the streets, she walked the half mile to the deli.

At ten minutes until four, she breezed through the deli's glass door. The men who finished their nights with morning plates of eggs, gefilte fish, and rye toast were long gone. Instead, a smattering of actors, bookies, and seedy theatrical agents sat at the tables. Errand boys and assistants crowded the counter and waited for takeout orders.

Without the aroma of coffee to mask it, the odor of grease wrinkled Freddie's nose. She'd need another bath and shampoo, and her dress would need a good airing.

"Mr. Hawley." She walked straight to his table.

"You're early."

"Only by a few minutes."

"Girls are never early."

"On occasion, women are."

He snorted and jerked his chin at a chair. "Sit."

Freddie pulled out the chair and sat. "Do you have what I asked for?"

"Straight to business." He stroked his chin.

"You didn't impress me as the type of man who wastes a minute." Except for the countless hours he spent drinking coffee in a deli.

Hawley chuckled and pulled at his collar.

"What did Walter Ames tell you?"

"I haven't spoken with him yet."

Freddie pushed away from the table. "I won't take more of

your time." Annoyance laced her voice. She'd walked all the way here in the afternoon heat. Yes, she'd spotted open taxis, but they wouldn't have been any cooler. "Please contact me at *Gotham* when you have a name."

Hawley's brows rose. "You work for *Gotham*?"

"I do."

"You know the woman who writes that column?"

"What column?" Freddie didn't like where this was headed.

"The one about clubs, and speaks, and who she saw where."

"I do." Her voice could freeze the Hudson.

Hawley ignored the chill. "I have a client. She's gonna be a big star. Bigger than Brice. But she needs exposure. Her name in that column would help."

"A Touch of Rouge is not Walter Winchell. The column is not Mainly About Mainstreeters."

"It's better than Winchell. Funnier. Sexier." Hawley was playing her for a sap.

"The deal was a role in *The Cocoanuts* for Ames."

"What if I can tell you where to find them?"

She cared more about learning the name than Hawley did about landing a role for Ames. She tamped down a sigh. "I'll ask what I can do for your actress."

"Ames is having dinner at El Rey."

Much as she wanted—needed—the woman's name, she refused to spend hours at El Rey hoping Walter Ames appeared. "Not good enough."

"Nine o'clock. The column?"

"After I get the name and address." Freddie headed for the door.

Before she reached the exit, a man the size of a log cabin

stopped her with a hand just smaller than a catcher's mitt on her arm. "Mr. Rothstein wants a word."

Arnold "the Brain" Rothstein was said to run the Jewish mafia from a corner table in this very deli.

Freddie approached his table with extreme caution. "Good afternoon, Mr. Rothstein."

"Nothing good about it. It's too hot to sleep." Arnold Rothstein was a dapper man with dark hair, thin lips, and cold eyes. He dabbed at his forehead with a white linen handkerchief. "Sit."

Freddie sank into the chair held out for her. "You wanted to see me?"

"You got a talent. That Touch of Rouge column is good, and the wife adores your fashion pieces."

"Thank you." Freddie's voice was faint. Sure, she'd met gangsters. But Arnold Rothstein wasn't *a* gangster. He was *the* gangster. And he knew far too much about her.

"I hate to see such talent wasted."

Freddie clutched her hands in her lap. Was he threatening her?

"Word is you think a dame killed Ewan Duncan."

She nodded.

"And Jake Haskell."

She nodded again.

"And Ephram Loeb."

"He's dead?" Brandt hadn't called. Unbidden, tears filled her eyes. "When?"

"He passed this morning."

She stared at the glass of milk sitting at Mr. Rothstein's place at the table. "He seemed like a good man. I'm sorry."

"Me, too. You find the woman who jabbed him, you let me know."

It was one thing to give Detective Sullivan the woman's name and where to find her. Quite another to give that information to Arnold Rothstein. "I don't know who she is."

"But it's why you're here." He grinned. If sharks could grin, they'd look like Arnold Rothstein. "You do business in my office, I hear about it."

Freddie swallowed. What else did he know?

"You find her, you come to me." Arnold Rothstein seemed pleasant enough. *Seemed* being the operative word. The man had people who crossed him bumped off.

"Yes, sir."

"I'll tell my wife I met you. She says you must be the most stylish woman in New York." He studied her with dead eyes. "What are you wearing?"

Her dress was a flowered chiffon trimmed with a contrasting ribbon. The hem ended just below her knee. She'd paired it with silk stockings and a strap pump the same soft yellow as her dress. On her head, she wore a poke hat of Bangkok straw. "Carmaux."

"I'll tell her. Nice meeting you, Miss Archer." It was a dismissal.

She stood. "Likewise."

Somehow she exited the deli without her knees giving out. On the sidewalk, she grabbed hold of a lamppost and breathed deeply until she felt certain she wouldn't collapse. Then she walked. So slowly that other pedestrians—New Yorkers in a hurry—muttered about her mental capacity.

She didn't care.

"Move it, lady."

She took shelter under an awning and pondered her day.

She'd promised Groucho Marx he could read her beloved play and then given the play to Dotty.

She'd discovered Nick cheated on her.

Arnold Rothstein had involved himself in her life.

Ephram Loeb was dead.

Obviously, Ephram's death was the worst item on a terrible list, but Freddie was hard-pressed to select the second worst.

El Rey didn't count among Freddie's favorite clubs. The place took itself too seriously. The gaiety seemed forced. The bland food never failed to disappoint.

Freddie sat alone at a table for two and alternated her gaze between her watch and the entrance. Not that she could see beyond her outstretched hand; the haze of cigarette and cigar smoke was too thick.

She sipped her drink and wrinkled her nose. Whoever owned the place had poured cut-rate swill into expensive bottles. There was no way the brown plaid in her glass was Glenromach. The liquor was rough as a cob. One taste, and her throat felt as if she'd swallowed broken glass.

She put her drink on the table and wondered about Brandt.

He hadn't called.

Tallulah had. "You're sure Brandt hasn't called?"

"Not a word." It was God's truth.

"Why not? He said he'd call."

Freddie had spent the next hour listening to Tallulah's worry over Ephram. She hadn't had the heart to repeat Arnold Rothstein's news. She'd wait for confirmation from Brandt before she told Tallulah that Ephram had died. Even if it meant her friend was in danger of falling in love with what might have been.

"Hey, doll. Buy you a drink?"

Freddie looked up from her musings. The man in front of her wore too much pomade, smelled of too much bay rum cologne, and had too many gleaming teeth. She shook her head. "No, thank you."

"Don't be that way." He offered her a dimpled smile as if a second glance at his white teeth might change her mind.

"I said no."

"But you don't mean it."

Oh, she meant it. "There are lots of women who'd be delighted to have a drink with you." She waved a hand at the crowded club. "I'm not one of them."

"That's just mean."

Mean? Since breakfast she'd been threatened, been extorted, had her belief in humanity shaken to its core, and shared a play that she feared revealed her deepest thoughts and fears. She was not in the mood for a cake-eater with an oversized ego. "My husband is joining me."

He eyed her bare left hand. "Sure he is."

What was wrong with this man? She'd told him no and lied to spare his feelings, and he wouldn't give up. "I'm not interested."

He stepped closer to her, and ugliness shimmered in his eyes. "You think you can give me the brush?"

Anger flared in her chest. What gave him the right to intimidate her? She'd done nothing to invite his attention. "Leave me alone."

He settled into the second chair at the table as if her rejection didn't concern him. "Name's Ben."

Freddie stood. It was half past nine, and Walter Ames hadn't arrived. Ben was welcome to her table. She collected her handbag, a smart Chanel clutch, and stepped away.

Ben's hand on her wrist stopped her progress.

"Let go."

"I don't think I will. Pretty girl like you needs company."

She tugged against his hold. "Let. Me. Go."

His eyes hardened. "You set that fine fanny in that chair. Now." Freddie had a strong sense of déjà vu. And thanks to her experience at Eloise's, she knew precisely what to do. If Ben stood, she'd knee him in the balls.

"Let the lady go." A man wearing a dark pinstripe suit glowered at Ben.

Ben shrugged. "Mind your own potatoes."

Ben was an idiot.

Her white knight radiated violence, and the lump under his jacket might easily be a gun. He cracked his knuckles. "Let the lady go. I won't say it again."

A fissure appeared in Ben's brash façade, and he gave a nervous hiccup. His grip on Freddie's wrist loosened, and she pulled herself free.

Her wrist ached, and she rubbed the skin where Ben had held too tightly.

"Did he hurt you?" The man who'd come to her rescue had drooping brows, a down-turned mouth, and big ears. His voice, when he spoke to her, was soft as velvet.

Freddie resisted hiding her hands behind her back. Who was this man? "It's nothing."

"Let me see." He held out an open palm.

She showed him her wrist. Even in the dim light, red marks were visible.

He brushed the marks with gentle fingers. "Apologize to the lady."

"She's just another dame."

Freddie's white knight grunted and released her wrist. Then he pulled back his arm and smashed his fist into Ben's face.

Ben crashed to the floor.

Shock widened Freddie's eyes. What had just happened? She looked at Ben. She looked at the white knight. She repeated the process. Ben was still on the floor. The white knight waited with a polite expression on his face.

"Thank you." She couldn't think of anything else to say.

"You're welcome." He stepped away from the crazy tableau he'd created. "Enjoy your evening, Miss Archer."

He knew her name? How? "Wait!"

He paused.

"Who are you?"

"Arnold Rothstein sends his regards."

The man who ran organized crime in New York had taken a personal interest in her? Had sent someone to follow her? Freddie shivered.

"Goose walk over your grave?" The white knight grinned as if he'd told a joke.

The extreme dryness in her mouth kept her from answering. She nodded.

He took another step.

"Wait!" she croaked.

Again, he paused. But this time, he raised a brow. The brow still drooped, but it reached higher on his forehead.

"What's your name?" she asked.

"My friends call me Legs."

Freddie clutched the table's edge. "As in Legs Doyle?"

"At your service."

Legs Doyle made frequent appearances in the papers. Charges

almost never stuck. And when they did, juries acquitted in record time. The man was a bootlegger, a gangster, a killer. And he'd just saved her.

Two palookas, fear and anger, duked it out in her chest. The winner got to beat gratitude into the ground. In the meantime, gratitude said, "Thank you again, Mr. Legs." She resisted burying her face in her hands. "I mean, Doyle. Thank you, Mr. Doyle."

"Mr. Rothstein said you needed someone to look out for you."

"He did?" Freddie squeaked. She cleared her throat and tried the question at a lower pitch. "He did?"

Legs nodded. "He didn't tell me you're a peach."

Freddie ignored the compliment. "Why? I mean, why does Mr. Rothstein care?"

Legs scowled. "Mr. Rothstein don't like strangers with bean shooters clipping his business associates."

Did he mean Jake or Ewan? And what about Ephram? Had he worked for Mr. Rothstein? Did Brandt? "What does that have to do with me?"

"Mr. Rothstein thinks you'll find the people responsible."

Freddie gulped. "He does?"

Legs looked her up and down, but not like a man appreciating a woman. More like a man wondering if she were capable of anything more taxing than elbowing shoppers at a half-off sale on silk stockings.

Those women were vicious.

"Mr. Rothstein don't make mistakes."

"There's an actor," Freddie explained. "He was supposed to be here tonight. He might know something about a woman I spotted when Ewan Duncan was murdered, but he's not here."

"Is she?"

She'd been so busy looking for Walter Ames that she hadn't bothered searching the club for the woman. She searched now.

There were dozens of pretty women in pretty frocks. Dozens of men in evening dress. A waiter helped Ben off the floor and escorted him to the exit. And in the corner, at a table for two, the mystery woman sat alone. Freddie's shoulders stiffened.

"You see her?"

"What happens if I say yes?" Freddie wanted no part of Legs Doyle using his bean shooter to clip the woman.

Legs tugged on his left earlobe. "Nothing."

"Nothing?"

The woman glanced at her watch, pursed her lips, and stood.

"She works for someone," Legs added. "Mr. Rothstein wants to know who."

"You won't hurt her?"

"You think I'd hurt a woman?"

"Of course not." Freddie's reply was immediate, and not entirely true. The woman had been out with Jake Haskell before he died, was present at Ewan's murder, and her dress, a Carmaux, matched the description Tallulah gave of Ephram's killer. Maybe Legs should hurt her. She tilted her chin toward the woman.

Legs touched her elbow. "She's leaving."

"We should go."

"Go?"

Freddie nodded. "We should follow her."

CHAPTER 14

A FTER THE DIM NIGHTCLUB, the streetlights' jaundiced glow
seemed ridiculously bright, and Freddie blinked rapidly,
even as the throaty growl of engines, voices, horns, and hawkers
assaulted her ears. She stumbled, and Legs Doyle grabbed her
elbow. "You okay?"

She nodded.

"Good. She's getting away." He pointed at a Checker cab,
shoved Freddie into a waiting taxi, and barked at the driver, "Follow that cab."

The driver grinned as if he'd waited his whole life to hear
those words and slammed his foot onto the gas pedal. The forward
momentum plastered Freddie to the back seat.

"Very dramatic," she murmured.

Legs chuckled darkly, and the light and shadow playing across
his face made him more demon than a man. "Ewan Duncan was
a friend. If that dame can lead us to his killer, I'm not losing her."

The cabbie swerved around a slow-moving vehicle, and Freddie fisted her hands. Had she lost her mind? Speeding across

Manhattan with an infamous killer really couldn't be good for her health. "I didn't realize you and Ewan were friends. What about Jake and Ephram?"

"Them, too. But Ewan and I—it's hard to explain." He grimaced and ran an open palm across his face.

Freddie understood. On paper, she and Dotty had only their writing in common. But they'd met and seen kinship in each other's eyes. "Sometimes people fit together like puzzle pieces."

"Exactly."

"Where do you think we're headed?"

He glanced out the window. "Downtown. Can you hide your pearls? Take off your rings?"

Freddie nodded and hid a rope of marble-sized pearls inside her dress. Then she took off her earrings and the sapphire ring she wore on her right hand and stashed them in her handbag.

Legs nodded his approval.

They drove toward Lower Manhattan. With each block, the streets grew more crowded. One block was awash in water from an uncapped fire hydrant. Children splashed in the spray, and their laughter filtered past other, less pleasant noises.

Freddie glanced at her watch. "It's late for them to be on the streets."

"Their apartments are hotter than ovens. And they sleep six or seven in a bedroom. When—*if* they go to bed, they'll sleep on the roof or the fire escape."

Freddie winced. Her apartment was stifling, but she had numerous fans and didn't share a single inch of her space. "Did you grow up here?"

"Nah. Hell's Kitchen. Less crowded. Just as rough."

"Rough?"

"Prostitution. Gangs. Murder. Poverty. Filth. Hopelessness." He frowned at her. "You ought to take off the watch."

She slipped the diamond wristwatch into her bag. "You escaped."

"Brown plaid. Bootleg scotch. The good stuff."

"Ah."

"There's a fortune in top-shelf scotch. The swells can't get enough."

Had Jake, Ewan, and Ephram been murdered over scotch? She drank it on occasion, but preferred gin with soda water and plenty of lime.

"Scotch and money." Legs closed his eyes as if he'd imparted precious wisdom. "They're the same thing."

"What about Brandt Abrams?" she asked.

He frowned at her. "What about him?"

"Is he in danger?"

Legs's eyes glinted in the darkness. "Could be. Could be he's responsible for his friends' deaths."

She didn't believe that. She refused to believe that. Not after she'd witnessed Brandt's grief. His rage. Brandt hadn't murdered his friends. "No."

"What makes you so sure?"

"I saw him with Ewan."

Legs grunted and fell silent.

The driver took them farther south and east until the view from her window was unrelentingly grim.

Had she completely lost her mind? No sane woman would venture into the Lower East Side. Not at night. A handful of Mother's friends volunteered during daylight hours. They taught English and adult literacy and urged city leaders to build schools and force immigrant children to attend.

Freddie looked at the crumbling, derelict buildings. The do-gooders should add decent housing to their list. "How many people live here?"

"More than half a million. Someone told me it's the most crowded place in the world."

"I believe it." She clasped her hands in her lap and composed a column.

A cab ride to the Lower East Side is like a fevered dream. There is the constant buzz of thousands of voices speaking in unknown tongues, the reek of decay, and the stench of desperation. The tenements lean against each other as if a strong breeze might blow them down. And laughter. The laughter comes from children in a fire hydrant's spray, from a shopkeeper, from two men sharing a cigarette. It's not the gay sound one finds in a midtown club—a sound as effervescent as champagne bubbles. Rather, this laughter is tempered like steel—a sound that defies a hardship.

"You're quiet."

"Am I? I apologize." It was a woman's job to entertain, and she'd failed. "I was writing."

"Writing?"

"In my head."

Legs scowled.

"Don't worry. I won't remember a word." And even if she miraculously recalled every syllable, Gus would never publish it. Her brief was as clear as fresh water. Did these people have fresh water? She wrote about all that was fun and gay and light. The dark, dank Lower East Side would never appear in A Touch of Rouge.

They passed a woman with tired eyes, tangled hair, and gaunt cheeks, who balanced a crying child on each hip. She stared at Freddie as if a mythical creature had arrived in her neighborhood. A unicorn or a fairy princess or a fiery phoenix.

Freddie had known there was poverty in the city, but need and misery had been abstract ideas. This? This was hunger and despair and illness and—

"Don't pity them." Legs's voice cut through her musings.

"Pardon?"

"I can see it on your face." He waved at the mass of humanity outside the taxi. "Don't pity them. They don't want it. They don't need it. And they'll despise you for it."

"I—"

"You're wearing the same expression every do-gooder I ever met wears. You think you can fix them, but you can't. They're people, not projects."

"But—"

"People. Different from you, but still people."

"People in need. Surely there's—"

"There you go. Do-gooder. What they need are decent-paying jobs. Can you do that for them?"

"No," she admitted.

"Know anyone who can?"

"I might."

"Then talk to them. These people aren't interested in pity." He radiated ire, and Freddie wondered if some well-meaning woman on a mission to improve his life in Hell's Kitchen had somehow made things worse.

The taxi in front of them turned left, and their cabbie followed.

"Where's she going?" Freddie asked. It was a safer topic.

"My guess? The docks."

"The docks?" Freddie might not have a criminal mind, but she could put two and two together. Three dead bootleggers. And their alleged killer was on her way to the docks. It meant the woman was muscling in on the dead men's business. "Were Jake, Ewan, and Ephram in business with Mr. Rothstein?" Her curiosity burned so bright it was a wonder Legs didn't see its light shining through her pores. A lucky wonder. Too much interest in Arnold Rothstein's business might earn her a pair of cement overshoes and a late-night sail on the East River. Maybe this wasn't a safer topic.

"It's not healthy to ask about Mr. Rothstein's business." It was as if Legs could read her mind.

"Forget I asked."

A smile ghosted across Legs's sinister lips.

The taxi slowed.

"What's wrong?" Legs demanded.

"Too crowded," the cabbie replied.

Freddie peered through the windshield at the crowded street. People spilled from the tenements onto the pavement. Their faces appeared wan and tired in the automobile's headlights, and they seemed disinclined to let the taxi pass.

Ahead of them, the woman's cab was also stopped.

Freddie stiffened as a back door opened and the woman exited the cab. "Look!"

"That's her?"

Freddie nodded, and Legs threw a few bills into the front seat. "There's more if you wait for us."

The driver's head swiveled as he took in the neighborhood and the crowd. "For how long?"

"An hour," Legs replied. "I'll make it worth your while."

The cabbie nodded. "One hour. Not a second more."

"She's getting away." Freddie opened the car door and stepped gingerly onto the pavement.

Legs joined her, grabbed her hand, and cut his way through the crowd.

"Where are we?" She didn't see any street signs.

"The Lower East Side."

Freddie rolled her eyes. "Which street?"

"Clinton. Runs straight to the river."

An unseen hand tugged on her dress, and Freddie tugged the fabric free. "You were right. She must be headed to the docks."

Legs nodded. "That or a warehouse."

The crowd watched them. Freddie's spine prickled as if thousands of people had her pinned beneath a microscope.

She stayed close to Legs. She liked to think she could take care of herself, but this neighborhood and these people stripped away her illusions. Without Legs's protection, she wouldn't last a minute. She gratefully accepted the damp heat of his hand surrounding her fingers.

"This way." He pulled her onto a sidewalk so crowded that progress was nearly impossible.

"She'll get away."

"She'll see us if we stay in the street."

How was the woman walking unmolested? She was young, pretty, and wore ropes of pearls. Meanwhile, Freddie cowered in Legs's shadow, certain she'd be knifed for the jewelry she'd stashed in her bag.

"Can you see her?" Freddie asked. She'd lost all sense of direction.

Legs, who stood taller than most, nodded. "This way."

She followed him. He might be leading her to a white slaver, or an opium den, or a quiet place to kill her. Strike that. There were no quiet places on the Lower East Side. Not that he'd need one. Freddie would bet a month's salary that not a soul among the crowd would admit seeing a thing if something happened to her.

Her fingers chilled in Legs's hand, and she stumbled.

"Keep up."

"I'm trying," she snapped. "Your legs are at least a foot longer than mine."

He replied with a scowl, and Freddie bit back further reply.

He led. She followed. What choice did she have? She'd made an epic mistake coming here, and in a life filled with poor decisions, that was saying something.

Legs stopped abruptly, and she bumped into him.

He glared at her, as if she'd intentionally smashed her nose into his back. "She went into that warehouse."

They were close to the East River. The scent of rotting fish and refuse overpowered the stench of unwashed bodies.

She peered around Legs's bulk. Two men armed with Tommy guns guarded the door to a square brick building. "What do we do?"

"We wait."

Here? "For how long?"

"Till she comes out."

Nothing happened. For what seemed like hours, not one interesting thing occurred. Meanwhile, Freddie's mouth was as dry as dust, and she felt a physical need to run or scream or fight.

Legs yawned and squinted at his watch.

"Do you know who owns the warehouse?"

"No." Legs's terse reply suggested that the hole in his knowledge annoyed him. Deeply. That, or she annoyed him. Deeply.

"Where are we?"

"I already told you. Clinton Street."

This time, she refrained from rolling her eyes. "The cross street?"

"Cherry."

She could work with that. Assuming she made it out of here. "How long do we wait?"

He scowled. "As long as we can. I'm not exactly popular here."

That confession did nothing to allay Freddie's fears. Legs might not be leading her to her doom, but she wasn't safe. Not by any measure.

They stood in the shadow cast by the corner of a decrepit building and watched the warehouse. Another thousand minutes passed, and Legs ventured to the building's edge. "Don't move." He poked his head out of the shadows.

Freddie heard a whoosh and a sickening thud, and Legs collapsed to the filthy pavement.

She stared at his body. This was bad. Worse than bad. This was cataclysmic.

Legs's assailant rounded the corner, and Freddie sank to her knees and fumbled inside Legs's suit coat with fingers near frozen from terror.

There!

Her hand gripped Legs's gun. The dratted thing weighed far more than she was used to, but she held it steady and pointed it at a man who reeked of cigarettes and cheap gin.

He grinned at her with rotting teeth. "You're a pretty piece."

"One step closer, and I shoot."

He smiled as if she'd offered him high-grade entertainment. "You don't want to do that."

"I do." She really did. He'd knocked out Legs and left her to deal with the Lower East Side alone. She left her handbag on the ground next to Legs and used both hands to aim the gun at the man who threatened her. They'd drawn a crowd, and she suspected any sign of weakness would mean the end.

He stepped.

Freddie shot.

The bang echoed off the surrounding buildings, and the man howled and gripped his leg.

Freddie took a deep breath and addressed the crowd. "This is Legs Doyle." She nodded toward the unconscious man next to her. "He works for Arnold Rothstein."

A few in the crowd muttered and backed away.

"Mr. Rothstein will reward the man who lets him know Legs is injured."

"Rothstein's got no power here." The man she'd shot had found a second wave of courage. And idiocy.

"Really?" She widened her eyes in mock surprise. "The man who runs New York has no power on the Lower East Side?"

The crowd's mutters grew louder.

"Are you standing by this man?" Freddie spoke with confidence she didn't feel. "Do you trust no one will tell Mr. Rothstein this story?"

"She's right," yelled a woman in the crowd. "We don't need that kind of trouble."

Next to her Legs stirred. At least she hoped it was Legs. If it was a rat (which seemed an all-too-real possibility), she'd scream and lose her credibility.

"Legs?"

He groaned.

"How bad?"

"I've had worse."

"Can you stand?"

"Give me a minute."

A dark-haired woman in a limp brown dress pushed through the crowd. "Is it true?"

Freddie focused on the woman. "Is what true?"

"You shot Ezra?" She pointed at the man Freddie shot.

"I did." Now was not the time for apologies.

The woman stared at Freddie for long seconds and then turned and slapped Ezra across the face. "Idiot. How will you keep a job with a bum leg?"

Ezra covered his face with bloody hands. And the crowd rumbled with laughter.

"You think you're a big man? A gangster? You're a failure." Her hands connected with Ezra's ears, and he stumbled backward and fell to the pavement. Then the woman glanced in Freddie's direction. "Those are Rothstein's people, you idiot. Do you know what the Brain will do if he finds out—when he finds out—you attacked them?" She shuddered.

Another woman, this one in a drab gray dress, stepped forward and offered them a tired smile. "We don't want trouble. Ezra and the boys were just playing with you. I'll see you back to your taxi, miss."

"We should take her up on that," Freddie whispered to Legs. "Can you stand?"

Legs pushed into a sitting position, and Freddie helped him from the pavement.

He held out her abandoned handbag and swayed.

Don't let him fall. Don't let him fall. Keep him upright, and I'll give up gin. Or scotch. I'll give up scotch.

Legs leaned against the building and took a restorative breath.

"Who owns that warehouse?" She used Legs's gun to point at the building.

Faces that had looked marginally less menacing shuttered.

"Never mind," she hurried to say. "It's not important." She had other ways of finding the owner.

Legs leaned against her and said, "I was supposed to protect you."

They could deal with that when they were safe. "Do you need a doctor?" she asked.

"Nah. Just an aspirin and a good night's sleep."

She didn't believe him but didn't bother to argue. Not now, anyway. They limped after the woman in the gray dress with what felt like ten thousand sets of eyes upon them.

When they reached the cab (the most gorgeous automobile Freddie had ever seen, and thank God, the fates, and her lucky stars that the driver had waited), she asked Legs, "Where should I take you?"

"The deli." Legs tumbled into the cab's back seat and laced his fingers across his skull. "I need to report to Mr. Rothstein."

Freddie's heart skipped a beat, but she climbed in after him.

The taxi surged forward, and a tiny bit (an extremely tiny bit) of the tension in her neck eased.

"You stood over my body," said Legs.

She nodded.

"You protected me."

She shrugged. "I protected us both."

"You shot someone."

She gave a second nod.

"You were brave. I owe you."

Now she shook her head. "Anyone would have done the same."

"Not true. You could have run. Like I said, I owe you." He offered her a dark grin. "Mr. Rothstein owes you."

Freddie didn't argue. Instead, she returned his too-heavy gun. Given how her life was going, having Legs Doyle and Arnold Rothstein in her debt wasn't a bad idea.

CHAPTER 15

GAIN?" ANNIE'S VOICE WAS as sharp as an assassin's blade.
Which brought poor Ephram to mind. Freddie groaned
and cracked her eyelids.

"Why bother keeping an apartment when you sleep in your office?" Annie's hands were firmly planted on her hips, and her brows were gathered in a disapproving line. She looked positively terrifying.

"Coffee?" Freddie croaked.

"On your desk."

Freddie stretched her arms above her head, rolled her ankles, and flexed her toes. "I don't suppose you'd bring it to me?"

Fire glinted in Annie's eyes.

With a sigh, Freddie pushed off the divan and crossed to her desk.

"Is that blood?"

"Where?"

"Your dress."

Given where she'd been, she hoped the brown stain on her dress was blood. "Oh, that. I'm not sure."

"Where were you last night?" Like a hunting dog with a sensitive nose, Annie always sniffed out the question Freddie didn't care to answer.

Telling Annie she'd visited the Lower East Side held zero appeal. Freddie could practically hear her squeal of dismay. Rather than answer immediately, she took a restorative sip of coffee. "A speak in the Village. There was a brawl."

"Were you hurt?"

"Not in the least."

"Then whose blood is it?"

"No idea." At least that was honest.

"Have you considered spending a night at home?"

"Where's the fun in that?" She sipped again. "This coffee is heaven. Thank you."

Annie regarded her through narrowed eyes. "Something's wrong."

"Wrong?" Freddie smoothed her hair.

"How much did you drink last night?"

"I didn't." Another honest answer.

Annie crossed her arms. "Then why are you here?"

"What do you mean?"

"You never sleep here when you're sober." It was official. Annie should be a crime reporter. She possessed the requisite cynicism, more than enough toughness, and a disturbing level of distrust.

"There's a first time for everything." She kept her voice light. And innocent.

"Not this."

After dropping Legs at the deli, Freddie couldn't face her empty apartment. Not the space. Not the luxury. Not the shadows. The divan in her office had seemed a better choice. Especially when Arnold Rothstein had assigned a no-necked man the size of Rhode Island to see her safely home. It had required only a half second of reflection to decide that life was simpler and safer if Mr. Rothstein didn't have her address.

"Which speak?"

"Pardon?"

"Which speakeasy?"

"The Village Inn," Freddie lied.

"Didn't you witness a murder the last time you went there? The place is too dangerous."

If Annie knew the truth, where Freddie had really been, she'd lock her in her office and throw away the key. They needed a new topic. "What time is it?"

"Half past eight."

"Is Gus here?"

"Not yet."

That was brilliant luck. Freddie drained her coffee. "I'll pop home and clean up, then I need to stop by B. Altman's."

"You were just there." Annie's arms remained firmly crossed, and her gaze held a decidedly suspicious cast.

"I need to look at a dress. I can't remember the designer." Yet another lie. Her soul blackened with each passing moment. But a supposed trip to B. Altman would give her an hour or two of unexplained time away from the office.

"It's not like you to forget a designer's name."

"When did you become so suspicious? Is this thanks to Detective Sullivan?"

Annie uncrossed her arms, and her hands returned to her hips. "He's convinced you're investigating without him."

Smart man. "*Moi?* Never. Do I have any messages?"

"Miss Bankhead called. She wants you to go to a wake with her."

"A wake?"

"Sitting shiva, I believe she called it."

"For Ephram Loeb?"

Annie sniffed. "She might have mentioned that name."

"Did she say when?"

"Tonight."

"I'll call her from home."

"There's a staff meeting at two."

"Got it."

"You're due at Carmaux at half past three."

"Perfect." She edged toward the door.

"Wait!"

Freddie paused.

"Were you truly in a brawl?"

"Why do you ask?" Freddie tried to look innocent. Really, she did.

"That dress is filthy."

Oh, dear. It wouldn't do to be spotted in a soiled frock. "Someone knocked me down. I should change before I leave."

Annie pursed her lips as if she doubted every word, and Freddie braced herself for further interrogation.

"More coffee?"

That was her question? Freddie swallowed a relieved sigh. "You're an angel."

Annie left her, and Freddie slipped out of her ruined dress. Such a shame. Perhaps she'd replace it when she stopped by Carmaux's. She slipped on a white cotton voile dress embroidered with

French blue polka dots, grabbed her handbag, and met Annie at her desk.

"Your coffee." Annie held out a second cup.

"I take back every unkind thing I ever thought about you. You are heaven sent, and you have my eternal gratitude." Freddie drank deeply.

Annie rolled her eyes and covered the beginnings of a smile with her palm. "You want to thank me? Don't forget the staff meeting. It makes Gus cranky when you're not there."

"I never forget."

"Then you miss them on purpose?"

Freddie winked. "Of course I do."

Annie shook her head as if Freddie were a hopeless case. "Go. Get cleaned up. And don't be late."

Freddie sailed out of the office, flagged a taxi, and rode home deep in thought.

How was Legs?

Who owned that warehouse?

What was the woman's name?

Would Brandt be at Ephram's wake?

The cabbie pulled to the curb in front of her building, and Bert opened the door for her. "Good morning, Miss Archer."

"Good morning."

"I have a package for you."

"A package?"

"Delivered not ten minutes ago." He disappeared behind his desk and handed her a box.

"Thank you." She tucked the package under her arm and rode the elevator, pretending not to notice Ernest's disapproving stare.

The elevator doors opened, and she hurried to her apartment. She had calls to make, but first she needed more coffee and a bath.

She dropped the package on the chest in the front hall, hurried into the kitchen, and put water on to boil. Then she ran hot water into a French press and let the glass warm. Coffee preparations begun, she wandered into the bathroom and turned on the taps in the tub.

Thirty minutes later, clean, fully caffeinated, and smelling like honeysuckle, she faced the day with actual enthusiasm. She settled at her home desk, picked up the telephone, and called John Burcham.

"Hello." John's voice was as familiar and comfortable as old shoes.

"It's Freddie."

"What's wrong?"

"Why must something be wrong?"

"You never call me."

"I don't?"

"Never."

"I'm sorry. I should." And she would. She adored John when he didn't act like a stick-in-the-mud.

"You attended a party at the Lardners' place." Disapproval positively dripped from his voice. "And you shoved Nick Peters into the bay."

Stick. Mud. And John wondered why she never called. "He had it coming."

"I don't doubt it."

That stopped her. Usually, John erred on the side of ladies behaving like ladies. "Did you know he cheated on me?" The question escaped before she gave it proper thought.

Long seconds passed before he replied. "I did not."

She wasn't sure she believed him. "But?"

"No *buts*."

"Oh, there's a *but*. I hear it in your voice."

John sighed. "But I'm not surprised."

"You never liked him."

"With good reason. You're too good for him."

"You're sweet."

"We both know that's not true. Now, what do you want?"

"I have questions." Freddie drummed her fingers on her desk's edge. "Jake Haskell, Ewan Duncan, and Ephram Loeb."

"What about them?"

"All murdered."

"Not a question, Freddie."

"Did they step on toes?"

"Why do you want to know?"

"I'm curious."

"You're familiar with the story about the cat?"

"I'm not that curious."

"Liar."

"Fine. I am that curious. Just tell me so I don't ask the wrong person."

John's sigh carried the weight of the world. "Someone wants their business. That, or Brandt Abrams got tired of sharing the wealth."

"Brandt Abrams is not a killer."

"You sound very sure."

"He's not. I was dancing with him when Ewan was shot." She positioned the fan so it blew directly at her too-warm cheeks. "When Ephram died, the poor man was destroyed."

"Even if he didn't kill his friends, he's still a bootlegger."

"What's your point, John?"

"He's not the man for you."

"You might be right." Ceding John's point was easier than arguing.

"Is that all?"

"No. If I wanted to find out who owned a building, where would I find that information?"

"City hall."

"Which department?"

"What are you looking for?"

"The owner of a warehouse."

"A warehouse?" She could hear his scowl. "Why? Where?"

"Now who's curious?"

"Where's the warehouse, Freddie?"

"At the corner of Clinton and Cherry."

John exhaled slowly, and Freddie pictured him pinching the bridge of his nose. "How do you know what's on a corner of two streets on the Lower East Side?"

"What do you mean?"

"That's a dangerous neighborhood, Freddie."

And how.

"I wouldn't expect you to be familiar with the buildings. Please tell me you're not going down there."

"I'm not going down there. Cross my heart." If she never returned to the Lower East Side, it would be too soon.

"That was too easy. Tell me you haven't been down there."

"I haven't been down there."

"You're lying."

"You told me to tell you."

"Why did you visit the Lower East Side?"

"I followed someone."

"You what?" he exclaimed.

"A woman. I followed a woman."

"By yourself?"

"Not exactly." This topic had been a mistake.

"With whom did you go?"

"You don't want that answer." John would have a coronary if he knew she'd spent an evening with Legs Doyle.

"I do."

"Trust me. You don't."

"Freddie—"

"John, I'm fine. I won't be returning. I just want the warehouse owner's name. If you can't—won't—help me, I'll ask someone else." Was her threat wearing thin?

"Knowing you, that means more trouble. I'll find the owners."

"You'd do that for me?"

"If it keeps you safe? Absolutely."

"Thank you, John." She added a heaping helping of sugar to her voice.

"You're welcome. I'll call when I have an answer. Now, for the love of God, write your little column, go to fashion shows, and stay safe." He hung up before she could take him to task. Her column might not change the world, but it was important to her. She didn't appreciate him calling her work "little."

She returned the receiver to its cradle and sipped her coffee. Then, rather than call Tallulah, she fetched the package from the front hall.

Jewelers, milliners, and stores of all sorts sent her gifts in hopes that she'd mention them in her column. But she couldn't be bought. She admired the gifts, wrote charming thank-you notes, and returned them.

She placed the box on her desk next to the typewriter and opened the top drawer in search of scissors.

The phone rang, and she picked up the receiver. "Hello."

"It's me." Dotty sounded deeply annoyed.

"Good morning," Freddie replied.

"Is it?"

"The sun shines. The birds sing." She hadn't died in the shadows of a Lower East Side warehouse. "I'd say it's good."

"The play."

Freddie's stomach clenched. "You hated it."

"It's brilliant. I hate you."

"Pardon?" Had she heard correctly?

"It's not fair. You get the looks and the happy disposition, and now you've written a fucking masterpiece. Without telling me."

"You like it?"

"I wish I'd written it."

"That's the nicest thing you've ever said to me."

"Don't let it go to your head."

"You wouldn't let me."

"True. Now, who will produce?"

"Produce?"

"You didn't write this to take up space in your desk drawer."

"No," Freddie allowed. Her dreams had been fluffy and tinged with rosy pink. She'd share the play with Nick. He'd love it. They'd produce it together. Those dreams were as ruined as last night's frock. "I didn't."

"Nick is completely out of the picture? This play is his cup of tea, and he'd do a good job with it."

"I'd rather jump off the top of the Flatiron Building than work with Nick."

Dotty laughed as if Freddie had delivered the punch line to an especially funny joke. "You must take this play to Alan Copley." Copley was a producer even more successful than Nick. "I absolutely insist."

"Nick hates Alan."

"All the more reason to do it."

"You make an excellent point."

"Of course, I do. Now, much as I'd love to inflate your ego with well-deserved praise, I must go."

"Thank you for reading the play."

"Thank you for sharing it with me. Don't forget. I hate you." She hung up.

Freddie smiled as she hung up the telephone. Dotty liked— loved—her play.

She stared out the window at the park and allowed herself to imagine a Broadway opening. Could it happen?

Idly, Freddie pulled the package closer, took up the scissors, and cut through the string. Inside the paper, a velvet box and sealed note tempted her. Box or note? Box or note? She opened the box and gasped. Nestled in black velvet was a glittering necklace. One her mother would call "important." She tore open the note.

Thank you ~ Legs.

Diamonds. So many diamonds. More carats than a farmer's garden.

Diamonds she couldn't accept.

How did one return a killer's gift?

With the greatest tact.

The morning sun on the stones cast a thousand rainbows and nearly blinded her. She closed the lid on the sparkling gems.

A knock on the front door drew her attention. Bert with another package?

She stepped into the small foyer and called, "Who is it?"

"Your father." Which explained why Bert hadn't called to warn her. Her father was a co-owner of the apartment (not because she needed his money, but because a single woman couldn't buy in the building without a man's guarantee).

Freddie glared at the door.

"You've been avoiding my calls."

"Because I have nothing to say to you."

"We need to talk."

Freddie did not agree.

"Please?"

The *please* kept her rooted. Gerald Archer didn't say *please*. He said *jump* and waited for people to ask him how high.

"Please, Freddie?"

That second *please* had her turning the lock and cracking the door.

"May I come in? Please?"

"Suit yourself." It was a graceless welcome, but she wasn't feeling particularly graceful. She felt stiff and awkward and angry, and *How could you?* danced at the tip of her tongue. She sealed her lips, led him to the living room, and sat.

Her father took the seat across from her. He crossed his legs. He laced his fingers together. "It was my first time there."

She studied the silver-haired gentleman on her couch. "I don't believe you."

"I attended a card game."

"I don't believe you."

"What would you believe?"

"That you went to a brothel and paid to have sex with a woman your daughter's age."

He winced.

"Maybe younger. If you had a remotely innocent reason for being there, you'd have helped me when Walter accosted me."

His cheeks turned the deep rose of aged colonial brick.

"I haven't said anything to Mother. Not yet." And she wouldn't. Telling her mother would cause nothing but pain. It wouldn't change anything substantive. Marjorie Archer would never consider a divorce.

He leveled his steeliest gaze at her. "Why were you there?"

"You're not asking the questions."

"If you'd let me explain—"

"That Mother doesn't make you happy? That some girl named Trixie or Dulcie makes you feel young again?" A shudder began at the base of her neck and ran down her spine. "Save it. Let's put this whole nightmare behind us and never speak of it again."

He sat back in his chair.

"Of course," she added, "we'll both avoid brothels in the future." She let the threat of telling Mother hang in the air like a menacing thundercloud.

"When did you get so hard?"

"When did you get so weak?"

The flush returned to his cheeks. "Fine."

"I have your word? No more brothels."

"You have my word." For what it was worth.

Freddie felt as if she needed a second bath.

"How do you know Eloise?" he asked.

"I met her at a party at Ellis and Ring Lardner's place on Long Island. She offered me a ride back to the city."

"You're not friends?"

"Acquaintances."

He nodded and stared at his hands. Seconds passed. "Your mother misses you. She says you never come to dinner."

"You told her you were coming to see me."

He nodded.

"Tell her to lay off the Elis."

"You'd prefer Harvard men?"

"I'd prefer dinner with my parents without Mother's friend's nephew who's a whiz at picking stocks or some scion who's just made partner at a law firm. They make indescribably dull conversation."

"I'll tell her."

The phone rang, and Freddie stood. "I should answer that."

Her father rose to his feet. "Thank you for seeing me."

She used one of his severe stares against him. "Keep your word."

"I promise. I'll see myself out."

When the door clicked shut, Freddie hurried to the telephone. "Hello."

"Where have you been?" Tallulah demanded.

"You wouldn't believe me if I told you."

"Did you get my message?" Tallulah's voice was thick as Tupelo honey. Not that Freddie had ever encountered Tupelo honey, but it came from Mississippi and was said to be heavier than honey from New York bees. "You need to come with me tonight. To the Loebs' home. I can't go alone."

Freddie sat. "Why not?"

"I don't know them. They don't know me."

"I'm aware."

"Ephram's family—"

Freddie rested her forehead in her hand. "They'll be delighted you care enough to pay your respects." That or they'd be bemused by the Broadway actress who'd spent a few hours with their son and felt compelled to sit shiva.

"You're coming." Tallulah was in a mood.

"Fine."

"No arguments. I need you."

"Fine."

"I mean it, Freddie. I need you for moral support."

"I said—"

"You were there. You understand. Ephram and I fell in love at first sight. You must come with me."

"Fine."

"You can't make me face them alone. I'll—"

"Tallulah!"

"What?"

"I'll go with you."

"You will?"

"Yes."

"Oh. Good. I'll pick you up at six. Wear something somber."

CHAPTER 16

FREDDIE STARED OUT THE Checker's window and frowned. "You didn't tell me we were going to Brooklyn."

"Where did you imagine we'd go? Sutton Place?" When Anne Vanderbilt had left her Fifth Avenue mansion for the up-and-coming enclave, the news made the papers.

Freddie didn't appreciate Tallulah's sarcasm. Not one bit. "I didn't expect Brooklyn." They might as well be on a bridge headed to New Jersey.

Their cabbie, a man who smelled of liver and fried onions, honked at the car immediately in front of him. That being insufficient, he stuck his head out the window and yelled. According to him, the other driver's mother had enjoyed intimate relations with a farm animal. At least that felt like Manhattan.

Tallulah tittered and then her expression transformed into a lily-faced mask, as if she'd remembered why they were in a cab in Brooklyn. Ephram's family was sitting shiva, and she was an uninvited guest. She smoothed her skirt, fiddled with the pearl bracelet on her wrist, then dug a compact mirror from her handbag. "Do I look all right?"

"You're beautiful. Ephram's mother will hate you on sight."

Tallulah flipped open the mirror and eyed herself. "You're not helping."

"What on earth is wrong with you?" Tallulah didn't get nervous. Ever.

"I'm a bit"—she measured a small distance between her index finger and her thumb—"apprehensive."

Tallulah could hold an audience of thousands in the palm of her hand. They cried or laughed or smiled at her whim. And now she was nervous? "Tell me why."

"There's a part of me that can't believe he's dead. We spent such a short time together, but it felt like...like flying. Like we'd leaped off a cliff together. And even though we fell, we soared. This is like meeting my in-laws."

Freddie bit back her initial response: *Are you kidding me? You barely knew him.* Instead, she reached for Tallulah's free hand and squeezed. Falling in love with a dead man couldn't be easy or healthy.

Actual tears wet Tallulah's lashes. "I wish we'd had more time. What if he was the one?"

"The one?"

"The one who'd make me forget everyone else. My soulmate. The person destiny planned for me."

"Since when do you believe in soulmates?"

"Since I met Ephram."

If Ephram were alive, Tallulah would learn his faults. He left his dirty socks on the floor or hogged the blankets. He drank too much too often or spent more than he made. Without a deeper understanding of his character, Ephram would forever remain the ideal man, and Tallulah would pine for an impossibly perfect ghost. "I don't believe there's one perfect man," Freddie replied.

"You have no romance in your soul."

Neither did Tallulah, but now was not the time to point that out.

The cabbie turned onto a lovely street filled with impressive houses, leafy trees, and an air of having arrived. He slowed and pulled to the curb in front of a large brick home.

Tallulah took in their surroundings. "See? Brooklyn's not so bad."

The cabbie, who'd left the glass separating them open, peered over his shoulder and stared at her. "This is Crown Heights. The rest of Brooklyn don't look like this."

Freddie leaned forward and asked, "How much to wait?"

The cabbie suggested a sum large enough to keep him in liver and onions for a decade.

"Five dollars," she replied.

"How long will you be in there?"

"An hour, tops."

He rubbed his chin. "I'll wait."

Freddie and Tallulah slipped out of the taxi and climbed the front stairs.

"I can't believe you asked him to stay," Tallulah complained.

"Look around. We'd never catch another cab." Theirs was the only taxi on the block.

"But only an hour?"

Sixty minutes seemed like too much time. A whole hour of avoiding Brandt. Maybe she shouldn't be so petty. After all, the man had lost his friend. But he'd promised to call. And that broken promise piqued her pride. "We go inside. We pay our respects. We visit for thirty minutes. We leave."

"But—"

"There are no *buts*. Not one. You and Ephram might have soared. Or not." She callously ignored Tallulah's wince. "You weren't a part of his life. The people inside are his family. We're strangers here." And Freddie guessed they wouldn't be welcome strangers. She stared at the leaded glass panels on each side of the front door. "How did you find the address?"

"I asked around."

Did boys from nice neighborhoods grow up to be bootleggers? "You're sure this is the place?"

Tallulah lifted her nose in the air. "Ye of little faith." Then she fisted her hand and rapped sharply on the door.

It opened immediately, almost as if the man who stood on the other side had watched them talking on his stoop. Finding fault with Tallulah's charcoal gray dress, the restrained strand of pearls at her neck, or her carefully coiffed blond hair seemed unlikely, but he stared at her with obvious disapproval, grimacing as if a patent medicine salesman had just invaded his home.

Tallulah thrust her hand forward. "I'm Tallulah Bankhead. Ephram and I were friends."

"You? And my son?" The man ignored Tallulah's manicured fingers and smoothed the lapels of his dark suit. "I don't believe it."

Tallulah flinched as if he'd slapped her.

Coming here had been a mistake, but it meant something to Tallulah. Freddie forced a polite smile. "Tallulah's a famous actress." Not a gold-digging chorus girl. "She's starring in a play in London's West End this fall."

"An actress? Ephram would never—"

"We've come to pay our respects," said Freddie.

"Who are you?" His gaze took in Freddie's navy faille crepe dress with a scalloped skirt, her matching pumps, and her smart hat made of Bangkok straw. "Another actress?"

"No, sir. I'm Freddie Archer. I'm a writer."

"Of novels?"

"Columns. I write for *Gotham*."

He closed his eyes, rubbed his forehead, and seemed disinclined to let them in. "How do you know my son?"

"Brandt Abrams introduced us."

A shadow passed over the man's features, and he turned and called, "Brandt."

This visit was not going as planned. Not for Tallulah, who'd no doubt imagined she'd swan into the Loebs' home, charm the family, and spend the evening dabbing her eyes with an embroidered handkerchief as she oohed and aahed over Ephram's baby pictures with his mother. Nor was it going as Freddie planned. Not with Brandt (handsome as ever) gaping at them.

He ran a palm over his mouth. "Freddie. Tallulah."

"You know these women?" An accusation, not a question.

Brandt grimaced. "I do."

"Ephram knew them?"

"He did."

With a disapproving grunt, the man opened the door wide and waved them inside.

Tallulah crossed the threshold immediately, but Freddie hesitated. They were strangers intruding on a family's grief. She'd wait for Tallulah here on the stoop or in the cab (the cabbie's liver-and-onions odor wasn't *that* overwhelming).

Brandt cleared his throat, and Freddie realized she'd kept both men waiting. Tamping down her reluctance, she entered a spacious foyer. To her left, chairs lined the living room walls. Chairs filled with curious mourners. Oscillating fans set in the corners tried and failed to make the heat bearable. There were too many people, too much raw emotion.

Perspiration trickled between Freddie's breasts.

A woman with red-rimmed eyes stood as Tallulah entered the room.

Tallulah stepped forward and introduced herself. "I was dancing with Ephram," she explained, "when—"

The woman cut her off with a wave. "Come." She grabbed Tallulah's arm. "Sit. Tell me everything about Ephram's last moments."

Brandt's lips thinned, and he closed his eyes, as if Ephram's mother's grief made him uncomfortable.

"I'm sorry for your loss," Freddie told him. Loitering in the foyer until Tallulah finished telling Ephram's mother about his last moments seemed a reasonable course of action.

Brandt opened his eyes and said nothing. It was as if he couldn't bring himself to speak to her.

"Nice house," she ventured. "Did Ephram grow up here?"

"No. He bought it for his parents last year."

Had she somehow offended him? Freddie searched his face but found only cold, angled planes. "When is the funeral?"

His lips thinned. "We buried him today."

"If I'd known…" She wouldn't have attended the funeral, not when she wasn't welcome, not when she might have missed her appointment at Carmaux's. But death and white lies were old friends. "I'd have tried to be there."

Brandt grunted.

She hardly recognized the man standing next to her. She didn't expect charm or sparkle, not as Ephram's family sat shiva. But this Brandt was a stranger. "What's wrong?"

"Whenever I see you, someone dies."

"What are you saying? That I'm bad luck?"

"Miss Archer, how nice of you to come." Arnold Rothstein appeared at her elbow.

"You know each other?" Brandt's gaze traveled between them.

"Miss Archer saved Legs."

"You? You're the woman who held off a crowd?" Brandt's surprise was downright insulting.

"She stood above Legs's body, armed with six bullets. Five bullets. She used one. And she talked down the crowd." Mr. Rothstein (she couldn't wrap her mind around calling him Arnold—not even in her head) sounded like a proud papa.

Brandt frowned at her. "You went to the Lower East Side?"

She nodded.

"You?"

She lifted her chin. "Yes."

"Why?"

"I wondered that myself, Miss Archer." Mr. Rothstein's voice was deceptively mild.

If only the room weren't quite so airless. "Might I have a glass of water?"

"Tell us," Brandt replied.

Freddie swallowed the dryness in her throat. "I—we—followed the woman from Ewan's murder, the same one I followed into Washington Square Park. The same woman Tallulah described from Ephram's murder."

Mr. Rothstein rocked back on his heels. "You saw a woman kill Ewan?"

"No." Freddie shook her head. "I saw her with Jake Haskell, then again at the Village Inn the night Ewan died."

"You're sure Tallulah saw the same woman?" asked Mr. Rothstein.

"Not a hundred percent, but there's a good chance. It's her dress."

Both men stared at her as if she'd given up speaking English for Greek.

"There's a designer here in New York," she explained. "Sophie Carmaux. She makes gorgeous clothes. They rival French couture. She also has a ready-to-wear line."

Mr. Rothstein shifted his weight from foot to foot as if his patience were limited. Brandt rolled his eyes toward the ceiling. That's when it hit her like a fist to the gut—Brandt didn't think her unlucky. He thought she might be responsible for his friends' deaths. The pain in her stomach spread through her body and stole her breath. She ought to be furious—absolutely livid. Brandt suspected her of murder! But she couldn't muster an ounce of ire. Instead, a leaden pall settled on her shoulders. A man she'd liked considered her capable of killing three people. How could he—

"You were saying, Miss Archer?"

She took a ragged breath and continued. "The woman I saw with Jake Haskell wore Carmaux. She wore it again when I saw her at the Village Inn. Tallulah says the woman who stabbed Ephram wore a Carmaux frock." She turned to Brandt. "You didn't call because you suspect I committed murder. It wasn't me. I didn't kill your friends."

"Of course you didn't," said Mr. Rothstein. "No one thinks that."

Mr. Rothstein was mistaken. It was exactly what Brandt

thought. Freddie stared at the Loebs' floors. Polished oak without a speck of dust.

"Freddie, I'm sorry—"

"Don't." The oak was stained a nice dark shade of brown.

"Would you two like to be alone?" asked Mr. Rothstein.

"No!" Freddie and Brandt spoke as one.

Mr. Rothstein's gentle smile carried a hint of danger. "There are men who believe women can't handle much more than cooking and raising children. Those men are idiots. A strong woman can do anything."

"You don't think—"

"That you killed our friends? I do not. But you're a strong, capable woman. Brandt agrees." The smile returned. "So does Legs. I hear he sent you a thank-you gift."

She met Mr. Rothstein's gaze. "It was far too lavish."

"You saved his life."

"His life wouldn't have been in danger if he hadn't come with me."

"Legs told me exactly what happened. Would you have exited that taxi without him?"

"No." She wouldn't have followed the woman without him. Not after that horrible feeling in Washington Square Park. And if she had, she definitely wouldn't have followed her past 30th Street. "Be that as it may, I can't keep it." All those diamonds.

"You'll offend him if you return it."

"What did he send?" Brandt demanded.

"A necklace." The diamond necklace was a problem for another day. Perhaps she'd sell it and use the proceeds to fund a literacy or housing program in the Lower East Side. She'd name the program after Legs. "Do you know who owns the warehouse?"

Mr. Rothstein's face went blank.

Brandt leaned forward. "What warehouse?"

"The woman disappeared into a warehouse on the corner of Clinton and Cherry."

Brandt stiffened. "That's not possible."

"I saw her."

"But it's not possible."

"She disappeared into the warehouse. Legs will back me up."

Brandt leveled a loaded glance at Mr. Rothstein. "You knew?"

"Since Legs showed up at the deli last night. You were busy burying Ephram." Mr. Rothstein adjusted his tie. "I figured the news would keep."

She was missing something. Something important. A prickle on the back of her neck had Freddie turning her head.

Mr. Loeb glared at her—at them—as if they'd snuck into the dining room and poisoned the food weighing down the table.

"I get the feeling I'm not welcome," she whispered.

"It's not you, Miss Archer. It's me. Moshe doesn't approve. I should pay my respects and leave." Mr. Rothstein nodded at her. "Always a pleasure." Then he speared Brandt with a telling gaze. "Abrams, we'll talk tomorrow."

Brandt bounced on the balls of his feet as if he could hardly wait for a new day to dawn. "Yes, sir."

Mr. Rothstein stepped into the living room, shook Mr. Loeb's hand, kissed Mrs. Loeb's cheek, and disappeared through the front door.

Everyone in the house seemed to relax when the door shut behind him. Everyone but Brandt.

"We need to talk." He claimed Freddie's arm and pulled her toward the front door.

She resisted. "I can't leave. Not without Tallulah."

Brandt glanced at the settee where Tallulah sat next to Ephram's mother. "She's fine."

"But how will she get home?"

"Isn't that your taxi?" The automobile idled across the street, impossible to miss with its yellow body and checkered trim.

"He'll only wait an hour. Tallulah has no sense of time. She'll be stranded." In Brooklyn.

"I'll handle the taxi. You tell Tallulah we're leaving."

"No."

"No?" His brows furrowed as if the word were unfamiliar to him.

"No," she repeated. "Who owns the warehouse?"

"I do."

Freddie stilled, and curiosity lifted its furry chin from its paws, perked its ears, and waggled its whiskers. This was why Eve bit into the apple, why Pandora opened the box. "What do you store in the warehouse?"

He glanced at the room filled with people. "What's your guess?"

"Glenromach."

"Good guess."

"How long since you inventoried what's inside?"

"Apparently too long. Come on. I'll take you home."

Part of her wanted to smile pleasantly and cede to his wishes. That was how women handled men. Small compromise after small compromise, until they ended up like her mother—comfortably married to a man who visited brothels. "No."

"Why not?" he demanded.

"You suspect I committed murder." She ignored the prick of

conscience that reminded her she'd also suspected him. She might have suspected him, but she hadn't admitted it.

"I'm sorry."

"That's not good enough."

He pinched the bridge of his nose. "What do you want, Freddie?"

"Do you trust me?"

"Trust doesn't come easy for me."

"So that's a no."

"It's not you."

"Do you trust Mr. Rothstein?"

"That's different."

"How?"

"Honor among thieves."

"Of course." Hurt bled into her voice.

"I am sorry. Losing Ewan, and this thing with Ephram. It's..." He paused as if he expected her to jump in and absolve him.

She didn't.

"You're not making this easy."

"Why should I?"

He frowned as if her question surprised him.

Why should she make his apology easy? Because he was a man? Because she was expected to support men, not challenge them?

"If I accused you of murdering my friends, would you forgive me?"

"It's different."

She wrenched her arm free. "How?"

"Dammit, I'm not sure. But it is." He raked a hand through his dark hair. "I like you. I like you a lot, and I'm not thinking clearly, and..."

She was sorely tempted to put a hand on his arm and tell him not to worry, she wasn't upset, everything was okay. All lies. But lies that might smooth the lines bracketing his mouth. She resisted.

"And I've never met a woman like you. But my world is dangerous. Especially lately. I should be mourning my friend or inventorying my warehouse or checking in on my clubs, but all I can do is think about you."

Freddie's mouth went dry.

"I don't know up from down, crooked from straight, or dark from light. There's no room in my head for anything or anyone but you." He brushed a lock of hair away from her cheek, and half her resolve melted away. "Please. Forgive me. Let me make this up to you."

Did he mean those things? "Okay," she whispered.

"What? What did you say?"

"Okay."

"You're sure?"

She nodded.

He swept her into his arms and kissed her.

CHAPTER 17

One is so often seduced by music and bright lights and gaiety that one forgets the absolute bliss of an evening spent at home.

FREDDIE TAPPED HER PEN against the small notebook, and a dreamy smile curled her lips. She could write neither about her evening at home nor the glorious way she and Brandt passed the time. Her job was to get people out of their homes, and if other women knew the things Brandt did to her were possible, they'd never leave their bedrooms. She wished she was still in bed with Brandt, not stuck in the back of a cab that smelled of goulash and feet.

"How long you two been together?" asked the cabbie. "A week? Two?"

"Pardon me?"

"You got the look of a woman in love," he explained.

"Do I?" It must be the sappy smile. She stuffed it into her handbag next to her compact and lipstick. Work, not Brandt Abrams, should be her focus. She tapped her pen once more and then wrote.

A good dress shop is a blessing. A truly fine dress shop is a balm to the soul. And Carmaux's is a truly fine dress shop.

The cabbie pulled to the curb and stated the fare.

Freddie paid him.

When he saw the tip, he grinned. "You be sure he treats you nice."

"I will." She walked into Carmaux's, where a gorgeous silk twill demanded her fingers test its smoothness. Creamy perfection, as expected. She breathed lilac-scented air and gave a contented sigh.

She ought to start every day at Carmaux's. Or maybe this sudden sense of everything being right with the world wasn't due to the shop but the man she'd left in bed.

A woman clad in a light jersey, two-piece cardigan ensemble in palmetto green (she'd paired the skirt and sweater with a white silk polka-dot blouse) smiled a welcome. "Miss Archer, good morning. Miss Carmaux is expecting you. If you'll come this way, please?"

Freddie followed the saleswoman through the chic shop and into Sophie Carmaux's equally chic, empty office.

"Miss Carmaux will be with you in a moment. May I offer you coffee?"

"Please."

"How do you take it?"

"Black."

"Right away." The saleswoman turned.

"Wait."

"Yes, Miss Archer?"

"You're new here. What's your name?"

"Paloma."

"A pleasure to meet you, Paloma."

"Likewise." She disappeared in an efficient whirl of green jersey.

Freddie settled into the chair facing Sophie's desk and checked her watch. She was early—as she should be after canceling yesterday's appointment at the absolute last minute. According to the mother-of-pearl dial, she had five whole minutes to think about Brandt Abrams.

Another sappy smile touched her lips.

He might not trust her completely. She might not trust him either. But last night had been splendiferous.

Her eyes drifted shut, she stretched like a cat in a sunbeam, and a happy sigh escaped her.

"Whatever it is, I want some."

Freddie opened her eyes to an amused Sophie.

"A man?" The designer, who wore a white linen dress with navy-blue piping, worried a pleat in her skirt. That was Sophie's curse. Her hands were never still. She was constantly sketching or pinning or sewing. Denied the tools of her trade, her hands fluttered like hummingbird wings.

"How did you know?"

"Freddie, darling, there is but one thing that brings such a smile to a woman's face, and it's not a new dress."

Freddie pressed her fingers to her cheeks.

"You look sated."

Freddie didn't argue. *Sated* was too apt a word.

"What's his name?"

"Brandt Abrams."

Sophie's elegant brows lifted, and her hands pressed together and released as if she were silently clapping. "The man with the scotch?"

"You know him?"

"By reputation. Rumor has it, he's the cat's meow." Her fingers stroked imaginary whiskers, and the curve of her lips was downright naughty.

Freddie's cheeks warmed from a low simmer to a full boil, and Sophie laughed. "Your blush is all the confirmation I need."

Freddie forced her hands to her lap. "Enough about me. I heard your fall collection can make angels cry with envy."

Sophie, whose parents were both born in France, gave a Gallic shrug—complete with tilted head, lifted brows, pursed mouth, and raised hands. "Who am I to argue with angels? *Bof.* Perhaps I tempt fate. Perhaps you will hate the collection." Her face showed not a hint of worry. "The models will be ready shortly. Coffee?"

"Paloma is fetching some for me."

Sophie pressed a hidden button, and a bright young woman appeared.

"Ask Paloma to hurry along with Miss Archer's coffee."

"Yes, Miss Carmaux."

"I saw one of your dresses a few nights ago," said Freddie. She was here. She had to ask about the mystery woman.

"Oh?"

"Light blue." Freddie smoothed the cornflower blue crêpe de chine of her own dress. "Gorgeous beading and a harlequin hem."

Sophie's hands froze. "How did you know it was mine?"

"Your work is distinctive."

She shook her head, and her lips thinned. "I never produced that design."

"But—"

"If I tell you something, will you promise not to print it?"

"I promise." She didn't want the information for her column.

"The design was stolen from me."

"Stolen?"

"A whole portfolio of drawings." She brought her fingertips together and then exploded them outward. "Gone."

"Who?"

"A saleswoman who worked here just long enough to learn my habits. Her name is Roxanne Smith."

"Light brown hair, round face, small nose."

Sophie gave a grim nod. "That's her. One day, I came into the office, and both she and my current sketchbook were gone."

Roxanne Smith. Could it be so easy? "Do you know how I can find her?"

"If I knew that, I'd have my sketchbook."

At least she had a name. "Was she friends with any of the staff?"

Sophie pressed the pads of her fingers against her closed eyes. "One of the models. Rose."

"Have you asked her?"

"Of course." She laced her fingers together and rested her hands on her desk. "She claims ignorance. Why are you interested in Roxie?"

"She may have harmed someone."

Sophie fiddled with a charcoal pencil, turning it with restless fingers. "Harmed?"

"Murdered."

"Well"—Sophie put the pencil on the desk, her hands dropped to her lap, and she sat back in her velvet chair—"how perfectly awful."

"May I speak with Rose?"

"She's modeling for you today. She's the tall brunette with the vivid blue eyes. Why are *you* looking for Roxie? If she murdered someone, the police should be looking for her."

"They are."

"But you don't believe they'll find her?"

The police wouldn't know to look if Freddie hadn't told them. "I do not."

"And you don't care if the search is dangerous?"

"I do not." She did. But she wouldn't admit her fear.

Sophie regarded her with serious brown eyes. "You are determined."

"I am."

She reclaimed her pencil. "If you find Roxie and see my book..."

"I'll return it to you immediately."

"Thank you. I had three collections sketched in that book."

A tap at the door had them both turning their heads.

"Come in."

Paloma opened the door and presented Freddie with a woefully tiny cup of coffee. Blast the French and their demitasse cups.

"Thank you," she murmured.

"That will be all, Paloma." Sophie waited until the office door closed. "I know you promised silence, but—"

"I won't mention or write about the stolen sketches. You have my word."

"Thank you. I trusted that woman, and she stole from me. It suggests poor judgment."

"My lips are sealed." Freddie put her empty cup (two sips when she needed a whole pot) on the corner of Sophie's desk. "Please keep my interest in Roxie mum."

Sophie mimed locking her lips and throwing the key over her shoulder.

A tap on the door claimed Sophie's attention, and she called, "Come in."

The door opened, and Paloma's head entered. "The models are ready, Miss Carmaux."

"Thank you, Paloma." She stood.

Freddie rose from her chair. "What do you have for me today?"

"Autumn. Gorgeous russet tones, sumptuous tweeds, the softest cashmeres."

"I can't wait." Freddie followed the designer into the cream and gold viewing salon.

They paused in the entrance, and Sophie whispered, "I'll point out Rose. She might actually talk to you. The girls are in awe of your column."

When the fifth model entered (wearing a fawn box-pleated skirt paired with a cashmere sweater set), Sophie said, "Rose, come closer so Miss Archer can see the embroidery on the cardigan."

Freddie dutifully admired the gold geometric pattern that elevated the sweater from mundane to extraordinary. "Hello, Rose." Her voice was flat as pavement.

"Freddie." Rose made the name into a mild curse.

"You know each other?" asked Sophie.

"From college," Rose replied. College, where Rose decided that Graham Mindlin was the man of her dreams. The only thing standing between her diamond ring, a date at the altar, and a house in Connecticut was Graham's pin on Freddie's sweater. Rose, unfettered by morality or a sense of fair play, got herself pregnant. In retrospect, Freddie counted herself lucky. If she'd married Graham, her life would be much different. And she liked her life.

"I see." Sophie's tone suggested she sensed the deep waters swirling beneath them. "Thank you, Rose." It was a dismissal.

When Rose retreated, Freddie murmured, "I'm the last person on earth with whom she'll share a secret."

"I sensed that. A bit of history?"

"Her husband. I knew him before they married."

"Her ex-husband." That explained why Rose was modeling and not at home in her garden or playing bridge or sitting on a committee at her country club.

The next model entered, and they turned their focus to the clothes.

"They're gorgeous," Freddie gushed.

"Each can be made to order. Rose's skirt and sweater in blue instead of fawn. That dress"—Sophie pointed at a willowy blonde in a sapphire-blue georgette evening gown accented with peacock feathers—"can be sewn using emerald green. The clothes you're seeing today—the fabrics, the colors—they will be our ready-to-wear line."

Freddie looked up from her pad. "I've made notes, but you'll send full descriptions?"

"They'll be on your desk by tomorrow. Now, may I treat you to a late breakfast or an early lunch?"

"I'd love to..."

"But?"

"I may have a way to find Roxie." It was possible Frank Case, the manager at the Algonquin, would recognize her name. Failing that, he might tell her if Ames had upcoming reservations.

Thirty minutes later, Freddie breezed into the Algonquin. Well, perhaps she didn't actually breeze. A humid whiff? A sultry waft? Summer heat had reduced the crisp pleats in her dress to wilted lines. The bounce in her hair had decamped for cooler weather, and she sported a bobbed helmet of damp locks. Her nose needed powder, and the rest of her needed a scented bath (sooner rather than later).

Nonetheless, she approached the check-in desk with a spring in her step. "May I please speak with Mr. Case?"

"Your name, please?"

"Freddie Archer."

"If you'll have a seat"—the gentleman behind the desk nodded to a cluster of chairs in the lobby—"I'll see if he's available."

Freddie withdrew to the chairs, selected one directly below a ceiling fan, and sighed. How hard life must have been before modern conveniences like electric fans and taxis and radios.

Of course, other things were less marvelous—Prohibition, exhaust fumes, and income tax—but one must take the bad with the good.

"Miss Archer?"

She stood and held out her hand. "Mr. Case."

Frank Case was a marketing genius. He'd established the Algonquin as *the* hotel for literary and theater types. Once aspirants learned that Dotty and George S. Kaufman and Robert Sherwood could be found at "the Gonk," they flocked like eager starlings. He shook her hand. "How may I help you?"

"Walter Ames."

His brows rose. "What about him?"

"He dines at a table close to the circle." Hoping someone would throw him a crumb.

"It's a common practice among aspiring young actors."

"How often is he here?"

"Once or twice a week."

"I'm here once or twice a week. I've never noticed him."

Frank Case shrugged as if to say her poor observational skills were her problem, not his.

He was right. She'd still be blind to Walter Ames's presence if he hadn't dined with Roxie Smith. "Do you expect him again this week?"

"He has a reservation for noon today."

"Does he?" Freddie glanced at her watch. That was less than twenty minutes from now. "For how many?"

"Two."

"Is Miss Smith accompanying him?"

"Miss Smith?"

"The woman with whom he dined a few days ago."

"Ah. Mr. Ames did not share his guest's name with me." So Frank didn't know her. "The police also had questions about the young lady." He scanned the lobby as if he were worried about eavesdroppers. "Should I worry?"

"Worry?"

"I must consider the hotel's reputation." Guests who received liquor deliveries to their rooms weren't keen on police in the lobby.

Frank Case had always been kind to her. He deserved the truth. "It's possible Mr. Ames has unsavory friends. It's also possible he's unaware of his friends' activities."

Frank blanched. "If you were me?"

"I'd give him the benefit of the doubt."

Frank nodded. "So you wouldn't misplace his reservation?"

Not today, she wouldn't. "No. Would you mind terribly if I waited here until he arrives?"

"Having a beautiful writer in the lobby can only enhance the hotel's cachet."

She wasn't beautiful, but she was a writer. "Thank you, Mr. Case."

"May we get you anything?"

"An iced coffee?"

"My pleasure." He bowed slightly and retreated to the front desk, where he issued an order.

Freddie took out her notepad.

> *A good hotel sees to its guests' wants and needs. An exceptional hotel anticipates its guests' whims. An unannounced delivery at three in the morning? Bicarbonate of soda and aspirin at eight? Ham and eggs at ten? An exceptional hotel sees to it. It also charms, seduces, makes promises, and keeps them (unlike a shocking number of young men).*

She tapped her pencil on her notepad. Not bad. A few lines about the hotel in the next issue were the least she could do to repay Mr. Case's willingness to share information.

"Miss Archer?"

She looked up.

"Your coffee." A waiter put a sweating glass on the table next to her. "Cream or sugar?"

"Black." She reached for her handbag and the money to pay him.

"Compliments of Mr. Case."

She gave him a quarter (far more than the coffee's actual cost). "Thank you for bringing it."

"My pleasure, Miss Archer."

Freddie lifted the glass to her lips. She could write a whole column about the delights of cold coffee on a hot day. She'd be amusing, even witty, but in the end, everyone already knew the divine relief iced coffee offered.

She held the cool liquid on her tongue before swallowing and refrained (barely) from pressing the cold glass to her forehead. Instead she chilled her fingers and then pressed them to her temples.

Walter Ames strode into the lobby. He wore a summer-weight suit and a silk tie, and his face was flushed from the heat.

He walked past her, and she checked her watch.

Walter was early for lunch. Eager to meet someone?

Clasping her purse in one hand and her iced coffee in the other, Freddie stood. "Mr. Ames?"

He stopped, and his brows rose in a do-I-know-you arch.

"I'm Freddie Archer." She extended her hand.

A furrow creased his brow. "I heard you asked about me."

"I asked about your friend," Freddie corrected. "Roxie Smith."

"Never heard of her."

"You had lunch with her. Here. In this hotel. Just the other day. I saw you with her."

"You're mistaken."

"A part in the new Marx Brothers' show says I'm not."

Longing, pure and unadulterated, flashed across Ames's face.

"It could make you a star." Or at least pay his rent and keep him in Glenromach and silk ties.

"I can't tell you anything."

"Can't or won't?"

He shifted his weight from foot to foot and scanned the lobby. "You don't know what you're asking."

"I'm asking where I can find Miss Smith. Is she joining you for lunch? Are you in love with her?"

His brow puckered. "What?"

"It's a simple question. Are you in love with her?"

"Lord, no."

"Then why are you protecting her?"

Walter paled. He looked over his shoulder as if he expected to find an ax murderer at his back. He scanned the lobby. His tongue wet his lips.

"You're frightened."

He shook his head with too much vigor. "I'm not. You're sure about the show?"

"Positive."

He glanced over his shoulder. "I'll tell you anything you want to know. But not here."

"Where?"

"Central Park. Four o'clock. Come alone."

Not in a million years. "Where in the park?"

"Oh. Right. The gazebo by the reservoir." Again his eyes searched the lobby.

"Don't be late, Mr. Ames."

"I'll be there."

"If you don't show, the deal is off."

"I'll be there." He turned on his heel and left her.

Freddie watched his disappearing back. What—or who—had him so frightened?

CHAPTER 18

Freddie sat on a park bench with Dotty beside her. They both held parasols. Well, Freddie held a parasol. Dotty held a dour black umbrella. Their shade did nothing to dispel the heat.

"He's late," Dotty groused.

"I know." It wasn't as if Freddie had any control over when Walter Ames made an appearance. Or if he made an appearance.

"Are you sure we're in the right spot?"

"Yes."

"Because you've made that mistake before. You've waited at the wrong café, the wrong speak. I'll never forget the time I waited at Jack and Charlie's, and you were at the Dizzy Club."

"That wasn't my fault. You said you wanted one of Jack's side-cars." Jack was the bartender at the Dizzy Club. "Bill is the bartender at Jack and Charlie's."

"Excuses," Dotty replied. "And it's not just speakeasies. You've caught the wrong ferry, the wrong train. I could go on..."

"This is the place." If Ames didn't show, she'd find another way to locate Roxanne Smith.

Dotty adjusted the angle of her umbrella and narrowed her dark eyes.

"What?"

"You're thinking."

"Is that a problem?" Freddie took a handkerchief from her handbag and dabbed her hairline.

"If I were a man, I'd worry."

"You're not a man."

"Which is why I'm not worried." Dotty lifted her pointed chin. "You're scheming."

She wasn't. Not really. She was just weighing the cost of Ames's information. "How can you tell?"

"The tilt of your head and the faraway expression in your eyes." Dotty glanced at her watch. "Are you sure he's coming?"

Not remotely. For the fifth time, Freddie scanned the park. No Ames. Just drooping mothers with lethargic children and an enterprising young man who held the leashes for five dogs. She nodded toward the dog walker. "Do you suppose that's a viable business?"

"Focus, Freddie. Where's Ames?"

"He said four o'clock."

"And it's a quarter past."

"Let's give him another five minutes."

"Then what?"

"We give up."

"We're out here melting because Walter Ames has information you want, yet you don't seem to care that he's not here." Dotty, who'd had the foresight to bring a fan, waved it vigorously. "He isn't coming."

"You may be right."

"One would think, after wasting your time and nearly dying of heat prostration, you'd be at least miffed. But you're not upset."

Why hadn't she brought a fan? The heat really was dreadful. "If he doesn't come, he doesn't get the part."

Dotty's eyes narrowed. "What part?"

"A role in the Marx Brothers' new show."

"Why would Groucho cast Ames in his new show?"

"As a favor to me."

Dotty scowled and rolled her wrist in a get-to-the-point gesture.

"If he doesn't get the part, I don't owe Groucho a favor."

"What does Groucho get?"

"He wants to read my play."

"Groucho? Your play?" Dotty sounded deeply outraged, as if Freddie had suggested she dry out for the rest of the summer or wear her glasses in public.

"He has a mistress."

Dotty's expression shifted from outraged to appalled. "Absolutely not. That play deserves a real actress, not Groucho's latest bit of fluff."

"That's why I'm not upset that Ames didn't show." Freddie stood.

Dotty's cheeks, already pink from the heat, darkened. "So you dragged me out here for nothing?"

Freddie stood. The way sweat glued her slip to the back of her legs was deeply unpleasant, but she forced a smile. "It could be worse."

"How?"

"There's a breeze." She pulled her slip away from her skin.

"Barely."

"You're with me."

Dotty rose from the bench and pointed her fan at Freddie's nose. "You refuse to fully explain what you want from Ames. 'Information' is extremely vague."

"I'll buy you a gin rickey."

"When?"

"Now?"

"I'm too cranky to drink."

"Gin might help with the crankiness."

"Doubtful. Besides, I need to write. How about tomorrow?"

"It's a date." She swiveled her head, looking for Ames. "He's not coming. Let's get out of here."

They strolled toward Fifth Avenue with the sun beating against their parasols' feeble protection. An unexpected shiver ran down Freddie's spine, and she glanced over her shoulder.

A man in rough trousers and shirtsleeves followed them.

Had Mr. Rothstein sent him? The alternative—that he was associated with the killer—was too terrifying to contemplate.

"What are you looking at?"

"Nothing."

Dotty peered over her shoulder. "Is that man following us?"

"Ignore him. Maybe he'll go away."

"Since when are you an ostrich?"

They left the park for the crowded sidewalk, and Freddie breathed easier.

"Just what are you involved in?" Dotty demanded.

"I'm not exactly sure."

"Why are you involved?"

"I'm not sure of that, either."

"Are you in trouble?"

"I don't think so."

"The man behind us says different. We should hail a taxi." Dotty waved her free arm, and a Checker cab pulled over. "The Algonquin," she told the driver.

They climbed into the automobile, and their shadow got lost behind them.

Freddie breathed a relieved sigh.

"Now what?" Dotty demanded.

"Now you write or take a cool bath or sneak off for a drink with Robert, and I go to the office."

"The office?" Dotty's eyes narrowed in disbelief.

"I left a column with Gus."

"Worried he won't like it?"

"Positive he won't like it."

"Promise me you won't do anything stupid?"

"Not unless I call you first."

"So I can talk you out of it?"

"So you can join me."

Dotty snorted as the cabbie pulled to a stop in front of the hotel. When she got out, Freddie gave the driver *Gotham*'s address before resting her head against the seat and dreaming of easy answers and cooler weather.

Ten minutes later, as she approached her office, Annie looked up from her desk. "Gus wants to see you."

"Ugh. Now?" She wanted a glass of tea and the pleasure of sitting directly below a ceiling fan in a dim room. Also, she felt... wilted. Her hair. Her dress. Her makeup.

"He doesn't like your column."

As she expected. "That column was genius."

Annie held up her hands in surrender. "Don't shoot the messenger."

"Fair enough." Freddie stalked toward Gus's office.

She tapped on the open door, and Gus, who'd rolled up his sleeves and loosened his tie, looked up from editing a piece.

"Come in. I'd tell you to close the door, but it will get unbearably stuffy."

Freddie left the door open, and Gus shuffled through a stack of papers. When he found what he wanted, he adjusted his glasses on his nose and read. "One wonders what this city would be like if women were in charge. This writer knows at least three grande dames who, if given free rein, could clean up the tenements, educate poor children, and have dinner on the table by seven. Instead, the tenements continue as blights, filled with despair, disease, and crime . . . " Gus took off his glasses. "Freddie, I can't print this."

"Because I don't recommend a boutique on Hester Street?"

"Very funny." He shook the page at her. "This is almost seditious."

"It's not. I truly believe a handful of empowered women could fix the problem. I'm not suggesting they run the city government or be paid for their labors."

"This isn't our kind of column. Give me something about hats or Club Monaco or the coolest rooftop. I know"—he dug through the stacks on his desk—"take these." He held out two tickets.

"What are they?" Freddie was cautious. *Beware of Gus bearing gifts* was the office slogan whispered behind his back.

"Tickets to a play."

"The theaters are closed for the summer."

"It's Off-Broadway." As if that were appealing. A terrible play in a hole-in-the-wall theater with no air circulation and no way to walk out without the entire audience and all the actors noticing.

"No, thank you." She backed toward the door.

"I insist."

"I'll write about hats. Or shoes. I'll write you a whole column about shoes!"

He put the tickets on the edge of his desk. "Go to the play, Freddie."

"It's sure to be dreadful."

"How do you know?" He stared at her with one brow lifted. Since he had miniature porcupines for brows, the effect was comic rather than stern.

"Summer." She ticked a finger. "Off-Broadway." She ticked a second finger. "I haven't heard a whisper about it, which means it's an amateur production." She ticked a third finger.

"You're going."

"I have plans."

"I didn't give you the performance date."

Drat!

"Freddie?"

Grateful for the interruption, she turned toward the door. "What is it, Annie?"

"There's someone here to see you."

She didn't ask who. She didn't care. "Coming."

"Freddie." Gus's voice stopped her. "The tickets?"

"Shouldn't Leyton do this? He is the theater critic."

Gus laced his fingers behind his neck and leaned back in his chair. "He's on vacation in Vermont."

"Vermont?"

"I don't book his travel. Now take the damn tickets."

She hesitated, and he picked them up and waved them at her.

"Fine." She took the wretched tickets from Gus's outstretched hand.

"I hope you like it."

She pursed her lips and narrowed her eyes. "If I go, will you run the column?"

"No. Go anyway."

"But—"

"No arguments, Freddie. Just do it."

"The woman from Carmaux's is waiting," Annie chided.

"From Carmaux's?"

Annie nodded. "I put her in your office."

"Who is it?"

"She said her name is Rose Mindlin."

Rose stood at the open window. The humidity had frizzed her hair and added a shine to her face.

Freddie lifted her hand and touched the brim of her straw boater. She'd lost her first love to this woman. Her pride wished for fresh makeup, a crisply pressed dress, and combed hair. Instead, she was as wilted as last week's daisies.

On days like this one, when the heat was nearly unbearable and the air was so damp it puddled in her lungs, she was grateful she didn't have a softly curled bob like Zelda Fitzgerald or Clara Bow. Humidity and curls were not friends. Thank heavens her ruler-straight hair didn't frizz. How did women survive summer with masses of hair? Was there a column there?

"Freddie?"

"Sorry." She focused her attention on Rose. "The heat has

melted my brain. Welcome." She took off her hat, sat behind her desk, and waited to hear what Rose wanted.

Rose claimed the chair on the other side of the desk. "Nice office."

"Thank you. May I offer you tea? Coffee?"

"Do you have anything stronger?"

Freddie opened the bottom desk drawer and pulled out a bottle of Glenromach. "If you prefer gin, I can ask Annie. The theater critic usually keeps a bottle, and he's in Vermont. He won't notice if I swipe it."

"Scotch is fine."

Freddie poured a finger into two glasses.

"Thank you." Rose accepted the drink, leaned back in her chair, and sighed, as if meeting in Freddie's office were a regular occurrence.

"Hot day," said Freddie.

"Brutal," Rose agreed.

They sipped and sat in silence, and Freddie studied the woman across from her.

Even with a sheen of sweat on her skin and frizzy hair, Rose was still impossibly pretty. When they were in college, Rose's cornflower-blue eyes burned with avid curiosity. In retrospect, perhaps that fire might have been greed. Greed for knowledge. For experience. For Graham Mindlin. Now, the expression in her eyes was brittle. "You're wondering why I'm here."

Freddie replied with a polite smile and a nod that encouraged her guest to get to the point.

Rose closed her eyes. "I'm divorced."

"Sophie mentioned that."

"Our marriage was never good. Then our daughter died."

"I'm so sorry." She meant it. The loss of her brother had nearly destroyed her, and her pain didn't hold a candle to the agony her parents had endured. The unhappy lines that bracketed her mother's down-turned mouth appeared after that terrible telegram. And her father? It was as if he'd distanced himself from his wife and daughter to protect himself from further loss.

"Graham and I didn't make sense after she passed. He only married me because I was pregnant. Only stayed because of our daughter."

Freddie sipped her scotch. If Rose expected sympathy for her failed marriage, she'd come to the wrong place.

"When we were in college, I was head-over-heels for Graham, and I was sure he'd come to love me in return." Her fingers wrapped tightly around her glass, and she lifted the scotch to her lips with both hands. "I sometimes wonder if Adelaide was crushed by the weight of disappointment. When I dropped out of school, my father disowned me. Then I married a man who was in love with someone else."

Was Rose suggesting Freddie had had a hand in ruining her marriage?

The memory of Graham's confession still retained its sharp edges. The sorrow in his eyes and the feel of his hand around hers as he confessed were still clear as day. She remembered the way the floor—the world—disappeared, and she felt herself falling into an abyss.

She'd staggered to her feet and run home to her mother.

Marjorie Archer did all the right things that night. She'd stroked Freddie's hair as she sobbed into a pillow. She'd promised the pain would end. She'd declared a man who cheated wasn't worth her tears.

The irony made Freddie wince.

"My coming here is probably a surprise."

Never, not once in that endless slew of tear-soaked nights, had Freddie imagined she'd one day sit across a desk from Rose and pity her. "Adelaide is a beautiful name."

"She was a beautiful girl."

"How long have you been divorced?"

"Four years." Rose's brow creased, and she stared into her glass. "I'm surprised Graham never reached out to you." Bitterness laced her voice.

"When he told me about the two of you, I told him—definitively—I never wanted to speak to him again." Although it was a surprise that her mother hadn't told her. Marjorie Archer and Graham's Aunt Enid were friends.

Rose brought her glass to her lips. "After the divorce, I had to get a job." She offered a rueful smile. "Turns out, I'm hopeless in an office."

"So you model."

"While I can. I won't be young forever." Rose was still pussyfooting around her reason for coming.

"What brings you to *Gotham*?" To her office? What could she possibly want?

"I overheard you and Sophie. You're looking for Roxie."

Freddie stared at Rose's hard eyes and the proud tilt of her chin and said, "I am."

"What if I know where she is? What's the information worth to you?"

So Rose was here for thirty pieces of silver? "Sophie would pay more than me." The designer wanted her notes returned.

Rose wrinkled her nose and gave her head a quick, decisive

shake. "Sophie is running a small business. She's barely scraping by. But you? You're an heiress."

That didn't mean she was rolling in dough. "How much do you want?"

"Five thousand dollars."

Freddie barely kept her jaw from dropping to her desk.

A flush colored Rose's cheeks. "New York isn't good for me. I want to get out, hop on a train, and head west until I find a place where my memories can't find me. Chicago. St. Louis. Maybe Denver."

Rose's memories would travel with her. But rather than point out the flaw in her plan, Freddie asked, "You have Roxie's address, her phone number?"

"I even have her real name."

"Which is?"

"Five thousand dollars."

Freddie glanced at her watch. "The banks are closed."

"The information will keep till morning. Meet me at Carmaux's with the money."

"Then what?"

"You get what you want, and I disappear."

"No."

"No?"

"I'll give you half in the morning and the other half when the information is verified."

"What's to stop you from keeping the second payment?"

Freddie laced her fingers together and rested her hands on the desk. "Of the two of us, I think we can agree, I have more integrity." Rose got pregnant to steal a man, and now she was selling out her friend. "Also, I can only pay you two thousand."

Anger flashed in Rose's eyes. "Four thousand."

Freddie shifted, as if she meant to stand and show Rose to the door. "We're at an impasse."

"Three thousand."

Three thousand dollars was a lot of money, what most men made in a year. But if paying Rose meant she didn't need Walter Ames's information, the price was a bargain. "In two payments."

"Fine," Rose ground out.

"I'll be there by nine thirty."

A small, triumphant smile curled Rose's lips.

"I hope, wherever you end up, that you find happiness."

Rose snorted. "No wonder he never got over you."

"Pardon?"

"Graham never got over you. He said you were smart, and funny, and kind."

"I try."

"He was right." Rose stood. "It makes it hard to hate you."

Why Rose would hate her was a mystery. Freddie wasn't the one who'd slept with Rose's boyfriend. "What will you do? In your new city, I mean."

"I don't know. Forget."

"In college, you were a talented writer." They'd had several English and creative writing classes together. "You could take it up again."

"Stop that."

"What?"

"Being kind."

She wasn't being kind. Not really. Rose had done her a tremendous favor. Without her pregnancy, Freddie might have married Graham. If she had, there'd be no column, no job at *Gotham*, and no friendships with women like Dotty and Tallulah. "I'll see you in the morning."

Rose nodded and walked out of the office.

Freddie swallowed her scotch in one enormous gulp, enjoyed the burn in her throat, and then let her head fall to her hands.

"Everything okay?" Annie stood in the doorway.

"Why are you still here?"

"I didn't like the looks of that woman."

"Oh?"

"I know her type. She'd smile while she slit your throat."

"Rose is more a stab-you-in-the-back girl."

"Be that as it may, I'm glad she's gone."

No need to tell Annie about their rendezvous in the morning. "Me too."

CHAPTER 19

The phone on Annie's desk rang, and both she and Annie scowled at the outer office. Neither made a move.

"Are you going to get that?" Freddie asked.

"What is that your friend asks callers? What fresh hell is this? Smart woman." With a curt nod and a lingering glare, Annie left Freddie in her office.

Alone in her office, Freddie stared at the bottle of Glenromach. She was sorely tempted to pour a second drink and went so far as to wrap her hand around the bottle, but she paused. To scotch or not to scotch? That was the question. And what a ridiculous question it was. She splashed an inch of amber liquid into her glass.

"Brandt Abrams is on the line," Annie called through the open doorway.

Her grip on the glass tightened. Brandt? What could she say to him? When it came to Brandt, she, a writer, was at a complete loss for words. She had more vices than fingers. She drank, and when she drank, she smoked. She spent too much money on clothes; surely that counted as vanity. If it didn't, the amount of time she spent on her hair and makeup did. She stayed out until the wee hours. She told the occasional fib. She kissed men. Often. What she didn't do was treat sex as a casual pursuit. How did one behave after what she and Brandt had done together? Tallulah would know exactly what to do, how to act, what to say. Freddie didn't. She was out of her depth. She took a restorative sip of scotch and croaked, "Put him through."

Seconds later, her extension rang, and she picked up the receiver. "Hello."

"Hello." Brandt's voice rumbled through her. "Are you free tonight?"

"I have tickets to a play."

"You have plans?" He sounded disappointed.

She stared into her scotch and gathered her courage. "Would you like to come with me?"

"Yes." He didn't ask which play or theater or actors, and his willingness to go with her, without question, soothed her nerves.

"It's Off-Broadway." It was only fair to warn him.

"I don't care."

"It's most likely dreadful."

"I don't care."

"Probably produced by amateurs who couldn't get jobs as social directors at the summer camps." During the summer months, creative types who failed to secure jobs in rehearsals for fall productions flocked to camps in the Catskills or Poconos.

"Freddie, I don't care about the play or how bad it is. I want to see you."

Bubbles fizzed in her blood like champagne, and a smile took hold of her lips. "Okay." She wanted to see him, too.

"When should I pick you up?" he asked.

Did "now" make her sound too eager? "Come at seven. We'll have a drink before we go."

"I can't wait to see you."

Likewise. She didn't say that. She needed a semblance of control. Instead, she swallowed, and an awkward silence claimed the line. "Seven o'clock," she croaked.

"I'll be there." He hung up.

Rather than replace the receiver, Freddie gazed at the clean surface of her desk and remembered waking up with Brandt. He was handsome and brave and smart and dangerous and made her heart beat double-time.

"Freddie?"

She lifted her gaze to Annie.

"Is everything all right?"

"Fine." She hung up the telephone.

"Mike—Detective Sullivan—is worried about you." Annie's eyes narrowed. "He suspects you're holding something back." She planted her hands on her hips. "But I told him, if you knew anything, you'd share the information immediately." She scowled. "I spoke the truth, did I not?"

"Annie..."

"I'm not interested in your reasons." She wagged her finger. With vigor. "He asked you to keep an eye out for that woman. Not follow her. Not look for her."

"That is what he asked," Freddie ceded. But Ephram was dead. And Ewan. And before Ewan, Jake Haskell.

"Tell Mike what you know, then go back to doing what you do best."

"Drinking at speakeasies?" Her nights seemed trivial in the face of murder.

"Writing columns that make people smile, that remind us there's fun and gaiety to be had. You convince us life isn't entirely bleak."

"You make the column sound like more than it is." She needed the light that came with dancing and drinking and laughter. That light pushed back the darkness. But only a fool believed the darkness was gone. It waited, biding its time, ready to feed. Freddie saw the darkness, and she bet her readers did, too.

"We need the reminder, Freddie." Worry creased Annie's forehead and cut twin channels between her nose and her mouth. "We need you. Don't get yourself into trouble you can't get out of."

She was the second woman today who'd told Freddie not to do anything stupid. Annie was just more polite than Dotty.

"I'll stay safe," Freddie promised.

Annie's eyes narrowed as if she doubted Freddie's sincerity. "And Brandt Abrams?"

"What about him? Gus insists I go to a dreadful play. Brandt is escorting me. That's all." A patent lie.

The hands Annie had planted on her hips fisted. "I didn't just fall off the turnip truck." She stared at Freddie without blinking. Her stare lasted long enough to make Freddie squirm in her chair.

"Annie—"

Annie held up her index finger, wagging it in Freddie's face. "Be home by a decent hour."

Since when did Annie suggest curfews? Freddie raised her brows.

"Spending the night with that man will cause you nothing but grief. Also, you have an appointment at nine thirty and need to stop by the bank before you go."

"You heard all that?"

"If you want a private conversation, close your door. I won't repeat a word, if"—Annie raised her index finger then went so far as to tap it on Freddie's desk—"if you promise to share the information with the police." She meant with Detective Sullivan.

"I will." But first she'd tell Mr. Rothstein. Detective Sullivan might not appreciate coming second, but crossing Arnold Rothstein could be deadly.

Annie sniffed and collected the dirty glasses.

Freddie returned the scotch to its drawer. "Are you done for the day?"

Annie nodded, and they located their handbags and hats and left *Gotham*'s offices together, pausing outside the building's doors.

"You'll be careful?" Annie asked. Not so much a question as a demand.

"I will."

"If it were anyplace other than Carmaux's, I'd insist you tell Mike right now."

"Why aren't you? Insisting, I mean."

"If Mike talks to that woman, she'll play dumb. You might glean actual information." Annie adjusted the brim of her hat. "People like talking to you. They tell you amazing things. Pola Negri told you that she and Valentino never share a bed."

An amazing revelation, but not one Gus would ever print. Not even Walter Winchell would print that confession. American women didn't want to know they held little appeal to the man of their fevered dreams.

Freddie had let the tidbit drop six months ago, and Annie still rubbed at it like a worry stone.

"A poof." Annie shook her head sadly.

"A man," Freddie corrected. "One who deserves his privacy. I shouldn't have told you." But Annie had talked endlessly (a solid week without stopping for breath) about her favorite actor and his role in *The Eagle*. Freddie had snapped.

Annie snorted. "Like I said, people tell you things."

"It's not the same. This is..." Life or death. "This is important." The heebie-jeebies skittered down Freddie's spine, and she glanced over her shoulder. "Also, I'm paying for the information."

Annie waved away Freddie's payment to Rose with a flip of her wrist. "I bet she'd tell you. Eventually."

When people were dying, eventually wasn't good enough. "What time is your train?"

Annie glanced at her watch and squeaked. "I need to hurry." They trotted to Fifth Avenue, stopping near the subway entrance.

"This is me." Annie gave Freddie a last behave-or-else stare before descending the stairs.

When she was certain Annie wasn't coming back, Freddie turned to the man following her. "Good evening, Legs."

He grinned. "Hot enough for you?"

Given that it was hotter than the hinges of hell, she nodded. "You're following me?"

He offered her an aw-shucks grin. "Wanted to check on you."

Should she thank him or tell him off for invading her privacy? "Was that your man in the park?"

His brows drew together. "My man?"

Freddie nodded. "Earlier today. The one who followed my friend and me."

The remnants of his smile ran away from his face. "Not one of mine. You're sure he followed you?"

Was she? Had she imagined a threat? The hair on the back of her neck stood at attention. "I was sure at the time."

He rubbed his chin. "Sounds like you actually need protection. I'll escort you home. Are you staying in this evening?"

"No. I'm going to a play."

"A play?" He sounded surprised.

Did Legs Doyle, bootlegger, bagman, and killer, understand the utter ridiculousness of opening a play in June?

"Who puts on a play in June?" He did understand. "What's it called?"

She hadn't looked, so she made up a ridiculous name. "*The Bee's Knees.*"

He tucked her hand into the crook of his arm and walked toward the curb. "Better than *The Cat's Pajamas.*"

"Good one. *The Bullfrog's Beard*?"

He snorted. "*The Clam's Garters*?"

She nodded her approval. "*The Tiger's Spots*?"

"Tigers don't have spots."

"Clams have garters?" she countered.

He grinned and hailed a cab.

"About the necklace." Her hand rose to the rope of pearls at her neck. They were a far cry from the diamonds he'd sent.

"You like it?"

"It's stunning. But when a man gives a woman jewelry like that..."

Legs's eyes twinkled. Like diamonds. "I don't need another mistress."

"You have more than one?"

A taxi pulled over, and Legs opened the door for her. "Don't take this the wrong way, but you're not my type. Too ritzy."

She didn't want to be Legs's mistress. Not by a long shot. But being told she was too high hat didn't sit well.

Freddie climbed into the automobile, and the cabbie asked, "Where to?"

She gave him her address.

And Legs, who'd climbed in after her, snorted. "Upper East Side. Ritzy."

She wrinkled her nose at him. "There are a lot of stones."

A grin split his face. "I got pals for twenty years who wouldn't have stood over me like you did. You saved my life. The stones are a thank-you. Wear the necklace. Don't wear the necklace. But keep it. When the world goes to hell again—"

"When?" She frowned at him. "That seems highly pessimistic."

"Read your history. The world always goes to hell."

Legs read history? She hadn't given him enough credit. She would have bet he perused the odds for the horses at Saratoga or Aqueduct or Belmont Park. Maybe all three. That, or he read newspaper stories about bootleggers. "You're an interesting man, Legs."

Again, his eyes twinkled. "I'm not sure that's a compliment."

"It is, Legs. It is."

Freddie ignored the butterflies waging war in her stomach and answered the door for Brandt at precisely seven. "You're right on time."

"I couldn't wait to see you."

The dratted butterflies were reenacting the Battle of the Marne, but her hands remained steady as she accepted a bouquet of pink roses. "They're lovely."

He offered her a gentle kiss, the merest brush of his lips against hers, but the butterflies sent salvos into her small intestines. She took a bumbling step back.

Brandt followed her. He caught her hand. "I missed you today."

Now the butterflies were using howitzers. "Make yourself a drink." She nodded toward the living room. "I'll put these in water." She needed a moment alone.

The amused flash in his eyes said he'd picked up on her nerves and knew he was the cause. "What can I fix for you?"

"I started without you." After the day she'd had—the park, Rose, Legs Doyle seeing her to her door, and the main reason, her feelings for Brandt—she'd deserved an early drink. "Just fix one for yourself."

When she reached the kitchen, Freddie turned on the tap, filled a vase, snipped the ends off the stems, and put the roses in water. Then she dried her hands and braced herself against the counter's edge. She forced deep breaths until the butterflies settled. Only then did she carry the flowers to the living room. "Thank you. Pink roses are my favorite."

"Your favorite roses or your favorite flower?"

"Roses." Red roses were too showy. White roses were too white. And yellow roses represented friendship, not something she wanted from him.

He nodded as if she'd said something profound. "What's your favorite flower?"

She pondered. "Lilacs or hyacinths or freesia."

"Scented to seduce...bees."

And how. She sank onto the nearest chair, reclaimed her gin and lemonade, and drained the glass. Somehow, she resisted fanning her face.

"What are we seeing tonight?" he asked.

She'd finally looked beyond the performance date and time on the tickets. "It's called *Life Goes On*."

He winced.

Life goes on. When his friends were dead. How insensitive could a woman be? "If I could skip the play, I would. My boss insists I go."

He shook his head. "It's fine. The title threw me."

"The title may well be the best part." She studied him. His face was as handsome as ever, but dark circles smudged the skin below his eyes, and he seemed taut, like a harp string wound too tight. Had something else happened? "I'll repeat my warning: It's sure to be dreadful."

He caught her looking and offered a brittle smile. "I'm glad to be here. With you. But my company may match the play."

"Don't be silly. The play can't fix me another cocktail."

He took her glass. "What are you drinking?"

"Gin and lemonade."

He lifted a brow.

"Don't judge. It's cool and refreshing, and I almost melted in the park this afternoon. I need cool and refreshing."

"I'll take your word for it." He added fresh ice to her glass, splashed two fingers of gin, and then poured lemonade. "A police detective called on me today."

Something inside her went still (not the damned butterflies—they'd devolved to wing-to-wing combat). "Oh?"

"Detective Sullivan. He wonders if I killed my friends."

"Did he say that?"

"Not in so many words." He handed her the cocktail.

"You have an alibi for Ewan's death. You were with me. We

heard the shots together." She gripped the cold glass with both hands. "And Tallulah will swear a woman stabbed Ephram."

"It's not hard to hire a killer."

"I wouldn't know." Although she suspected she need only ask Legs if she wanted someone bumped off.

"I didn't kill my friends." He drank. Deeply. "I didn't hire anyone to kill my friends."

"I believe you."

"I asked Sullivan about the woman, but he was cagey."

"I don't suppose police detectives share details with suspects." Brandt winced.

Ouch. She was better with words than that. "You didn't kill Ewan or Ephram. You're innocent. But until the killer is caught, you're a suspect."

"Or until the woman comes after me."

Freddie stared. She hadn't considered that. She liked Brandt more than she'd liked any man in ages. Given time, she might more than like Brandt. But to discover those feelings, they needed romantic evenings and walks in the park and whispered secrets. They wouldn't have any of those experiences if Roxie killed him.

"She killed Jake and Ewan and Ephram," he continued. "I'd be an idiot not to assume I'm next."

"If you knew how to find the woman, what would you do?"

"She murdered my friends."

"So you'd exact revenge?" She couldn't tell him she had a lead. Not if he might kill Roxie.

His lips thinned. "Death is too good for her. I'd make sure she rots in jail."

Air snuck back into Freddie's lungs. "You have faith in the police and courts?"

"Don't you?"

She shrugged.

"The Volstead Act has made us a country of scofflaws. It's too bad, because society needs law and order." This was the Brandt who'd served his country. Honorably. Not the bootlegger with a warehouse full of illegal scotch.

Freddie swirled her drink.

"I see what you're thinking." Bitterness tinged his voice.

"Oh?"

"You're easy to read, Freddie."

She didn't like that idea. Not at all. "What am I thinking?"

"That I'm a hypocrite."

"Wrong."

"You weren't thinking I'm a bootlegger? A man who breaks the law on a daily basis?"

Maybe a little bit. "It's a terrible law, designed by do-gooders to deprive the Germans their beer and the Irish their ale. I was thinking it made criminals of all of us."

"There's a difference between drinking at a speakeasy and importing scotch." He'd voiced one of Freddie's private thoughts.

"Both should be legal." In that moment, she meant it.

The smile he gave her melted the butterflies' cannons. "Why do you ask about that woman? Do you know where she is?"

He didn't want to kill Roxie. He wanted her in jail. Freddie's grip on her glass tightened. "No. But I have a lead. I'm meeting a woman who can tell me where to find her."

His dark brows drew together in a single line. "Sounds dangerous."

"Not at all. I'm meeting her at Carmaux's in the morning."

"Carmaux's?"

"A dress shop on Park."

"I'll go with you."

"I'm more likely to get the information if I go alone." She took in his thunderous expression and held up her hands. "It's a dress shop. There will be salesgirls and models and Eunice."

"Eunice?"

"The alterations lady."

"Is she your source?"

"No. One of the models. Rose."

"And when you have the information?"

"I'll tell the police." And Mr. Rothstein.

He stared at her as if she were naïve. "I don't like it. What time are you going?"

"Nine thirty." She glanced at the crystal clock on the library table. "If we hope to make the opening curtain, we should leave for the theater."

"Which theater?"

"The Puffin. It's tiny. If we're late, we'll be noticed." She stood and crossed to the console, where she'd left her handbag and the tickets.

Brandt finished his drink and rose from the couch. "You're sure you wouldn't rather stay in?"

The butterflies launched an offensive maneuver, and Freddie folded her free arm over her stomach. "I'd much rather stay in." Somehow, she kept her voice steady. "But Gus expects a review. To do that, I need to see the play."

CHAPTER 20

One wonders how one's precious time is best spent. In a dentist's chair? In a hot subway train, stalled between stops? With one's accountant? In a queue, desperately waiting for headache powder? This summer's production of Life Goes On *offers a tepid alternative to those options. The play, a purported comedy, was at least brief. The actors have adopted a new technique: They competed to see who could say their lines the fastest. For those who must seek entertainment in this heat, one suggests a visit to the morgue (where the temperatures are cooler, and the cast is livelier) over a trip to the Puffin Theatre.*

REDDIE SLIPPED THE SMALL notebook and pen into her handbag and crossed her fingers that Gus didn't have a cousin or in-law in the play. Writing about the horrible performance had calmed her frayed nerves and eased some of the worries that hounded her.

The cab pulled to a stop in front of Carmaux's, and the cabbie, whose blue eyes danced with mischief, looked over his shoulder and told her the fare. "You have a nice morning, miss." His accent was pure County Mayo. Or Cork. Or Tipperary.

"Where are you from?" she asked.

He grinned. "Castlebar in County Mayo."

"How long have you been in New York?"

"Going on ten years." The driver scanned the busy sidewalk for his next fare. "You need help with the door, miss?"

"No, thank you." She paid him, adding a hefty tip for his friendly smile.

Pausing in front of Carmaux's, Freddie took a deep breath before pushing through the shop's door.

The new girl, Paloma, greeted her with a bemused smile. "Miss Archer, is Miss Carmaux expecting you?"

"No, not today."

The young woman looked relieved, as if Freddie had saved her from voicing an unpleasant explanation. "How may I help you?"

"I'd like to speak with one of your models, Rose Mindlin."

A furrow plowed through Paloma's delicate forehead. "Rose?" She hesitated, as if she expected Freddie to explain why she wanted to see the model. When Freddie remained silent, she offered a tight smile. "I'll see if she's available."

"Thank you."

Paloma disappeared into the back of the boutique, and a chiffon frock positively called to Freddie. The fabric was a soft lemon hue, and wearing the dress would be like draping a sunbeam over her shoulders.

Freddie smoothed the whisper-thin lavender linen of her own

frock. She'd paired the dress with a white chiffon scarf dotted with lavender and silver polka dots and a boater with a grosgrain band. She looked cool and crisp and ready for the day. Well, until the heat melted the pleats from her dress.

A midnight blue evening gown with scalloped beading demanded her attention. She owned a similar gown, but it was black, not blue, and it wasn't a Carmaux.

She nodded at a saleswoman. "Do you have this in my size? And the yellow?" She pointed at the sunbeam.

"I'll check, Miss Archer."

"Thank you."

She let herself imagine an evening with Brandt. She wore the blue gown. He wore a tuxedo. They danced in a rooftop garden strung with fairy lights. They drank champagne, and the bubbles tickled Freddie's nose. They laughed as if life were a giddy whirl. No darkness. No death. No murder.

"Miss Archer?" Paloma pulled Freddie from her daydream.

"Yes?"

Paloma clasped her hands together. "We can't find Rose."

"Can't find her?"

"She arrived on time this morning. Her handbag is here, and Luella spoke with her not fifteen minutes ago, but she's missing."

"Did anyone see her leave?"

"I've been on the sales floor." Paloma nodded at the mannequins and then the glass front door. "She couldn't have left this way."

"Is there another exit?"

Paloma wrinkled her nose. "The back door leads to the alley."

"Show me."

Paloma hesitated.

"Sophie won't mind." Not if finding Rose meant she got her sketchbook back.

"There's no reason she'd be in the alley." Paloma raked a hand through her Marcel waves, and her soft brown hair fluffed around her head. "It smells out there."

"Be that as it may, I'd like to see for myself." Dread wedged itself into Freddie's throat, and her voice came out unnaturally high.

"As you wish."

Paloma led her past the private salon and into a room where electric light bulbs illuminated tidy worktables, spools of thread in every imaginable color covered an entire wall, and a rack of dresses hung next to a sewing machine. "This is where Eunice works."

Eunice, who wore a cotton smock over a light summer dress, looked up from sewing a button. "Good morning, Miss Archer."

"Good morning." Freddie forced a smile for the best alteration lady in New York.

"Have you seen Rose?" Paloma asked.

"She stepped outside to smoke."

Maybe Rose was nervous, too. "This is quite a workroom." Freddie waved at the wall of thread. "Are the clothes made here?"

Eunice flashed a slightly superior grin. "There's piece work with seamstresses on the Lower East Side. Miss Carmaux also keeps an atelier in Brooklyn."

"Brooklyn?"

Paloma shrugged her chic shoulders. "The rent is cheaper." She paused with her hand on a doorknob. "Here's the alley."

"Open it," said Freddie. "Please."

The alley smelled of coal and cabbage and cigarette smoke. It was brick and wide enough for a delivery truck to pull up at the buildings' loading doors. Freddie glanced down at the cobblestones before stepping outside. For an alley, it was surprisingly clean.

A few business owners had even put benches by their back doors. Rose sat on Sophie's bench with her hands folded in her lap.

"Rose," said Paloma, "Miss Archer is here to see you."

Rose didn't move.

"Rose!"

The model remained still, and Freddie squeezed past Paloma and took a small step into the alley. "Rose?"

Rose ignored her, and Freddie took a deep breath. What was that metallic scent?

She glanced at the cobblestones where Rose's shoes rested in a dark puddle.

"Rose?" Louder this time. But Freddie knew. She felt the horror in her belly, in the staccato beating of her heart. She reached out, touched Rose's shoulder, and watched as Rose's body tilted off the bench.

Behind her, Paloma screamed.

The sound bounced off the bricks and hung in the humid air. Loud enough for Freddie to be grateful she hadn't started her day with a hangover.

"Paloma," Freddie barked.

Mercifully, the woman stopped shrieking. Instead, she posed on her toes, ready to run. Her eyes looked too big for her face, and beneath the rouge on her cheeks, her skin was as white as milk.

"Call the police," Freddie told her. "Ask for Detective Sullivan."

"She's . . . dead?" Paloma held her palm over her mouth as if she might vomit.

Freddie empathized. Her own stomach was in full revolt.

"The killer?" Paloma's saucer-like eyes scanned the alley.

"We're the only ones here."

Paloma's hand slipped from her lips to her throat. "What killed her?"

Freddie forced herself to look at Rose's body.

The dead woman wore a green dress, the front of which was almost pristine. That meant the pool of blood beneath Rose was caused by a wound in her back.

Surely someone would have investigated a gunshot. Although no one came running when Paloma screamed. "I don't know." The admission cost Freddie nothing. "We need the police."

Paloma remained rooted.

"Should I call?" Annoyance crept into Freddie's voice.

"Call?" Paloma sounded far away.

"The police," Freddie snapped.

"Oh. Right. Detective O'Sullivan?"

"Sullivan."

"You're staying here?"

"It seems wrong to leave her."

Paloma stared at Freddie for seconds that lasted years, gave a brief nod, and then escaped into the building.

Freddie examined the wall, determined she might soil her frock if she leaned against it, and gathered the strength to remain upright without support.

Tough when guilt slashed at her like fresh razors. She'd convinced Rose to sell out Roxie, and now Rose was dead.

Murdered.

Collapsed in a pool of her own blood.

If Freddie had kept her mouth closed and her curiosity in check, Rose might be alive.

Tears filled her eyes, but she refused to let them fall. When Detective Sullivan arrived, he'd find a strong, observant woman, not a weeping mess.

Observant. She could be observant.

How had the killer knifed Rose in the back if she was sitting on a bench that backed up to a wall?

Had Rose been standing? Pacing? Worried that Freddie might not show?

Had she known her killer? Turned her back on a murderer? Or had the killer snuck up behind her, stabbed her, and lowered her body to the bench?

Freddie pinched the bridge of her nose.

Why kill Rose today? Did Roxie know Rose was about to spill? If so, how had Roxie found out? Who'd known that Freddie was coming to Carmaux's for the information?

Annie. But Annie was a veritable vault.

And Brandt.

He'd declined her invitation to come in for a drink and kissed her goodnight. The kiss had curled her toes and left her longing for tangled sheets and the burn of his lips on her skin. She'd barely stopped herself from begging. Had he left her to spend the wee hours planning a murder? She shook her head. He wanted to see Roxie in jail. Rose's death was the opposite of helpful. But... would Brandt kill Rose to get Roxie's address? To stop Rose from sharing the address with the police?

She covered her face with her palms. She was being ridiculous. Rose could have shared her plans for the morning with anyone. Brandt was innocent. *Then why don't you trust him?* She shushed the voice in her head. Brandt was a target, not a killer. *Of course you'd think that. You're falling for him.*

Freddie skirted the pool of blood and stared at Rose's body. She looked almost peaceful. Yesterday's bitterness erased by death.

"Miss Archer."

Freddie jumped away from the body. Detective Sullivan had surprised her.

He joined her in the alley, and she felt the need to make herself smaller. The man took up acres of space, and his disapproval radiated like a second sun. "What happened?"

"I found her." Her gaze caught on Rose's ruined shoes.

"Who is she?" His voice was gentle, at odds with his rhinoceros size.

"Her name is Rose Mindlin. She's a model at the shop."

Detective Sullivan crouched next to Rose's body, lifted her shoulder, and examined her back.

Freddie waited for him to say something.

After an interminable minute, he said, "She's been stabbed."

Freddie swallowed. She'd been right.

"You don't look surprised," the detective observed.

"No."

"Any theories?"

"We were to meet this morning. She was going to give me Roxanne's address."

Detective Sullivan's already ruddy face darkened six shades, and he stood, towering over Freddie. "I told you to stay away from this investigation. It's too dangerous for a woman." He jerked his chin at Rose as if her dead body proved his point.

"Rose would never have shared what she knew with the police." Mainly because the police couldn't afford her rates.

"Maybe not," Detective Sullivan ceded. "But she might still be alive."

She felt guilty enough without his assistance. Ire warmed her blood. "You blame me?"

He grunted.

"The person who killed her is responsible. Not me."

The detective's lips thinned. "I made a mistake involving you, Miss Archer. One I deeply regret. I insist you stop inserting yourself in this investigation."

He insisted? Well, if a man insisted, she'd better do as she was told. A hundred smart replies rose to her tongue. She swallowed each one. Mainly because the detective looked as if he might arrest her if she offered him any sass.

"Are we clear?" he demanded.

If men knew how insulting it was to treat women like recalcitrant children, would they still ask questions like that?

She suspected they would. They enjoyed their authority.

"Are we clear, Miss Archer?"

She absolutely understood what he wanted, and she absolutely refused to comply. Not that she'd share that. Instead, she nodded. "Crystal."

His eyes narrowed as if he doubted her sincerity. Smart man.

"If there's nothing further, I'll leave you to your investigation."

"I need a statement. Wait inside until I have time to question you."

Detective Sullivan was insisting. Again.

She turned her back on him and opened the door.

Inside Sophie's shop, the staff was in tears.

"What happened, Miss Archer?"

"Rose is dead."

The women gathered around her gasped as if Paloma hadn't already told them.

"How?"

"Murdered," she replied. "Stabbed." Which led to more gasps.

"Why?" asked Eunice.

Freddie studied the staff's red-rimmed eyes, the quivers in their powdered chins. She listened to their sniffles and swallowed sobs. What could she tell them? "Were any of you friends with Rose? Outside of work, I mean."

The women's heads turned, and a blonde stumbled forward. "We went for drinks on Friday nights."

"Where?" Freddie asked.

"A speak on 52nd."

"The name?"

"The Dizzy Club."

"Did Rose have a fellow?" Freddie dug a handkerchief from her handbag and offered it to the blonde.

"No." The woman accepted the handkerchief and wiped under her eyes. "Least not one she told me about."

"What about Roxanne?"

"What about her?"

"Were she and Rose still friends?"

The blonde sniffed. "I don't know."

This was a disaster. Rose was dead, and Freddie's best lead on finding Roxie was gone.

An hour later, Freddie sat at her desk with her fingers steepled. She stared out the window as if the answers to all her questions might appear on the building across the street.

A disapproving Annie sat across from her.

"Why would a killer take a job at a dress shop?" Why had Roxie bothered?

Annie made a placating sound in the back of her throat. "Your friend Dotty worked at *Vogue*."

Dotty had wasted her days writing captions, but Freddie couldn't help but repeat her favorite. "'Brevity is the soul of lingerie.' What's your point?"

Annie glanced at her hands folded in her lap. "The job paid the bills, and she gained experience."

"Dotty learned from her job," she admitted. "What did Roxie hope to gain?" Freddie tapped her fingers to her lips. "Access."

Annie's head tilted to the side. "What do you mean?"

The thought wasn't fully formed. She needed to talk it out. "Rich women shop at Carmaux's. Women who entertain. Women whose husbands drink good scotch, and Roxie supplied it. The job gave her access to customers."

Annie gave a grudging nod. "Why are you smiling like Christmas morning?"

"If I can find one of her customers, I may be able to get a phone number."

"And then?"

"Then I'll order a delivery and see where it leads me."

"No."

"No?"

Annie's brows knit together in a determined line. "You'll tell Mike your theory. And if you don't, I will. A woman was murdered this morning, a woman who sat in this office yesterday afternoon."

"I'll be fine."

"Really?" Anne infused the word with both doubt and disdain.

"I have Le—" Better if Annie didn't know Freddie had a new shadow or that said shadow was a killer. "I'll be fine."

"You have?"

"Nothing. No one. I'll be careful. I promise."

"You and I have different definitions of *careful*."

"Annie," she wheedled.

"I mean it. Tell Mike, or I will."

"Fine."

Rather than bask in her triumph, Annie waved a handful of messages. "Your mother has called. Six times."

Oh, dear.

"Six times," Annie repeated.

"I heard you the first time. Did she say what she wanted?"

"Yes. Then we traded recipes for rum balls and discussed hemlines."

Marjorie Archer treated the help like help. She was polite, firm, and fair, but never friendly. Freddie's attempts to convince her that Annie wasn't a servant had fallen on deaf ears. "I take your point. I'll call her."

"Call Mike first."

"He'll be at the crime scene."

"You can leave a message. I'll wait."

"You don't trust me."

"I'll wait."

"That's hurtful."

"Make the call, Freddie." With Annie watching, she called the police station and left a detailed message for Detective Sullivan. When she hung up, she glared at her assistant. "Happy?"

"Yes."

"Here." Freddie opened her handbag and took out her note-pad. "Please type this up and give it to Gus."

"Where are you going?" Suspicion wrapped around each word.

"To see my mother. If she called six times, something is wrong." Had she discovered where her father spent his free time? Freddie stifled a groan.

Annie, who'd opened the notebook, caught her lip in her teeth. Her eyes widened, and a small gasp escaped her lips.

"What?" Freddie demanded.

"You didn't like the play."

"I did not."

"Or the actors."

"Nope." She popped the *p*.

"You didn't recognize anyone?"

Uh-oh. "Who?"

"Gus's sister-in-law."

"He can choose not to run the review, but I stand by what I wrote. Was she the bumbling ingenue?"

"Where should I tell him..."

"Tell him there was a family emergency." Freddie hurried to the elevator. Gus's sister-in-law? She'd been bad, but not nearly so terrible as the leading man.

The doors opened, and she stepped inside. What a day this was shaping up to be. Horrible.

Freddie winced. How could she complain (even to herself) when Rose was on her way to the morgue?

She took a taxi to her parents' house, climbed the front steps, and let herself inside.

The dreadful heat lost its power in her parents' home—pushed back by open windows hung with the summer curtains and the relentless whirl of ceiling fans. Her chiffon scarf fluttered like sunlight filtering through the leaves of a shade grove, and her heels clacked against the parquet floor in the foyer. She stepped into the sitting room, where a palace-sized Oriental rug muffled her steps. Above her, a basket-style crystal chandelier from Italy sparkled brighter than diamonds. An enormous bouquet sat on a gilt console table, adding color and scent to the room.

A set of matching club chairs flanked a marble-fronted fireplace, above which a mirror in an elaborate frame showed Freddie she needed fresh lipstick. Ming vases decorated the mantel.

Impressionist paintings—a Monet, a Manet, and three Degas ballerinas—hung on the walls.

The room was elegant, just like Marjorie.

"Mother?"

Silence answered.

Freddie returned to the foyer and called, "Mother?"

A maid appeared. "Miss Archer, good afternoon."

"Helen, where's Mother?"

"The pool."

Of course she was. Marjorie Archer adored swimming, and if she couldn't be at the beach, the pool was the next best thing. "Thank you. Would you please ask Sally to make me a sandwich?"

"Yes, miss."

Freddie gathered her courage and walked to the pool.

Her mother, still glistening from a dip in the water, lounged on a chaise beneath the shade of a sun umbrella. She eyed her daughter for long seconds and then said, "Freddie, what a delightful surprise."

"You called six times."

"I didn't expect you to show up. What's wrong?"

"Why do you think there's something wrong?" Marjorie was the one who'd left six messages.

"Because, darling, you only visit when something or someone is bothering you."

"That's not true," Freddie argued.

Marjorie waved a manicured hand at Freddie's objection and wrinkled her small, straight nose. "I don't mind. A mother is supposed to be her daughter's safety net."

"You're more than a safety net."

"It would be nice if you came when you didn't have a problem." For an instant, so fast Freddie almost missed it, something vulnerable shone in Marjorie's blue eyes.

"I have news."

"Oh?" Clearly her mother was expecting the sky to fall.

Rather than tell her about murders, diamonds from a killer, or Brandt, a man of whom her mother was sure to disapprove, Freddie blurted, "I wrote a play."

"How clever of you."

"Dotty read it. She says it's marvelous."

Her mother took a slow sip of iced tea. "Congratulations. Does this mean you're leaving *Gotham*?" Hope made her voice rise when she said the magazine's name.

"What? No."

"You're wasting your youth in speakeasies and clubs, drinking and dancing until dawn. You won't always be young and pretty." And when the bloom was off the rose, she'd have difficulty finding a man. That was what her mother meant.

Freddie reminded herself that, for her mother's generation, happiness meant a husband, a stable home, and children. Mother didn't understand the new generation of women who wanted—needed—to accomplish more than a perfect dinner party, a satisfied spouse, and a perfect rubber of bridge. "Sorry to disappoint."

"Oh, Freddie. I am not disappointed. But I worry."

"Worry less, I'll visit more."

"I'll try."

A corgi raced up to them and barked for Freddie's attention.

She crouched and scratched behind his ears. "Hey there, Charlie."

The dog grinned at her.

"What is it, Helen?" Marjorie asked the maid, who hovered nearby.

"Miss Freddie, your lunch is ready. Would you like to eat in the dining room?"

"The kitchen is fine."

"Freddie." Mother scolded with just a word.

"I haven't seen Sally in ages." The cook had been her steadfast friend during childhood. Freddie turned toward Helen. "Please tell her I'll be there in a few minutes."

"Yes, miss." She hurried inside.

"Why did you call?"

Her mother raised her brows.

"Six times."

"That many?"

"Yes."

"You should sit."

Uh-oh. Freddie sat.

"Your father is having an affair."

"I'm sorry."

"Why are you sorry? You're not the other woman."

Freddie blinked.

"We've decided to take a vacation."

"Europe?"

"No. The Adirondacks. We'll stay for the rest of the summer."

"You're going to the cabin?" *Cabin* was too small a word to describe the fourteen-room (not counting the staff's quarters) house. "But—"

"He's my husband. I love him. And he loves me. He needs time away from that woman."

Freddie ran a palm over her eyes. "I'm surprised."

"By his affair or my decision to stay? I refuse to blow up my life for one mistake."

Freddie tamped—stuffed—down the urge to tell her about the girl at Eloise's. Instead, she nodded.

"I didn't want to leave town without telling you."

"When will you go?"

"Tomorrow. You'll stay for dinner?" It wasn't a question. "We'll come back in early September, right after Labor Day."

"Are you closing the house?"

"We'll leave a skeleton staff. You're welcome to use the pool."

"Thank you."

"Give me a hug, then run along to the kitchen, but don't spoil your appetite. Ask Sally to put together a basket for you."

"A basket?"

"Perishables that won't survive the trip. Fruits. Vegetables. I believe she has an extra lemon cake. That's your favorite."

"Say no more." Sally's lemon cake deserved odes, and love poems, and lights on Broadway.

"Darling." Her mother's voice quavered.

"Yes?"

Marjorie stood. "Give me a quick hug then run along. I have packing to do."

They embraced, and Marjorie whispered, "I love you."

Freddie tightened her already fierce hold on her mother's slender shoulders. "Love you, too."

CHAPTER 21

REDDIE SAT AT THE kitchen table with a sandwich and a glass of iced lemonade in front of her. "Sally, this looks wonderful."

Sally rested her hands on her ample hips. "Ham and Swiss with that mustard you like." She frowned. "No cookies made."

Freddie winced at the sharp pain that came with those words. How many times had she and Gray tiptoed into the kitchen and begged their big-hearted cook for sweets? From the day she was old enough to toddle to the day Gray left for war, she and her brother had been the lucky recipient of Sally's baked goods. A wave of loneliness swamped her—tightening her throat and wetting her eyes. She dabbed her tears with the luncheon napkin and forced herself to speak. "How do you feel about going to the Adirondacks?"

Sally sniffed. "The kitchen's not much." A tap on the door made her turn, and she tilted her head in confusion. "I called the butcher and the grocer. There shouldn't be any deliveries."

A second tap, and she opened the door.

"Bumpy." She stepped aside for a man holding a large box. "I didn't realize you were coming."

Bumpy was built like a grizzly bear, and the box looked tiny in his massive hands.

"Over there." Sally pointed to the butcher-block table near the stove.

Bumpy? How did one acquire such a nickname? Was he clumsy? Or did he bump people off?

When Bumpy deposited the box on the table, Sally peeked inside. "Six scotch and six gin."

"That's right. Plus there's champagne in the cases on the stoop." Bumpy nodded at an additional two crates stacked outside the door.

Sally's usually sunny smile turned suspicious. "The Glenromach is real?"

Bumpy nodded again.

"You're sure? Mr. Archer can tell the difference."

"On my mother's grave. It's the real McCoy."

Sally sniffed her doubts. "The Archers are leaving town. Would you please carry the crates to the garage?"

Bumpy the grizzly grunted his assent.

"I'll show you which car."

He reclaimed his burden and followed Sally out the door.

Freddie sat. For three seconds. Then she grabbed half her sandwich and jumped to her feet. Glenromach? She hurried outside to the truck and peeked into the cab.

Aside from a pack of Lucky Strikes, the cab was pristine. Neither crumb nor ash marred the truck's interior. And the vehicle smelled of new leather, not smoke. When Bumpy lit a Lucky, he didn't smoke it in the truck.

Surely there was a delivery list. Had he left the list in the back of the truck? Freddie hesitated. She could ask Sally or her father where the liquor came from. There was no need to snoop.

The smart, careful option was to return to the kitchen and the other half of her sandwich, but niggling curiosity insisted she take a quick look.

Wooden slats rising six feet from the truck bed obscured the contents.

She gobbled the last of her sandwich, gathered her courage, and climbed inside.

Cases of liquor pressed against the sides of the truck.

Was it scotch? Glenromach? With trembling fingers, Freddie lifted a crate's lid and found bottles of English gin.

She peeked inside a second crate and pulled out a dark bottle with a brown label marked with a green rooster. Portuguese madeira.

She returned the bottle and opened yet another crate. Champagne. Real champagne. Her fingers brushed against the muselet, the wire cage that held the cork in place.

Someone, presumably lots of someones, had ordered expensive liquor.

The sudden roar of an engine froze her in place. The truck lurched, and Freddie bounced off a crate and landed on her bottom. She stayed there for a few seconds as her situation sank in. She'd snuck into a bootlegger's truck, and she very much doubted Bumpy would appreciate her joyriding with his deliveries.

What would she say when he found her? *I'm sorry for the inconvenience, but while I'm here, I simply must ask, do you work for a killer?*

Not that.

What would Bumpy say? He seemed a man of few words. Perhaps he didn't need them when he had hams for fists.

She scrambled toward the tailgate, but the vehicle was already moving too fast for her to jump out.

Although maybe a busted ankle was better than getting caught.

There was traffic. There were stop signs. The truck would slow, and as soon as she could safely hop out, she'd make her escape.

But the truck didn't slow. Instead, it achieved the impossible—an unimpeded ten minutes of driving in Manhattan. Where was she? She peeked through the slats. How would she get home?

The truck came to a sudden halt.

For a second time, Freddie found herself on her tuchus. She landed hard enough to jar her spine, and her teeth cut into her unsuspecting tongue.

Neither her spine nor her tongue mattered. The truck wasn't moving. Now was her chance!

Except the vibrations that had rattled her bones since the truck left her house were gone. The engine was silent.

Was this another delivery? If so, Bumpy would pull back the canvas and find her. Her mouth dried, and she sprang to the front of the truck and hid behind a crate.

Just in time.

Bumpy pulled back the canvas that hid the truck's cargo. He squinted at a clipboard, claimed a crate, and grunted at its weight. Then the canvas fell back into place.

Freddie crept toward the tailgate with her heart in her throat and her lungs unable to manage more than shallow breaths.

She reached for the canvas and peeked through a tiny gap. She was in an alley and the truck driver was nowhere in sight.

She jumped onto the cobbles and hurried toward the safety of the street and its sidewalks.

She'd blend in, hurry home, and ask where her parents bought their liquor. What she should have done in the first place. It was a good plan, filled with good intentions, but what did they say about the road to hell?

The walk home was sweltering.

She had neither hat, nor gloves, nor handbag. Also, she'd misplaced the new silk scarf she'd bought at B. Altman's.

And her shoes pinched.

She imagined a ski slope, ice skating, and a ride through Central Park in an open carriage as big fluffy snowflakes settled on her like a mantle.

Imagining didn't help. Not one bit. It was hot. She was hot. Everyone around her was hot. And they gave her side-eyed glances as if her lack of a proper head covering was responsible for the heat.

She trudged on. How was she only on 73rd Street? She'd walked for what felt like a solid hour.

She crossed an intersection with a cluster of New Yorkers, mostly men. She could tell they were natives because they didn't gawk at the gorgeous buildings. They strode with purpose, even importance. They might be stuck here, sweltering, sweating, working, but they were good providers. They labored so their wives and children could frolic at the seashore or on the banks of a lake.

The butter-and-egg men who crowded into the city were a mystery. Why leave a town where concrete didn't trap the heat? Where breezes weren't blocked by skyscrapers? Where one might swim in a river without concern for the water's cleanliness? Why visit New York in the summertime?

Another block. Three more and she'd be at her parents' home.

An older woman, clearly scandalized by Freddie's lack of hat or gloves, curled her lip.

Freddie's already hot cheeks warmed with embarrassment.

There was a column there.

She spent the next block writing in her head.

> *Who decides what is appropriate attire for a summer afternoon? Are women but slaves to fashion? One hopes not. But if a woman isn't a slave to fashion, then she's a slave to other women's expectations. Fashion seems a kinder master. Who decided one should wear gloves when the temperature is high enough to melt the varnish from one's nails? Fickle fashion or judgmental women? One rather suspects the latter.*

Two blocks away.

She paused beneath an awning and thanked heaven for the shade.

The doorman offered her a kind smile. "Call you a taxi, miss?"

"I'm only two blocks from home."

"But a hungry man could fry an egg on the sidewalk." The doorman made an excellent point. "And if you don't mind my saying, you look like a boiled owl."

Who boiled owls? And why? Also, did it matter when the nice man was offering an escape from the mean streets of the Upper East Side?

She didn't have a dime on her, but could run into the house, retrieve her handbag, and pay the cabbie. "Please."

The doorman's shrill whistle pierced the city's sounds, and a cabbie jerked his automobile to the curb.

Freddie climbed in, gave her parents' address, and sighed. "Hot enough for you?"

"Is it possible we've relocated to hell?"

The cabbie chuckled. "Come late September and October, there's no better place on earth."

She ceded his point with a tiny nod. "Too bad about November, December, January, February, and March."

"April's no picnic, but May can be nice."

"Can be," she allowed. "It can also be rainy or hot." May made no promises.

"Then there's June, July, and August." He sighed.

"So we stick around for six weeks of autumn."

"I wouldn't live anywhere else." He grinned over his shoulder and pulled to a stop at the curb near her parents' house. "Here you are, miss."

"I need to fetch my purse. I'll be right back." Freddie hurried inside, collected the straw clutch, and then stepped back into the heat and paid the cabbie.

When she returned to the shadowed coolness of the house, her mother waited for her. "Where have you been? And without a hat or gloves?" Her blue eyes narrowed. "You look as if you've been pulled through a rat hole."

"Thank you."

Her mother's lips pinched. "Go. Take a cool bath. You can borrow a dress for dinner."

Freddie didn't argue. Instead, she climbed the stairs to her childhood bedroom and ran the prescribed bath. The cool water felt like heaven. She washed with rose-scented soap and shampoo and emerged feeling like a new woman.

The sense of all being right with the world lasted until she saw the dress on the bed. Why would her mother lay out an evening gown? She wouldn't. Not for just the three of them.

Freddie was half-tempted to don her soiled frock and escape via the trellis next to the bedroom window. She'd done it before. But she'd given the last of her cash to the cabbie. And the thought of hoofing it home? Well, that was even worse than dinner with an Eli.

Did the men her mother procured find these evenings as awful as she did?

She towel-dried her hair and then ran a comb through it.

The dress, an emerald-green chiffon with a bateau neckline and a plunging back, fit perfectly. Freddie powdered her nose; applied blush, lipstick, and mascara; and readied herself for her mother's meddling.

It wasn't the poor man's fault her mother served up Yale men like the first course. He, whoever he was, probably had a mother pushing him to find a nice girl and settle down. Dinner at the Archer house couldn't be his preferred way to spend an evening.

A sigh rose from deep in her soul. After the afternoon she'd had, she longed for a good book, a cool breeze, and time alone. Instead, she descended the stairs.

She heard two male voices—her father's and that of the poor sap her mother had dragged to dinner. Fixing a polite smile on her face, she entered the living room.

The stranger was tall, with broad shoulders, dark hair, sparkling blue eyes, and chiseled features. Dreamy, if one went for that type. Who was she kidding? Every woman on earth went for that type.

"Freddie." Her father gave an apologetic shrug. "Meet Parker Van Dyne."

"A pleasure," she murmured.

"The pleasure's all mine." He stepped forward, claimed her hand, and brushed the barest of kisses across her knuckles.

"I thought I knew all the Van Dynes."

"My black-sheep father married a girl from Chicago. I was raised in Lake Forest."

"I see. What brings you to New York?"

"Work."

Another stockbroker or bond man or lawyer. "Oh?"

"Mr. Van Dyne is with the Bureau of Investigation." Her father offered her an indulgent smile and then added, "Freddie writes for a magazine."

Her mother swept into the living room looking elegant in a black gown paired with ropes of pearls. "That's right. She writes clever little columns for *Gotham*."

Little columns? At least she'd called them "clever."

Parker's gaze was speculative. "About what?"

"Nightlife and fashion. The occasional theater review. What do you investigate?"

"This and that. Tell me, as you do nightlife research"—his eyes positively twinkled—"have you heard anything about a war brewing among the bootleggers?"

"Freddie, Marjorie, drink?" Her father, who fancied himself a bartender, waited next to the bar with his fingers poised to mix any drink their hearts desired.

"Champagne," said Mother.

"Two."

"Freddie, I can't tempt you with a sidecar or a white lady?"

"No, thank you. Just champagne."

With disappointment pulling at his brow, he poured their simple, no-mixing-required wine, and then turned to Parker. "A war?"

"An astonishing number of bootleggers have been murdered these past weeks."

Freddie accepted a champagne flute from her father and took a sip to calm her nerves. "You don't say."

"The most recent victim was dancing with an actress when he died."

A coincidence. This was New York. Surely bootleggers died every day.

"Tallulah Bankhead is her name."

Freddie froze with her next sip of champagne halfway to her lips.

"Tallulah? Freddie and Tallulah are great friends. Her grandfather was a senator from Alabama." Marjorie smiled brightly as if Tallulah's esteemed grandfather somehow made up for his granddaughter being an actress.

Parker flashed her a grin. "Perhaps you could encourage her to speak with me?" The sharp gleam in his eye suggested he already knew that she and Tallulah were friends.

"Tallulah is leaving for London. She's set to star in a play on the West End." Did he know she'd been at the club with Tallulah and Ephram? What exactly was the Bureau of Investigation? And what did they investigate? She resisted the urge to pinch the bridge of her nose. "Tell me, Parker, how did you meet my mother?"

"I play tennis with Parker's aunt. When Eleanor told me her nephew was new to town, I volunteered to introduce you."

Perhaps he wasn't digging for information. Freddie let the champagne bubbles fizz on her tongue. "Well, welcome to New York. It's hot now, but come fall, the weather will be glorious."

"I'm from Chicago. We understand hot. And cold."

"That's right. The Windy City."

"So named by New Yorkers."

"Oh?"

"The meat-packing plants needed workers. When men from Chicago met the immigrants getting off the boats, they painted rosy pictures of the opportunities available in Illinois. The New Yorkers who wanted those same immigrants in their factories said the Chicago recruiters were full of wind."

"You don't say?" said her father. "I always figured Chicago got its name from the wind off the lake."

"True story, sir."

"Were they?" asked Freddie. "Full of wind, I mean."

"Chicago is my city. I'm not a fair judge."

"But you came to New York."

"My extended family is here."

"Your aunt Eleanor." Who was a dragon of the first order. The woman could scare anyone, even Marjorie Archer.

"And my cousins."

"I know your cousins."

He lifted a brow.

"I'm not sure I'd move halfway across the country to be near them."

"Freddie!" Her mother was scandalized.

But Parker grinned.

"Have you discovered anything?" she asked.

"About my cousins?"

His cousins were dull as ditchwater. "The murder you're investigating."

"I'm looking at a whole string of murders. I have a source who swears the killer is a woman."

Marjorie pressed a hand to her chest. "A woman?"

Parker tilted his head. "You don't think women can kill?"

"Of course they can. But killing someone who's dancing is brash. Violent. It seems like a man's crime." Marjorie turned her gaze to Freddie. "Did Tallulah say anything to you?"

"No." Because she'd been there. "Not a word."

"I find that difficult to believe."

"Perhaps she doesn't want to talk about it." Freddie didn't.

Parker offered another grin, this one appealing enough to charm the panties off a chorus girl. "I don't suppose you'd ask if she has time to talk to me before she leaves?"

Parker Van Dyne was here for information, not to meet her. Freddie was sure of it. "I'll ask, but don't hold out much hope."

"A little hope is better than none at all."

Freddie wrinkled her nose. Hope hadn't brought Gray home. She had little faith in hope.

Her parents' butler, a man who should have retired ten years ago, chose that moment to shuffle into the living room.

"Is dinner ready, Carson?" asked Marjorie.

"No, ma'am. There's someone here to see Miss Freddie."

"At this hour?" Marjorie *tsk*ed. "Who is it?"

"Miss Bankhead, ma'am. Miss Freddie, are you available?"

Tallulah, here? Whatever could she want? "I'll see her." Freddie strode toward the door, very much aware the dress her mother had selected gave Parker a view of her naked back.

"You'll ask her about an interview?"

Her shoulders tightened. "Of course." Right after they finished their snowball fight in hell.

How had Tallulah found her? And why? Freddie paused in the foyer.

"Ask her to stay for dinner," Marjorie called. "Carson, set another place."

"I asked your guest to wait in the morning room, Miss Freddie."

"Thank you, Carson." With worry trickling through her veins, Freddie hurried toward the room where her mother took her morning coffee. "Tallulah?"

Tallulah leaped off the love seat. Her blond hair was messy, her crêpe de chine dress was wrinkled, and her face was a mask of relief. "Thank heavens, I found you. We need to go. Now."

"What's wrong? What happened?"

"It's Brandt."

Freddie's heart plummeted.

"He's been arrested."

CHAPTER 22

THREE WALLS OF WINDOWS (all open in the hopes of a breeze),
two whirring ceiling fans, a tropical forest of ferns and palms
and flowering plants, and still the morning room seemed airless.
Stifling. Freddie struggled to breathe, and black dots danced at the
edge of her vision.

Tallulah clasped Freddie's shoulders and shook. Hard.

With her teeth rattling in her head, Freddie escaped Tallulah's
grasp and drew humid air into her lungs. The black dots faded.
"Arrested?" There was an outside chance Brandt had been caught
selling liquor. She crossed her fingers. "For what?"

Tallulah glanced at Freddie's fingers and grimaced. "It's ridiculous. The police are idiots."

Except they weren't. Freddie might not appreciate Detective
Sullivan's patronizing airs, but the man was not an idiot.

"What are the charges?"

"Brandt needs a lawyer." Tallulah raked her fingers through
her already messy hair. "A good one."

"The charges?"

"Murder."

As she'd feared. Her mouth dried, her fingers chilled, and she fought the urge to run or throw a punch. Neither would help Brandt. Instead, she stumbled to the nearest chair and sank onto its cushions. She needed to be logical. Deliberate. Except her mind whirred in circles like the ceiling fans.

"Freddie?"

She looked at her hands in her lap. Her fingers were still crossed. A fat lot of good that had done.

"Did you hear me?"

"Yes."

"Brandt needs a lawyer."

He did. But finding a lawyer was not the problem. "Let me think." Brandt hadn't killed his friends. She was one hundred percent sure of that. Ninety percent sure of that. But what about Rose? Had he killed her?

Brandt was one of the few people who knew Rose's plans the morning she died. Although one might assume Rose would go to work.

Had the killer known that Rose planned a betrayal, or was the timing of her death a coincidence? Freddie had heard innumerable people say there was no such thing as coincidence. Those people were wrong.

She regularly exchanged letters with her dear friend Camilla, who had married and moved to San Francisco. Neither of them mentioned traveling in their missives, but they'd bumped into each other, literally, at the train station in Cleveland. She'd been seated next to a grade school chum at Maxim's in Paris. She'd exchanged waves with a former beau from a gondola in Venice.

Coincidences happened.

But Rose's murder, ten minutes before she was supposed to hand over Roxie's information? That was too much of a coincidence.

"Freddie, talk to me."

She drew another deep breath. "I don't know what to say. Whose murder?"

"I assume Ephram's."

"Brandt wasn't on the dance floor."

"They'll say he hired someone." Tallulah was right.

"How did you find out?"

A flush touched Tallulah's cheeks. "I was at the police station when he was brought in."

"Why were you at the station?" Freddie asked. Tallulah wouldn't risk arrest. Not when she was set to sail for London.

"Zelda. She went skinny dipping in Pulitzer Fountain."

"Where's Scott?"

Tallulah grimaced. "Who knows?"

"Those two. If they faced their demons, maybe they wouldn't have to be so damned gay." There was absolutely nothing wrong with being gay, but the Fitzgeralds used relentless gaiety to paper over their problems.

"Scott is a writer. He faces his demons."

"Have you read Scott's work? He doesn't face his demons. He jams blond wigs on their heads, gives them upper-crust pedigrees, then sets out to woo them."

Tallulah pulled a face. "You might be right."

"I'm definitely right."

"Scott and Zelda aren't the problem."

Freddie lifted a brow.

"They're not today's problem."

"You just said Zelda was in jail."

"I bailed her out. Forget the Fitzgeralds. We need to talk about Brandt and what you're going to do."

"Me?"

"Who else?" Tallulah rolled her eyes as if Freddie were being deliberately obtuse. "You're the one who's half in love with him."

Before she could formulate a response, the click of high heels on the black-and-white marble tiles that led to the morning room alerted Freddie to her mother's approach.

Marjorie paused in the doorway, taking a few seconds to study the two of them. "Freddie, we have a guest, and you've been gone too long." She shook her head sadly as if the lapse in her daughter's manners were a heavy cross to bear. "Tallulah, it's lovely to see you. I've asked Carson to lay a place at the table for you."

Tallulah's eyes widened. "Thank you, Mrs. Archer. It's very kind of you to invite me, but I can't stay."

"Of course you can. I won't take no for an answer. Come along." An incipient threat gleamed in Marjorie's eyes. Freddie and Tallulah would comply. Immediately. Or else.

"Perhaps Tallulah doesn't want to be interrogated over oysters Rockefeller."

Tallulah's brows rose. "Interrogated?"

"Mother invited someone from the Bureau of Investigation to dinner. He wants to interview you about Ephram's murder."

"Oh, no." Tallulah pressed her hands to her cheeks. "I'm sorry, Mrs. Archer, but I can't—"

"I'll ban talk of murder at the table." With an elegant flip of her hand, Marjorie dismissed Tallulah's concerns. "Besides, I'm sure such topics are bad for the digestion."

"Mother, Tallulah has other plans."

Marjorie leveled a gimlet eye her way. "Winnifred, I went to a great deal of trouble to get that young man here. You will march yourself into the dining room, and you will smile at him, and you will laugh at his jokes, and you will be the charming young lady I know you can be." Marjorie's gazed turned to Tallulah. "And you will go with her."

Marjorie hadn't used Freddie's given name in years. The use of *Winnifred* was a dire warning.

"I'll go, but you can't force Tallulah to dine with us. She only came by to share some news about a friend. She needs to be on her way."

"Yes." Tallulah nodded as if her life depended on escaping Marjorie Archer's house. "I do."

Marjorie looked down her nose. Tallulah, the granddaughter of a United States senator, had failed an important test. Flighty manners and a family name might pass muster in Alabama, but here, in New York, the center of the universe, things were done differently. "Well, then, if you'll excuse us, dear. The first course is on the table."

There was no arguing with her mother. Not when she was like this. Freddie deeply regretted not escaping via the trellis. "Tallulah, I'll walk you to the door."

Marjorie pursed her lips. "Freddie, the soup is getting cold."

"You served hot soup? It's a hundred degrees outside."

Marjorie blinked. Once. Then she regrouped. "The chilled soup is getting warm."

Barking a laugh might be hazardous to her health. Instead, Freddie forced a mild smile, rose, and took a step toward the door. "I won't be a moment."

Her mother huffed. "I didn't just fall off the turnip truck. Don't even think of leaving this house with Tallulah."

The thought hadn't occurred to her. She was slipping, because leaving was an excellent idea. "You wound me."

"I mean it, Freddie. I want you at the table."

"Mother, this is important."

"So is dinner."

"Five minutes." This was her line in the sand. She refused to be pushed any further.

Marjorie glanced at the delicate diamond watch on her wrist. "If you're not seated within five minutes, I will find you." A full-fledged threat. "Your time starts now."

Together, Freddie and Tallulah walked to the front door.

Tallulah glanced around the elegant foyer and shuddered. "Your mother is terrifying."

"And how."

"What will you do about Brandt?"

"He'll have to tough it out for one night." He was in jail, not prison. "I'll find him a lawyer in the morning. We'll figure it out." She crossed her fingers again.

"How long will your mother hold you captive?"

Freddie rolled her eyes. "The agent? He's a Van Dyne." Which meant there was a fortune lurking in his background. Young. Handsome. Rich. A trinity, second only to the Father, Son, and Holy Spirit. "She won't let me escape without a struggle. It could take hours. Where are you going?"

"I need a drink. Or three. Club Napoleon."

Why couldn't Tallulah have picked Tony's or the Dizzy Club or Jack and Charlie's? Club Napoleon, with its dramatic gold and ivory décor, was frequented by theater people. People like Nick. "I'll try to stop by." She didn't mean it. Seeing Nick would be the rotting cherry atop a frightful sundae, and she'd had quite enough awful for one day.

Tallulah gave her a quick hug, exhaled as if she'd narrowly avoided a head-on collision with a speeding car, and then slipped through the front door to freedom.

Freddie watched her trot away. Then, with leaden feet and a sickly, sweet-as-pie smile on her lips, she headed toward the dining room.

"I apologize for keeping you waiting." Freddie stepped into the dining room, where the chandelier blazed like a thousand glittering stars and a Battenberg lace cloth covered the table's walnut and marquetry surface. A member of her parents' staff had removed the leaves from the table, which could seat twenty. Tonight it was set for a more intimate gathering.

Parker stood and pulled out her chair. "I hope your friend is all right."

"She received some bad news." Freddie slipped into her seat, took in the flatware, and suppressed a groan. Two forks to the left (dinner and salad), two knives (dinner and fish) and two spoons (dinner and soup) to the right. At least five courses—soup, salad, fish, an entrée, and dessert. Then coffee. Then brandy. She'd be here for hours.

Marjorie picked up her soup spoon and lifted a taste of gazpacho to her lips, the signal they could begin eating.

"When will Miss Bankhead have time to speak with me?" *When*, not *if*. Parker Van Dyne was very sure of himself.

"She's not ready to talk about the murder."

"I see." He didn't sound pleased. "I wouldn't ask if it weren't important."

"Freddie will ask her again. I'm sure, when Tallulah's over the shock, she'd be delighted to speak with you."

Freddie stared at her mother. Marjorie was making promises Freddie had no intention of keeping. She hadn't been the woman in Ephram's arms when he died, and if it was difficult for her to talk about that terrible night, it was even harder for Tallulah. Besides, telling a man that the woman—the killer—wore a Carmaux dress wasn't exactly helpful.

"I'd be very grateful," said Parker.

Gerald paused with his spoon halfway to his lips. "Tell us more about the string of murders."

"They were all bootleggers?" asked Marjorie.

"That's right."

"Criminals." Marjorie sounded smug.

"There was a criminal named Bumpy in your kitchen this afternoon."

"Freddie!"

Did Marjorie believe the wine she drank with dinner magically appeared in the cellar? "You have to buy your liquor somewhere."

"I stored enough wine and scotch for a few years." Gerald gave a what's-a-man-to-do shrug. "I never dreamed this foolishness would last so long."

"Parker." Marjorie bestowed her most charming smile on her guest. "Tell us why these men are being murdered."

"Scotch," said Freddie. "The good stuff."

Three sets of eyes settled on her, but it was her Parker who asked, "How do you know that?"

Whoops! "One hears things." She tried to sound light and airy.

"Where?" Parker's voice was sharp.

"At parties. At clubs." So light and airy as to be effervescent.

"What else did you hear?" asked Parker.

"Nothing specific. Marvelous gazpacho, Mother."

Marjorie frowned at her. "What kind of parties are you attending, and with what kind of people that you hear details of murders?"

Freddie glanced at her father. She couldn't help it.

Gerald's cheeks flushed, and he took a sip of wine. "Who are the victims?"

"Thus far, Ephram Loeb, Ewan Duncan, and Jake Haskell."

"Jake Haskell?" Marjorie's brows rose on her forehead. "Oh, no. You must be mistaken. I met him at a party at the Merriweathers' party this spring. You remember, Gerald. He was the young man who brought Glenromach as a hostess gift. Elizabeth was so pleased. Such a nice young man."

Bootleggers couldn't be nice young men? Brandt was. "Jake Haskell was a bootlegger."

Again, three gazes landed squarely on her person. Whoops.

"Don't be silly, Freddie. Bootleggers are unsavory sorts whose last names include odd letters and too many vowels."

"Like Luciano?" Freddie suggested.

"Exactly. And that dreadful little man who left New York for Chicago."

"Capone." Freddie smiled at Parker. "Chicago's most famous citizen is a New Yorker."

"I'd call him infamous," Parker replied. "Have you ever been to Chicago?"

"Only in fiction."

He winced. "Don't tell me. *The Jungle*?"

"Is that a book?" asked Marjorie. "What's it about?"

"Grinding poverty and meat-packing plants," Freddie replied.

Marjorie wrinkled her nose. "I don't believe I'd care for that. Let's return to Mr. Haskell. If, and that's a rather large *if*, he was killed over scotch, I don't understand why. Fishmongers aren't killed over who gets to sell us fish."

"No disrespect to fishmongers, but they're not going to become obscenely rich selling halibut. But selling scotch and gin and French wine?" Parker paused as Carson cleared his soup bowl. "There's a chance for men to become as rich as a Rockefeller."

"I had no idea."

"Importing real scotch is big business."

"How big?" asked Gerald.

"Tens of millions a year. And that's just for New York and New Jersey. Boston and Philadelphia have their own bootleggers."

Gerald rubbed his chin and leaned forward. The topic obviously interested him. "So when someone kills a bootlegger, he takes over their smuggling routes?"

"And their distribution. Even if the killer doesn't take over the dead man's routes, at least he's eliminated his competition." Parker lifted a glass filled with white wine and nodded at Gerald. "It's quite a business."

"Be that as it may," said Marjorie, "it's a shame that thugs are killing nice young men like Mr. Haskell."

"Bootlegger, Mother. Jake Haskell was a bootlegger."

"As you say, Freddie." Her disbelief was evident. "It's still perfectly awful."

Her mother, who was invincible and clear-eyed when in the

company of women, bent like a willow and talked like a nitwit in the company of men.

They fell silent as Carson served the fish course, a baked halibut garnished with lemon and parsley.

Freddie refused to act like a lob just because a handsome man sat at the table. "What exactly do you do for the Bureau of Investigation, Mr. Van Dyne?"

"Please call me Parker."

"As you wish." She waited for an answer.

None was forthcoming. Instead, Parker directed his attention to the fish on his plate. "This is delicious, Mrs. Archer."

"I'm so glad you're enjoying it. You must come again when we have more time to plan. Our chef is a genius when she has a few days to prepare."

"Parker," said Freddie, "you were telling me what you do."

"Was I?" He grinned. "I investigate."

"Murders?"

"Yes."

"Isn't that a job for the police?"

His grin widened.

"Detective Sullivan is leading the investigation into Jake Haskell's death."

"How on earth do you know that?" asked Marjorie.

Freddie ignored her. "Are you working with the detective?"

"We've spoken." The grin widened to Cheshire cat status.

"Freddie, how do you know the details of a murder investigation?" Her mother would not be ignored.

"I mentioned Mr. Haskell in my column. Shortly afterward, he was murdered. Detective Sullivan called on me at work and asked if I remembered any additional details."

"Did you?" asked her father.

"Mr. Haskell had a date for the evening. She wore pearls and a fabulous dress. That's all I remember."

"You and Miss Bankhead live interesting lives."

He didn't know the half of it. "One must keep busy."

Impossibly, Parker's grin widened even more.

"One must steer clear of the law," said Marjorie severely.

Freddie opened her eyes wide and tilted her head. Did her mother only hear what she wanted? Was she being deliberately obtuse? "Parker is the law."

"Of course he's not." Deliberate or not, Mother was definitely behaving like a nitwit.

"He is."

"Freddie, we have white wine on the table. And champagne. If Mr. Van Dyne was tasked with enforcing the law, he'd arrest us."

"Having and drinking alcohol is not illegal," Freddie replied.

"I beg to differ," said Marjorie.

"We can drink all we want." Freddie held up her glass. "We just can't buy or sell a single drop."

Marjorie frowned. "Is she right?"

"She is," said Parker.

"Which part?"

"All of it. The having, the drinking, the buying, the selling."

And the law enforcement. "Mr. Van Dyne has bigger fish to fry."

"That's right." Marjorie patted her lips with her linen napkin. "What does your aunt have to say about your murder investigation?"

He grimaced, as if displeasing his aunt pained him. "She'd rather I traded stocks."

Freddie understood the pain of disappointing her family and the necessity of following her path, regardless. Apparently, Parker was familiar with the same pain. She liked him better for it.

After his revelation, dinner was quiet.

Marjorie barely apologized for serving chilled lobster salad as an entrée.

Gerald drank steadily.

Dessert, pineapple upside-down cake, disappeared in less than a minute. A testament to Sally's culinary skills or their eagerness to leave the table?

"Coffee?" asked Marjorie.

"No, thank you," Parker replied.

Marjorie covered her mouth with her fingers as if hiding a yawn.

"Departure time?" asked Freddie.

Marjorie sighed. "Early."

"Departure?" asked Parker.

"We're going to the Adirondacks," Marjorie replied.

"And I've kept you at the table too long."

It had been the shortest dinner of Freddie's life.

Marjorie's lips curled into the barest hint of a smile. "On the contrary, having you with us has been delightful."

"Thank you for your hospitality." He turned his gaze to Freddie. "Are you traveling as well, Miss Archer?"

"No. I'm staying in the city."

"May I see you home?"

"What a wonderful idea," said Marjorie.

Which was how Freddie found herself in Parker's coupe.

He sped through the dark city. "Your parents are charming."

"It's nice of you to say so."

He chuckled, and the cheeky grin returned. It stayed on his face until he pulled to the curb next to her building. "May I see you again?"

"I'm not sure our lifestyles mesh."

"Ah. The Bureau of Investigation."

"I do spend half my time in speakeasies."

"I don't care if you drink in speakeasies."

"You care about murder?"

His expression turned serious. "When it's part of something bigger."

"What's bigger than murder?"

Parker got out of the car, circled the vehicle, and opened her door.

"What's bigger than murder?" Her question deserved an answer.

He offered his hand and helped her from her seat. "It was a pleasure meeting you, Miss Archer. I'll explain over dinner. Saturday night."

"Has anyone ever told you you're infuriating?"

"Never." His eyes twinkled in the streetlights' yellow glow. "I'll pick you up at eight." He didn't wait for her answer. Instead, he got in his car and drove away.

Freddie watched his taillights disappear. As a word, *infuriating* wasn't big enough to describe Parker Van Dyne. *Aggravating* and *vexing* were also required.

She tossed her hair, turned toward her building, and took a few steps toward the closed door. Where was Franklin, who replaced Bert in the evenings?

A man she didn't recognize stepped out of the shadows and

pointed a gun at her. He jerked his head toward a black Packard. "Let's go."

She stared first at the light reflecting off the gun and then at the man's dispassionate expression. Her racing heart rose to her throat. Getting in the car was a terrible idea.

"You've got the wrong girl." She raised her hands and backed up. Into a wall of muscle. And the world went dark.

CHAPTER 23

TEN TIMES MORE PAINFUL than the worst hangover she'd ever had (and she'd had some doozies), Freddie's head threatened to explode. She didn't dare move. Not so much as an eyelid. Who knew what might trigger the end?

What had she done last night? Too much champagne? Too much gin? Both?

Then came the memory of Parker's taillights and the man with the gun.

Her current headache was not self-inflicted. And she was in dire trouble.

She listened. Hard. And heard not a sound. But she'd have a hard time hearing the clang of ten fire trucks over the frantic beating of her heart.

She opened her eyes. Barely.

Wherever she was, at least the light was dim. Thank heavens for that. If her headache met bright light, she might upchuck her dinner. And this place smelled bad enough already (a foul combination of stale sweat, cigarette smoke, and grime).

She allowed herself one minute for self-pity and fear. Her head hurt. That was the understatement of the century. Her kidnappers had tossed her into a squalid room. She might die. Soon. Bleak. That was how she'd describe her current circumstances.

Still, she was alive.

She wiggled her toes. Then she shifted legs. Working order. She repeated the process with her fingers and arms. Those operated as they should.

Better yet, she wasn't tied up.

Slowly, as if she had all the time in the world, she pushed up to sitting.

Her head objected, and she paused for long seconds to let it get accustomed to its new upright status.

When she was sure her head intended to stay attached to her neck, she stood. And swayed. She felt as unsteady as a pie-eyed fraternity boy out for his first night on the town.

One glance at the divan where she'd awakened made her skin crawl. Even in the dim light, she could make out stains and rips and more stains.

Slowly, so as not to interfere with her head's tenuous connection to her body, she shuffled toward the door.

Locked. Had she really expected her captors to leave her in an unlocked room?

She glanced around the small space and spotted nothing but a desk, a chair, and the filthy divan. No weapon. No convenient key.

She pressed her hands to the side of her head. Who had kidnapped her? And why? For ransom?

After tonight's dinner, her mother might not pay her ransom. She tried the door a second time. Still locked.

The door was sturdy, solid oak, built to last, with a frosted glass window. The dratted thing was a holdover from a time when her prison was new and clean. If she rammed it with her shoulder, she'd break her shoulder.

But she couldn't stay here.

Whoever had taken her hadn't killed her. Yet.

Such a funny little word, *yet*. "Yet, yet, yet," she whispered. It got funnier with repetition. Funnier and darker.

She staggered to the desk, yanked open the top drawer, and groped inside. She found a nickel wedged in the back corner, a pencil stub, a gum eraser, a dried-up bottle of ink, and three paper clips.

Why had she never learned to pick a lock? Somewhere, there was a clever girl who could fashion those paper clips into a key. Freddie was not that girl.

She took the nickel and opened the next drawer. It was empty. As were the next three.

Her head throbbed, her eyes watered, and she steadied herself against the chair. It was large and ugly, with a sprung, cracked leather seat and worn arms. She perched on its edge, rested her elbows on the desk, and let her head fall to her hands. If she did escape this dreadful room, what then? She was alone and weaponless, with only a nickel to her name. The situation was hopeless.

No. She'd already taken a moment to wring her hands. She would not despair. She was made of sterner stuff.

The chair squeaked as she straightened her back and shoulders.

The chair.

She glanced at the door and then got up and tipped the chair on its side.

Fingers crossed this worked. She brought her foot down on the chair's leg. When the chair didn't break, she tried again.

It took five attempts, but the wood finally splintered, and she was armed with a sturdy club.

She approached the door. How should she do this? Channeling her inner Babe Ruth, she closed her eyes and swung.

Glass shattering was a deafening sound. Her suffering brain positively cringed. But she didn't have time to baby her gray matter. Her captors might have heard the glass break. How could they not?

She didn't have much time. She used the chair leg to knock out the remaining shards. But the opening was too high. With a desperate groan, she dragged the chair's remains to the door. Then she used them as a precarious step and escaped through the broken window.

Escaped was optimistic. She was in a dark warehouse. So dark that the shadows had shadows. Her best bet was to find a wall and follow it until she came across a door. And then what? She possessed a killer headache, a chair leg, and five cents (which would fund two phone calls if she could find a box). She didn't know where she was in the city, or if she remained in New York.

In the darkness, she heard a scurrying sound.

Rats? There were rats?

Her spine tightened, and her mouth went dry. She was half tempted to return to the office.

If Gray were here, he'd mock her fear of rodents. Then he'd stride into the unknown with his head held high. She could almost hear his voice. "Are you coming? Or are you going to stand there and wait for the rats to get you? Perhaps you'd prefer the kidnappers?"

She gathered the thin strands of her courage and ventured forward.

Freddie paused in the inky shadows cast by towering crates and wished Gray were actually with her.

He'd have a plan. Hell, Gray would already be out the door, on the street, and whistling a jaunty tune.

She wiped away a tear. If she wanted to escape the warehouse, she couldn't afford the distraction of sorrow.

Who had taken her?

Her abduction was somehow related to the murders. She had poked that hornet's nest too many times for it to be anything else. But why now?

It wasn't as if she knew anything. Rose had died before she spilled the proverbial beans.

But Roxie didn't know that. Was she worried that Freddie knew her secrets?

The woman had shown herself to be an efficient, cold-blooded killer. So why wasn't Freddie dead?

That funny little word popped into her head for a reprise. "Yet, yet, yet."

Freddie tiptoed into another pool of deep shadow.

Between the darkness and the height of the stacked crates, she had no idea if she was headed toward an exit or deeper into the warehouse. She didn't care. A chilly tingling between her shoulder blades insisted she keep moving.

Freddie tightened her grip on the chair leg and crossed an aisle wide enough to accommodate a wagon. Safely on the other side, she leaned against a crate and felt the delicate fabric of her dress catch on the rough wooden surface. A ruined dress, even if it did belong to her mother, was the least of her problems. If she survived, she'd replace the frock. If she survived, she'd buy her mother ten frocks.

She lifted her foot to take another step, but the tap of heels on the stone floor froze her in place.

"Bumpy." A woman's shriek sliced through the remnants of Freddie's brain.

She edged away from the voice.

"Bumpy!" Louder this time.

The sound of a man's boots on the floor reached her.

Something skittered over her foot, and Freddie clapped a hand to her mouth. She had bigger problems than rats.

"Where is she?" the woman demanded.

Bumpy answered with sullen silence.

"You don't know how long she's gone?"

"No." Bumpy's response was grudging. Resentful.

"You didn't hear the glass break?"

"No."

"First you let her sneak into your truck, then you let her escape? You're an idiot."

How did the woman, presumably Roxie, know Freddie had hitched a ride in Bumpy's truck?

Freddie touched her neck. Was that where she'd lost her scarf?

If so, how did Roxie know it was hers?

"Where is she?"

"Gone." Bumpy didn't sound as if he cared.

"Find her!"

"Where?"

"If you don't find her, the boss will wear your balls on her charm bracelet."

Charm bracelet? Just who was this boss?

"You want to be careful in a warehouse like this," Bumpy replied. "A crate falls? It could flatten you. Like a pancake."

When their voices faded, Freddie headed in the opposite direction. She found a wall. She found a door locked from the inside. She stepped into an alley and breathed deeply.

A mistake. The air stank of rotting fish and other even more horrible things. The cobbles beneath her shoes glistened with wetness unassociated with rain.

Still, she was free. Free in a strange neighborhood where nice young ladies in borrowed evening gowns never ventured.

Free did not mean safe.

She crept forward, keeping to the shadows, jumping every time she heard a noise. And there were plenty of noises. A woman yelled in the distance, a dog barked, a baby wailed, and trucks rumbled.

Surely, she'd be safer on the street.

Unless that was where Bumpy was searching for her.

She didn't have good options. Stay here in the stinking alley and hope a vagrant didn't accost her, or head to the nearest street, figure out where she was, and find a way to get home.

She massaged her temples. She'd had bad nights, but this one? It took the cake.

Reluctantly, she chose the street.

"Miss Archer?"

Her shoulders tightened.

If Dotty were in her shoes, she'd ask, "What fresh hell is this?"

Freddie lifted her skirts and prepared to run.

"Mr. Doyle is looking for you."

Legs? She paused.

"Says there's a reward for the one who finds a pretty lady in a green dress. That's you. Got to be."

How did Legs know she was missing?

"Come with me, miss?"

Follow a stranger? Freddie was running low on faith and trust. "What's your name?"

"Ira. It means watchful. I reckon that's why I found you." Ira was a boy of not more than fifteen.

"You found me. Now what?"

"We go to the Corlears Hook."

"Where?"

"The park, miss. Mr. Doyle is waiting there."

Hope bloomed like springtime. Did she dare trust the feeling?

"Half the Lower East Side is searching for you." Ira puffed his chest. "And I'm the one who found you."

Following Ira beat remaining in the alley. It also beat braving the streets by herself. "Lead the way."

He grinned as if he'd sensed her doubts and was happy to prove her wrong.

She followed Ira through a worrisome maze of dark alleys. Just when she was convinced he was leading her to her doom, they reached a riverside park.

She couldn't help but think of her nighttime foray into Washington Square Park and her mad dash to Barney Gallant's club.

Despite the neighborhood. Despite the company. Despite the fact that Roxie and Bumpy were looking for her. She felt safer now.

"Mr. Doyle?" Ira called. "I found her."

Legs stepped out of the shadows, and a wave of relief weakened Freddie's knees.

"Careful there, miss. The ground ain't even."

Legs claimed her elbow. "Are you hurt?"

"My head. Maybe."

His grip on her arm tightened.

"I'll be fine." After a bath, a bottle of aspirin, and two days' sleep.

"Mr. Rothstein wants to talk to you."

So much for her wish list. She was not the woman to keep Arnold Rothstein waiting. "That's fine. But first, Ira is due a reward."

Ira grinned. "I took her the back way, so nobody grabbed her."

Legs's lips quirked, and he reached into his pocket and pulled out a bill.

She glimpsed Ben Franklin's portrait. That hundred-dollar bill was probably more money than Ira had ever seen.

The boy stared at the money with his mouth hanging open.

"You got a job, kid?"

His gaze did not waver. "No, sir."

"You do now," said Legs. "You got brains, kid. You come round Lindy's tomorrow. You know where that is?"

Ira nodded, his gaze still fixed on his reward.

"I'll let Mr. Rothstein know you're coming." Legs released his grip on the bill.

Ira held the money in his hands as if he couldn't believe it was real. "Thank you, sir."

"Come on, Freddie. Let's get you someplace safe."

Legs led her to a waiting car, helped her into the back seat, and then climbed in beside her.

Without a word, the driver put the car in gear.

Why had Legs come looking for her? Not that she was

complaining. The opposite. She was endlessly grateful. "How did you know?"

"Saw it happen." His voice was grim. "I was too far away. They had you in the back of a truck before I could get to you. I'm sorry."

"Sorry? You just rescued me." She reached for his hand and squeezed. "Thank you."

He grunted.

The driver took them to an apartment building on Riverside Drive, and Legs helped her from the car.

Freddie winced at the brightness of the streetlights.

"We'll get you some aspirin."

A doorman, who didn't bat an eye at her disheveled state, ushered them inside and called the elevator.

She and Legs rode to the top floor. Then he escorted her to the only door and knocked.

A woman in a flowered bathrobe answered.

"Good evening, Mrs. Rothstein. Would you please tell Mr. Rothstein I'm here with Miss Archer?"

She gasped. "You're Miss Archer? You poor, dear girl, what happened? I'm so relieved Legs found you."

"We found her on the Lower East Side."

Carolyn pressed her fingers to her cheeks and stepped aside. "Come in, come in. What may I get you?"

"A glass of water, please. And two aspirin, if you have them."

"Coming right up. Legs, you know where he is." She hurried off.

Legs escorted Freddie to a terrace overlooking the river. The breeze off the water was cool, and the lights from New Jersey (Freddie had no idea which town) looked almost magical.

Mr. Rothstein's cigar glowed in the darkness. "He found you."

"A kid found her. He's coming round Lindy's for a job tomorrow."

Mr. Rothstein nodded at the chair across from his. "What happened?"

Freddie sat and smoothed the ruined dress over her lap. "Earlier today, my parents received a liquor delivery. I peeked into the truck and went for an unexpected ride."

"Were you caught?"

"No, sir."

The ghost of a smile touched Mr. Rothstein's lips.

"I got out of the truck and had dinner with my parents. One of their guests took me home. That's when Bumpy, the truck driver, knocked me out, kidnapped me, and took me to a warehouse filled with liquor. Well, I assume the crates held liquor."

Mr. Rothstein's cigar glowed brighter. "Where?"

"The Lower East Side. Ira could probably take you right to it."

He laced his fingers together, and a chilly smile curled his lips.

Mrs. Rothstein joined them on the terrace and pressed two pills into Freddie's hand. "Your aspirin, dear." She held out a glass. "And your water."

"Thank you, Mrs. Rothstein."

"I'm Carolyn. Mrs. Rothstein is my mother-in-law."

"Well, thank you."

Mr. Rothstein shifted in his chair. "How did you get away?"

"I broke a window and climbed through." She swallowed the pills and drank deeply. "I heard Roxie talking to Bumpy."

Mr. Rothstein's eyes glittered in the darkness. "And?"

"She threatened him. She said her boss would..." Embarrassment warmed Freddie's cheeks.

"Yes?"

"She said her boss would be furious because Bumpy lost me. She said the boss would wear his balls on her charm bracelet."

"Roxie's working for a woman?" Legs sounded disbelieving.

"That's what I heard." That's what she'd tell Detective Sullivan when she called him in the morning.

"Arnold." Carolyn leveled a severe look at her husband. "Miss Archer has had a traumatic evening. She needs a bath and rest. The poor girl has been through hell."

"As always, you're right, my dear." Mr. Rothstein fixed a cool gaze on Freddie. "My wife will set you up."

"Set me up?"

"Set you up. With a bath and clean clothes. You're staying here tonight."

Freddie looked at the man who ran the city and didn't argue.

CHAPTER 24

FREDDIE STUMBLED INTO *GOTHAM*'s offices wearing Carolyn Rothstein's Chanel suit. The cardigan jacket was nothing short of revolutionary, and Freddie promised herself a long visit at the designer's atelier the next time she went to Paris.

Annie looked up from opening the mail. "You look pale. And since when do you wear suits?"

Freddie ignored the first comment. While last night's blistering headache was but a ghost of its former self, determined hammers still pounded at her temples, and she felt as limp as yesterday's handkerchief. "The suit is Chanel." Carolyn Rothstein had insisted she wear it. Since they were close to the same size and the jacket was the latest in chic, she'd agreed. Also, Chanel.

"And you picked a day when the temperature hit ninety before nine in the morning to wear a black jacket?"

"I can't take it off." Truth was, she'd been sorely tempted to take off the jacket as the Rothsteins' driver brought her to work, as she rode the tightly packed elevator, and as she made her way to

Annie's desk. The only thing stopping her was the tightness of the sleeveless cotton blouse across her breasts.

"Hmph."

"What makes you so suspicious?"

Lord knows, Freddie had given Annie plenty of reasons. Reasons she conveniently ignored.

"You're here before nine without spending the night on the divan in your office."

"That's what you call suspicious behavior?" She crossed her fingers that Annie didn't notice the satin pumps on her feet. Carolyn's shoe size was much larger than hers, and she wore her evening shoes. "Sounds like a dedicated employee to me."

The way Annie rolled her eyes was quite insulting.

Quickly, before Annie could notice the shoes, Freddie nodded at the stack of mail on her desk. "Anything I should know about?"

"Invitations, sales flyers, letters from readers, and this." Annie held out an envelope marked personal and confidential.

"There's no postmark," Freddie observed.

"It was hand-delivered. There!"

The hammer in Freddie's head reacted to Annie's sudden yelp. It whacked hard enough to bring a lesser woman to her knees. "What?"

"Your expression. You're worried about something."

She worried about Brandt, who, as far as she knew, still sat in jail. She worried about murder, most especially her own. She worried her head might yet throw in the towel and leave her neck. Rather than reply, Freddie held out her hand. "May I please use your letter opener?" Seconds later, she pulled a single piece of paper from the envelope.

"What is it?" Annie demanded.

"Nothing." Except her heart had joined last night's pumps on the floor.

"That's why all the color drained from your face? Over nothing? You're in trouble. I'm sure of it."

Freddie squeezed her eyes shut. "Is Gus here?"

"No. He's out of the office until Monday."

That was unexpected good news. Gus usually put in an appearance on Saturday mornings. "It's possible I should speak with your detective. If you talk to him, would you please ask Detective Sullivan to swing by?"

Annie didn't waste a second. She picked up the phone and dialed.

Freddie left her to find coffee. She returned with a full cup. Every single one of her worries trailed behind her like a row of ducklings.

Annie extended her hand and stared pointedly at the page still clutched in Freddie's fingers. "He's on his way. Now, let's see that letter."

Freddie gave it to her, and Annie quickly perused the page.

"It's just names and addresses."

Yes. Her closest friends' names and addresses.

"What's this at the bottom?"

Are they as resourceful as you?

The kidnapper knew her friends and where to find them. Presumably, they were in danger if she talked. They were in danger if she didn't. And she'd already talked. To Arnold Rothstein.

She could hardly withhold information from the police. Plus there was an outside chance she could use her abduction to negotiate Brandt's release.

"I believe I'll work until the detective arrives."

"You didn't answer my question."

"I'm not exactly sure what that line means." Freddie wandered into her office and sank into her chair.

Annie was right. Even with the ceiling and oscillating fans whirring like mad, it was too hot for Carolyn's couture jacket. She took it off and hung it on a velvet hanger. Then she picked up a pen.

> Not so long ago, ladies suffered through summer in corsets and gussets and yards of fabric. One wonders how those brave souls survived. Now hems are short, dresses are loose, cardigan jackets are chic, and we owe our undying gratitude to the genius designer found at 31 rue Cambon.
>
> Cotton and linen and crêpe de chine are lovely in the heat, but jersey deserves a paean. It is cooler and more comfortable than what came before. Plus, one can breathe and move and even dare a tennis game without acquiring more wrinkles than a crushed paper bag. Visit the finer stores on Fifth Avenue, and one finds jersey in magnificent hues—soft yellows, bright greens, and midnight blues.
>
> Which shade to choose? Coco Chanel once said, "The best color in the whole world is the one that looks good on you." Unless that color is chartreuse. One has yet to meet a woman flattered by chartreuse. Bon mots aside, Chanel may be counted upon for simplicity, comfort, and individual elegance.

Freddie tapped the end of her pen against her desk and scanned what she'd written. It wasn't perfect, but it wasn't terrible. And writing was infinitely preferable to thinking about her upcoming interview with Annie's detective.

"Freddie?" Annie poked her head into the office. "Detective Sullivan is here." She bit her lip as if she had more to say.

"And?"

Annie stepped inside the office and closed the door.

"What?"

"You might want to powder your nose and put on fresh lipstick."

"When Detective Sullivan met me, I had a hangover the size of New Jersey, no shoes or stockings"—she tucked her feet farther under the desk—"and smudged mascara."

"He's not alone."

Apprehension dried her mouth and chilled her fingers. "Tall, handsome, arrogant smile?"

"You know him?"

Freddie slumped in her chair. "We met last night."

If you're sad, add more lipstick and attack. More wisdom from Chanel.

Did that work for nerves, too? She added more color to her lips, just in case.

She stood when they entered. "Detective Sullivan, good morning. Agent Van Dyne, I wasn't expecting to see you again so soon."

Parker's eyes sparkled as if she'd said something terribly droll.

You live but once, you might as well be amusing. If Chanel gave up designing, she could write witticisms and give Dotty a run for her money.

"Please." She gestured toward the two chairs facing her desk. "Have a seat. Coffee? Iced tea?"

"No, thank you," said the detective.

"Coffee. Cream. Two sugars." The government agent looked as fresh as a daisy. Then again, he hadn't been abducted, and presumably, he was wearing his own clothes.

"Annie?" She lifted her empty mug. "Please? And two aspirin?"

"Of course." Annie exited the office, which suddenly seemed far too small.

Freddie blamed the two large men.

Detective Sullivan leaned forward. "You have information, Miss Archer?"

There were to be no pleasantries? All right, then. "I was kidnapped last night."

"What?" Parker sat straighter. "When?"

She swallowed. "Immediately after you dropped me off, I was abducted and hauled off to a warehouse on the Lower East Side."

"How?"

"Someone knocked me on the head." Gingerly, she touched her still-tender scalp. "I woke up in a filthy office."

Parker, too, leaned forward. "You said you were taken to a warehouse."

"The office was in the warehouse."

"Where?" the agent demanded.

"I just told you. The Lower East Side."

Parker frowned at her as if she were the simpleton in this conversation. "The address?"

"No idea." It was the truth. She could afford to be airy.

He crossed his arms. "Yet, you're here."

"I crawled through a window and escaped."

"And you wandered down Orchard Street? By yourself?" His pursed lips said he found her tale outlandish.

"I met a young man named Ira. He helped me get to safety." She strongly suspected mentioning Legs would do more harm than good.

"Ira's last name?"

"I didn't ask."

"Coffee." Annie pushed into the office and offered a steaming cup to Parker. Then she put a fresh mug on Freddie's desk and dropped two pills into the palm of her hand.

"Thank you, Annie." Freddie waited until she left, swallowed the pills, and then said, "While I was in the warehouse, I heard a woman, who I assume was Roxie Smith, talking about her boss. Also a woman."

"Did you see the woman?" asked Detective Sullivan.

"I did not."

"Then how do you know another woman wasn't talking about Roxie Smith?"

Freddie sat back in her chair. "I didn't think of that."

Detective Sullivan gave the impression of a blundering rhinoceros, but there was a good brain inside that enormous melon.

"What did this mystery woman say?" asked Parker.

"She threatened the man who abducted me."

"Why?" asked Parker.

"Because I escaped." With her pointer finger, she pushed the letter across her desk. "Also, this arrived this morning."

The detective picked it up. "What is this?"

"A list of my closest friends and where they live."

His brow furrowed. "You think it's a threat?"

"I know it is." She took a bracing sip of coffee. "You realize what this means?" When he didn't reply immediately, she provided the answer. "Brandt Abrams is innocent."

Detective Sullivan tilted his head as if she'd presented him with a puzzle. "I wouldn't say that."

"Brandt didn't knife or shoot his friends. And if the boss is a woman, he's not the one who hired someone to kill them."

Parker laced his long fingers together. "How do you know Abrams?"

"We met the night Ewan Duncan was killed." The absolute truth. Well, part of it.

"And Ephram Loeb?"

"What about him?"

"Did you know him as well?"

"We'd met."

"Your friend, Tallulah, was with him the night he died."

"Yes."

"Were you?"

"Yes."

"What did you see?"

"Nothing. I was at the table, not the dance floor." She shifted her focus to Detective Sullivan. "Will you release Brandt?"

Detective Sullivan and Parker exchanged a telling look.

"You're very invested in the fate of a man you barely know," Parker observed.

She kept her expression neutral. "He's innocent. Wouldn't you go to bat for a man you knew to be wrongly accused?"

"Of course." Parker stretched his legs. "But I wouldn't lie for him."

"Lie?" She hadn't told the whole truth, but she hadn't told a single lie.

"Lying to the police is never a good idea, Miss Archer." Parker studied her expression. "If you were abducted—"

"*If?*" Outrage made her voice shrill, and she winced. Her fingers found the knot on her head. "I suppose I gave myself this goose egg?"

"You expect us to believe"—Parker waved his hand at her—"that you, dressed as you were last night, walked unscathed from the Lower East Side to wherever you managed to find a taxi?"

"I explained that. Ira helped me."

"A boy whose last name you didn't bother to learn? He didn't ask for a reward? He just helped you out of the goodness in his heart?"

"Not exactly."

Parker smirked.

There was no avoiding telling more of the story. "Legs dealt with Ira."

"Legs Doyle?" The temperature in her office dropped twenty degrees. Parker could rent himself out to hostesses with that trick.

"Yes," she admitted.

"Why would Legs Doyle deal with Ira?" He spoke slowly, enunciating each word.

"Legs and I are acquaintances. He owes me a favor, and he saw Bumpy kidnap me."

"Bumpy?"

"The kidnapper."

"How did Doyle come to owe you a favor?" Parker demanded.

"That's not relevant."

"I think it is."

She could tell him. But if he won this little skirmish, he'd roll over her like a Mark V tank. She smiled sweetly. "The last thing I remember seeing were your taillights. Mr. Doyle happened to be passing by, saw what happened to me, and put the word out."

"Happened to be passing by?"

She shrugged.

"The word?"

"A reward for my safe return."

"Which Ira collected."

"He did."

"Why were you abducted, Miss Archer?"

She glanced at the detective. "I've been asking questions."

He tugged at his collar. "You were told to stop."

"Do you do everything you're told, Detective?"

"I'm a man."

"And I'm a woman."

"We noticed." Parker's gaze paused briefly on the tightness of her blouse.

Their casual assumptions—that she couldn't take care of herself, that her looks were more important than her brains or her courage, that she should sit quietly and let men handle the world's problems—had her clenching her hands beneath the cover of her desk.

"Mr. Doyle took you home?" There was a hard edge to Parker's voice.

If he asked Franklin, the doorman who worked evenings, Parker would learn she hadn't returned home last night.

"No."

"You spent the night with a gangster?"

"No." *Yes.* But not the one they were asking about. "He took me to a friend's apartment."

"Her name?"

"Carolyn."

"And then you came to work as if nothing happened?"

"Columns don't write themselves, Agent Van Dyne." She drank the last of her coffee. "One wonders what brings you here."

"As I mentioned last night, Detective Sullivan and I have been sharing information."

"And you just happened to be in his office when Annie called?"

He grinned. "Lucky me."

"Hmph." She made herself look away from Parker's laughing eyes and cocky grin. "Back to Brandt."

"He's a bootlegger, Miss Archer."

"That's not why he was arrested."

"But we can hold him for it."

"Three of his business associates are dead, and Roxie had me kidnapped."

"Your point?"

"He wants the person who murdered his friends caught as badly as you do. He probably wants it more." She rested her elbows on the desk and thought back to the conversation she'd had with Mr. Rothstein as she left his home.

"Thank you for your hospitality."

"You're welcome. I've been thinking. Whoever wants you won't give up."

Not what a girl wanted to hear before her second cup of coffee.

"You need to make yourself a target."

She'd stared at him. Gaped, really.

"Go out. We'll watch. When Roxie, or whoever she works for, makes her move, we'll be there."

"I'm bait?"

He'd grinned. *"Like a worm on a hook."*

She hadn't loved the idea, but she couldn't think of another. She looked at the men taking up all the space in her office. "If

Brandt and I were to go out for dinner, dancing, what have you, we might draw out the killer."

"Absolutely not," the detective barked.

Parker leaned back in his chair and crossed his arms. "You'd do that?"

"It's no hardship to have dinner with Brandt." She relished his answering scowl.

As long as you know men are like children, you know everything. That Coco Chanel was a wise woman.

"It's too dangerous," the detective insisted.

"Apparently, walking from the curb to my building is dangerous. This needs to end."

"Where would you go?" asked Parker.

"A rooftop garden for dinner."

"And then?"

"Club Napoleon." If she was going to bring trouble to a club, better one she didn't particularly like.

"Fine," said Parker.

"Wait a minute," said the detective. "We can't put a civilian in danger."

"I'm already in danger."

Parker nodded. "She has a point."

"I won't be safe until you catch whoever is behind this."

Detective Sullivan gave a reluctant nod.

"Wonderful. We have a plan. Now, if you gentlemen will excuse me, I have calls to make and a column to finish." She offered them her brightest smile. "Have Brandt pick me up at eight."

CHAPTER 25

THE PHONE RANG AT precisely eight, and Freddie snatched the receiver from its cradle. "Hello." She sounded breathless. Nervous.

"Miss Archer, there's a Mr. Abrams here to see you."

"Thank you, Franklin." She lowered her voice an octave. "Please send him up."

Freddie opened the door to her apartment in anticipation of Brandt's arrival. Given all that was at stake—Brandt's freedom, their lives—she could almost pretend fear (and not the man) made her heart beat like a kettle drum.

The elevator doors opened, and Brandt stepped into the hallway. Their eyes met. And magic shimmered in the air. Bright as an unbroken promise. Alluring as a first kiss.

He held out a ridiculously large bouquet. "These are for you."

Freddie's smile was so big it hurt her cheeks. "They're beautiful. Thank you. Come in."

He followed her into the kitchen and crossed his arms over his chest as she took a vase from the cabinet. "You got me out of jail."

She'd assumed he wouldn't mind taking risks to catch his friends' killer. But she hadn't asked. And tonight was an enormous risk. "You're not mad?"

"Why would I be mad?"

She searched his face for signs of temper. "Because we're bait."

"That." Now his expression darkened. "I wish I could go alone. That you'd stay safely at home."

Her shoulders tightened.

"But that's not you. You're not the sort of woman who sits on the sidelines. I admire that."

She turned away from him, sure that her eyes would reveal too much, and filled the vase with water. "Thank you."

"For what?"

"For saying that." Her whole life, people had told her how to act. *Sit with your ankles crossed, Freddie. Laugh politely at young men's jokes, Freddie. Refuse young men's advances, Freddie.*

And when she did as she liked, she was found wanting. No one, especially not her family, admired her departure from the path that they'd plotted for her. No one saw her.

Not until Brandt.

She put his flowers in the vase. "I worried about you."

"I've been through much worse than a night in jail." Brandt leaned against the counter. "It looks like rain."

"Maybe a storm will break the heat." The weather? Why were they discussing the weather when there were other more important things to say?

"Rain will make rooftop dining problematic. I reserved us a table at Club Napoleon."

"The chef does an excellent Chateaubriand." Now food? Why couldn't she just spit out what she was thinking? Even if she couldn't bring herself to discuss her mixed-up feelings, she should tell him about being abducted and all that had happened since.

"Does he?"

"And Harry, the bartender, makes the best champagne cocktail in the city."

"I've never had one."

"You drink scotch."

"Exactly. What's in it? Besides champagne."

"Harry saturates a lump of sugar with bitters, adds an ice cube, and fills the glass with champagne. Then he adds a squeeze of lemon and stirs. He garnishes with a twist." She'd seen him mix the drink a thousand times.

"Perhaps you and Harry will convert me." Brandt glanced at his wrist. "Our reservations are for eight thirty."

"Then we should go. I'll grab my bag." She'd planned her ensemble around the petit point handbag with the jade clasp. She made to move past him, but he stopped her with a touch.

"You look gorgeous tonight."

She didn't. She wasn't beautiful like Tallulah. Or glamorous like Louise Brooks. She smoothed her dress over her hips. "This old thing?"

"Not the dress. You." His hands closed around her bare shoulders. "The dress is fine. You are stunning."

"Thank you." Her voice came out husky. "The same to you." Brandt, in a tuxedo, was handsome enough to make her rethink the whole "bait" plan. They could stay home. Disappear into her bedroom and not come out until September.

"We should go," he said.

"We should."

Neither moved.

Outside, a clap of thunder warned of the coming downpour.

"You made reservations."

"I did."

They didn't move.

"We're the bait. There are people counting on us." She'd spent half her afternoon discussing every possible scenario with Parker Van Dyne, and the other half discussing the same thing with Legs.

Brandt grimaced. "You're right."

They didn't move.

Lightning forked past the window, and Freddie jumped, breaking the spell that held them in place. "There are umbrellas in the brass stand by the front door. I'll just grab a rain cape." She freed herself and walked toward the door.

"Freddie."

She glanced over her shoulder. "What?"

"There's nothing I'd rather do than stay in tonight."

"Likewise." She forced her feet forward.

"Promise me something?"

She lifted a brow.

"Be careful tonight."

She tossed her hair. "Likewise."

He frowned. "I mean it."

"I do, too." They held magic in their hands. The kind of enchantment that made sleep unnecessary, put a song on her lips, and turned her somewhat cynical smile dreamy. She didn't want to lose him.

"We'll both be careful."

"Fine." She didn't believe he'd be careful. She'd seen him run toward danger. But he probably didn't believe her either.

Minutes later, Franklin hailed them a taxi.

They held hands on the way to 56th Street, but they didn't speak. Instead, Freddie watched the raindrops dance on the taxi's windows. If things went poorly tonight, this could be her last ever ride in a cab.

Brandt squeezed her fingers as if he sensed the dark turn of her thoughts.

All too soon, they arrived, and the doorman welcomed her. "Good evening, Miss Archer. It's a pleasure to have you with us again."

"Thank you, Pete."

They swept inside, where Freddie took off her cape and Brandt handed it and the umbrella to a coat-check girl. Then they climbed the stairs to the second floor, and the maître d' led them to a table in the dining room.

"So nice to see you, Miss Archer."

"Nice to see you, too, Hamilton."

When he left, Brandt cocked a brow. "Come here often?"

"Not anymore."

"I sense a story."

"A dull one. Not a single original line. When Nick and I broke up, I got our literary friends, the Dizzy Club, and Jack and Charlie's. Nick got our theater friends, Sardi's, and this place."

"So why are we here? You chose Club Napoleon."

If Roxie or Bumpy started shooting at her and if she didn't die, she might not be welcome anymore. "I don't want to be banned from a place I frequent."

"What about Harry's champagne cocktails?"

Freddie released a wistful sigh. "I'll miss them."

A waiter appeared at their table. "Good evening, Miss Archer."

"Good evening, Jimmy."

"Champagne cocktail?" he asked.

"Two," Brandt replied.

"Right away, sir."

Brandt sat back and surveyed the dining room. His gaze rested on two young men pushing an upright piano from table to table.

"They sing naughty songs," Freddie told him.

"How naughty?"

"Naughty enough to make Tallulah blush. And I didn't think that was possible."

Jimmy served their drinks, and Brandt lifted his glass. "To you."

"To us."

"I'll drink to that." He tasted his drink. "It's good. Better than good."

Freddie took a sip. "Now, we wait."

While they waited for the killer, they dined on poulet en cocotte served with glazed carrots and a green salad dressed with vinaigrette.

"It's a shame," said Brandt.

"What is?"

"That we'll soon be banned. The food here is excellent."

"Freddie!" The voice was too loud. Too brash. Too arrogant. "What are you doing here?"

She tightened her grip on her fork.

"Let me guess." Brandt frowned at someone over her shoulder. "Nick?"

"Exactly." She'd have said more, but Nick parked himself beside their table. He brought with him the scent of cigarettes and scotch. Per usual, he was impeccably dressed, but something about him seemed off. Too much scotch so early in the evening? She wrinkled her nose.

Nick scowled. A deep scowl. One he usually reserved for actors who muffed their lines on opening night. "Who's this?"

"Nick, this is Brandt Abrams. Brandt, meet Nick Peters."

The two men eyed each other, and Freddie forced herself to put down her fork.

"Be careful with this one," said Nick. "She'll tear your heart out."

Brandt's eyes widened. "I'll take my chances."

Nick shrugged. "Your funeral."

She would not pick up the fork and stab his leg. She would not. "Nick, be a dear and go away."

"You shouldn't be here. We had a deal."

More of an unspoken agreement. "Which should have kept you away from the Lardners' party."

He opened his mouth as if he wanted to argue, but snapped it shut when he realized he didn't have a leg to stand on.

"I wanted one of Harry's champagne cocktails." Not that she needed to justify her presence.

"And you brought him? Why not Tallulah or Dotty?"

Stabbing him in the leg with her fork became more appealing with every word he said. "You don't get the right to—"

"You left my ring on the bedside table." That was his wounded pride talking. He'd replaced her too quickly for his affections to have been genuine.

"Let's not do this, Nick." *Not now. Not ever.*

"Why, Freddie?"

The pain she saw in his eyes made her answer. "You didn't want me. Not as I am. You wanted a woman who'd sit in Connecticut and wait up for you. There are hundreds—thousands—of girls who'd settle for that."

"Marrying me was settling?"

"If I had to give up everything that mattered to me? Yes."

"Nicky! Your dinner is getting cold."

They all shifted their gazes to a marcelled blonde in a satin gown.

"Off you go, Nicky. Your dinner is waiting."

With a last fearsome scowl, he strode away.

Long seconds passed before Brandt asked, "Do you want to talk about it?"

"I don't. It's over. There's nothing to say."

"Dessert?"

"I couldn't." Nick had stolen her appetite.

"A drink at the bar?"

"Please." Bait. She was bait. Freddie scanned the dining room before she stood. If anyone was watching her (other than Nick, who shot daggers with his eyes), they were incredibly discreet.

They crossed the upstairs hallway to the bar, which was somehow both brighter and darker than the dining room. The tables were mostly full, and the bar was just shy of crowded. A trio played jazz in the corner.

"Champagne cocktail?" asked Brandt.

"Please." The spot between her shoulder blades tingled, and Freddie glanced back to the entrance.

No one was there.

"Shall I see about a table?"

"Let's stand at the bar." She tightened her hold on her evening bag and let him escort her to Harry's domain.

The bartender possessed an impressive nose, a diminutive chin, and the unfortunate habit of dousing his dark hair in excessive pomade. He eyed her. "The usual?"

"Two," said Brandt.

"I converted you?"

"They're excellent."

Behind the bar, Harry grunted.

High-pitched laughter drew their attention. Three girls, each with a dress more scandalous than the barely there satin number Nick's date wore, posed at the entrance to the bar. Eloise Silver stood with them. She said something, and the three girls separated. Each one moving through the room, pausing to chat with men who were without female companions.

"Business must be slow," said Brandt.

"You know Eloise?"

"We've met." His voice was flat.

"Not a fan?"

"No." Brandt grimaced. "If she comes over, try that 'Be a dear, and go away' line."

"I save that one for Nick."

"The man's a fool." Brandt grinned. "Lucky for me."

"Freddie." Eloise's hand closed around Freddie's wrist. "What a lovely surprise." Eloise wore a gown the same shade of lavender as the scarf Freddie had lost in Bumpy's truck.

"What a stunning dress." And not in a good way.

"What are you drinking? Champagne cocktails? Let me buy you a round."

"That's not necessary," said Brandt.

For a half-second, Eloise looked as if she'd smelled something rotten. Then she smiled. "Mr. Abrams, I heard you were in jail."

"You were misinformed."

"Was I? Freddie, dear, didn't I just see Nick Peters? Such a charming man."

Freddie knew the dig was meant for Brandt, but she still felt its sting. "I believe he's dining with an actress."

"Men can be such children. But you could get him back. Easily."

"I don't want him back."

Eloise shrugged. "You're sure I can't buy you a drink?"

"No, thank you."

"Harry." Eloise rapped the bar with her knuckles. "Champagne cocktails for me and my girls."

Harry, who was busy pouring a Glenromach for a banker type, pretended not to hear her.

"That man." She pursed her lips. "My money is just as green as an actress's or a producer's. I'm not la-di-da enough for him."

More likely, Harry didn't appreciate Eloise bringing her girls into his bar. Freddie kept that thought to herself. "You must tell me, where did you find your dress?"

"Altman's. I bought it the day we had tea. Do you remember?"

"Of course. That's the day..." A memory floated to the surface of her mind, and her breath caught.

"Is something wrong?" Eloise frowned at her.

The day she'd bought the scarf, Eloise had been there. With shaking fingers, Freddie reached for her handbag on the bar and asked, "Why?"

Eloise tilted her overly powdered chin. "What do you mean, dear?"

"You might not have pulled the trigger, but you're responsible. Why kill all those people?"

Eloise's eyes narrowed.

Brandt's jaw dropped.

And Freddie felt something cold and hard through the fabric of her dress.

Eloise had a gun. And she'd pressed its muzzle against Freddie's ribs.

"Why?" Freddie repeated. She needed an answer. "So much pain. And death. For what?"

"You should understand. If a woman wants to be anything but a doormat, she needs power."

Freddie wasn't buying it. "Power? Or money?"

Eloise shrugged. "Can't it be both?"

Where were Parker's people? Where were Mr. Rothstein's people? Didn't they notice the gun jabbed into her side?

Probably not. The pistol was tiny. But even a tiny gun could kill her.

Her heart hammered against her chest. "You won't shoot me. There are a hundred witnesses." If only she felt as confident as she sounded.

"Not a single person in this bar is paying attention to us." Eloise was right. The patrons were all transfixed by an impromptu floor show. One of Eloise's girls stood on a chair and played with the thin straps that kept her dress from pooling at her ankles. The girl held everyone rapt. "Abrams, your gun. Take it out and put it on the floor."

Brandt had a gun?

"Now. Or I shoot her." Eloise's voice was as cold as the gun's muzzle.

Brandt reached behind his back and then slowly crouched to put a large revolver on the floor. The black-handled gun was nearly invisible against the dark floor.

"Good. Now you two are coming with me."

Where were the men who were supposed to be ensuring her safety? She'd agreed to be bait because she had assumed someone would be there to catch the fish.

The girl on the table dropped a strap, and every eye in the room was on her bared chest.

"We're leaving."

Freddie didn't move, and Eloise poked her hard enough to leave a bruise.

"Move!"

Freddie looked at Brandt.

Brandt looked at Eloise's gun.

And Eloise looked at the door.

"You can't think Mr. Rothstein will let you take over," said Brandt.

"Because I'm a woman?"

"Because you're trying to cut him out," he replied.

"Dutch will take care of me."

"You trust Dutch Schultz?" Brandt shook his head at her foolishness. "Dutch will kill you soon as look at you."

"Never."

"He's not your only problem. I work with Arnold and Lucky. I import. They take their cut. You think they'll let Dutch Schultz and a cheap madam reach into their pockets? If Dutch doesn't knock you off, they will."

"Cheap?" Eloise poked Freddie a second time. Harder.

If she lived through the night, there would be an ugly bruise.

"Move." Eloise shoved Freddie toward the door.

Clutching her handbag as if her life depended on it, Freddie took a single step. "What about Roxie?"

"What about her? She works for me. A pretty woman with a talent for murder."

"She killed Jake and Ewan and Ephram?"

"Yes."

"On your orders?"

"Yes."

"Where is she?"

"Waiting outside. She can't wait to make your acquaintance."

Where was Parker? Where was Legs?

"Move."

Freddie and Brandt exchanged a loaded glance. Then she said, "No."

Eloise scowled. "I will shoot you."

"And if I go outside, Roxie will shoot me. I prefer my chances here. Also, if you think Harry hasn't noticed you, you're crazy. There are witnesses."

Eloise glanced at the bartender.

Freddie gathered her courage. "You know my father. Do you really think you'll get away with killing me?"

For the first time, Eloise's confidence seemed to wane. She bit her lower lip, and the pressure against Freddie's ribs eased a bit.

"You!" Nick's date had snuck up on them. Now she stood inches away. She jabbed Freddie with the tip of a varnished nail. "You think you're so special."

Freddie gaped at the woman.

Eloise and Brandt did, too.

"Nick doesn't care about you. He never did." The woman exhaled, and Freddie nearly passed out from the gin fumes. She smelled liked she'd used Seagram's as perfume. "He needs a woman who understands him. Supports him. Someone like me." Nick's date, who was decidedly lit, jabbed again, before tripping over her own feet. She fell into Freddie, and the feel of Eloise's gun disappeared.

Using the distraction, Freddie slipped her fingers into her handbag. They closed around the pearl-handled revolver Legs had given her. The gun was almost pretty, but Legs assured her it was deadly at close range. She pointed it at Eloise.

"Oh my God! She's going to shoot me!" Nick's date managed to distract half the room from the slow striptease on the table.

Freddie had the childish urge to roll her eyes. What a Dumb Dora. "Where did Nick find you?"

"I starred in *Bachelor Brides.*"

"I saw that play. A farce with a short run. You were not the star."

"What do you know?" The woman batted her eyes at Brandt as if she expected to win his affections. Then she pressed the back of her hand to her forehead and swooned.

He let her crash to the floor.

"You saw her," the woman screeched. "She pushed me."

"I did no such thing," Freddie snapped, suddenly aware that half the bar was gaping at her and not the girl on the table.

Eloise opened her mouth, but no words came out. Her kidnapping had been hijacked.

Dumb Dora, who still sat in an undignified heap on the floor, reached for Brandt's gun.

"Don't touch that," Freddie warned. Too late.

The sound of the gun firing echoed through the room. Someone shrieked like there was no tomorrow, and there was a mass stampede for the door.

Brandt crouched and gently took the gun from Dumb Dora's shaking hands as he looked up at Freddie. "You're okay?"

"Fine." Fine if one didn't count a galloping heart and the nearly uncontrollable urge to sob. "You?"

"Not a scratch."

"Are you hurt?" she asked Dora.

The woman grinned. And winked. "Mr. Rothstein sends his regards."

Freddie gaped at her as men with badges poured into the room.

Parker and Detective Sullivan rushed into the bar, spotted her (with nary a bullet hole), and slowed their steps.

Freddie searched the emptying room and spotted Legs at a table in a shadowy corner. At least one man who'd promised to watch over her had kept his word.

Legs gave her a nod and then sauntered out.

It was Parker who took the gun from Eloise's hands.

It was Detective Sullivan who helped Not-So-Dumb Dora off the floor.

And it was Brandt who took Freddie home.

CHAPTER 26

PARKER VAN DYNE AND Detective Sullivan sat side by side on the couch in Freddie's living room, and neither of them looked happy.

The situation called for happiness. The murders were solved. Eloise had been arrested. Brandt was free. Freddie was alive and well.

But the agent and the detective were focused on the trivial.

"Where did you get the gun, Freddie?" Parker had already asked her that. Twice.

Did he expect her to change her answer? "A friend lent it to me."

"What friend?"

"I don't think that matters. I didn't shoot the gun. I didn't use the gun to commit a crime. I didn't even complain when the police confiscated the gun."

Parker raked his fingers through his hair. "It matters because you could have been hurt."

"Isn't that the nature of bait?"

He growled.

"You caught Eloise. You caught Roxie. You even caught Bumpy." According to Detective Sullivan, the police had arrested Roxie and Bumpy on the sidewalk outside Club Napoleon prior to the gunshot that brought them running.

"If you'd come outside as we discussed, we could have avoided that circus in the bar." Poor Parker. The bags under his eyes were enormous.

"Did you sleep?" she asked. "You look tired."

That earned her a second growl.

Freddie took a sip of her coffee and stared out the window at the bright, shiny, blessedly cool morning. The rain had washed away weeks' worth of grime. The weather was cool. New York was at its best.

"How did things go so wrong?"

"You'd know that if you were watching like you promised."

"We were arresting Roxie and the driver."

"How was I supposed to know that? To me, it looked as if you weren't there."

"You arrived early, and you didn't go to the rooftop as we discussed."

"It was raining. Who eats on a rooftop in the rain?"

"You didn't notify us of the change in plans."

"Because I assumed you'd have people in place at Club Napoleon. Also, I thought an agent of the Bureau of Investigation would realize alfresco dining during a thunderstorm was problematic."

"Fine. You dined at Club Napoleon."

"The chicken was excellent."

Parker pressed his fingers against his temples.

Freddie suppressed a smile.

"And then?"

"Nick's tomato accosted me." She skipped over the woman's relationship with Mr. Rothstein. He meant what happened with Eloise, but playing dumb was fun. Especially when it put a thunderous expression on Parker's face.

He scowled at the papers in front of him. "Doris Bond."

"Is that her name? I should file charges." In truth, Doris deserved a generous reward.

"Arguably, she saved your life."

She pretended to consider his point. "Fine. I won't file."

"What happened?"

Freddie swirled the coffee in her mug. "I realized Eloise was behind the murders."

"How?"

"I lost my scarf in Bumpy's truck."

Both men stared at her.

"It was after I lost the scarf that I was kidnapped." She spoke slowly. Perhaps they were so tired they couldn't understand.

They still stared.

"How did Roxie know it was mine? I'd never worn it before. But Eloise? She was with me when I bought it."

"And you realized this last night?" asked Parker.

"Exactly. It was Eloise's dress that reminded me. The same shade of lavender as my scarf."

Detective Sullivan rubbed a hand across his eyes.

Parker growled. That was three times now. "And you thought confronting her was a good idea?"

"I didn't plan that. It just happened."

"She could have killed you."

"But she didn't. And you arrested her. And Roxie. And Bumpy."

The morning called for champagne. But she could wait for bubbles until she met Brandt for lunch.

She smiled at the men across from her. "All's well that ends well. More coffee?"

Parker waved off her generous offer and said, "You were in danger."

And it had been thrilling.

"I'm not the sort of woman who sits idly by."

"I realize that."

"I made a difference. You caught a killer because of me."

"True. But—"

"But nothing. You wouldn't carry on like a spinster aunt if I were a man."

"A spinster aunt?" Parker looked to be grinding his teeth.

Detective Sullivan covered his mouth with his catcher's mitt of a hand.

"A nervous one at that."

"You're not a man."

"But being a woman doesn't make me less capable."

"But it does make you more important."

She stared at him.

He stirred in his seat.

Detective Sullivan tugged at his collar.

"What's that supposed to mean?"

He flashed his arrogant smile and stood. "You figure it out. I'll see you Saturday night."

He walked out her front door before Freddie could tell him what she thought of his high-handed pronouncement. Before she could tell him that pigs would fly before she went out with him.

Detective Sullivan also stood. "We wouldn't have caught her without you."

"Glad I could be of assistance."

"Abrams, he's a dangerous man."

"I suspect Agent Van Dyne is as well."

Detective Sullivan grunted. "I was right about you. You notice things."

"If you ever need my help again, just ask."

He stared at her for long seconds and then nodded. "I will, Miss Archer. I will."

AUTHOR'S NOTE

I don't remember how I discovered Lois Long, the columnist who wrote as Lipstick for *The New Yorker* in the 1920s. What I do remember is falling in love with her writing. She was funny and arch and utterly entertaining.

I wanted to travel back in time and join her for a gin rickey at one of the speakeasies she frequented. I wanted to stroll Fifth Avenue with her as she gave her opinions on the latest fashions in the windows. I wanted to join her table at the Cotton Club as she listened to her favorite musician, Duke Ellington.

Time machines being sparse, the only way I could hang out with Lois was to base a character on her. She is the inspiration for Freddie.

I like to think that Lois, who was always up for fresh fun, would approve.

ABOUT THE AUTHOR

USA Today bestselling author **Julie Mulhern** is a Kansas City native who grew up on a steady diet of Agatha Christie. She spends her spare time whipping up gourmet meals for her family, working out at the gym, and finding new ways to keep her house spotlessly clean. Truth is, she's an expert at calling for takeout, she grumbles about walking the dog, and the dust bunnies under the bed have grown into dust lions. Action, adventure, mystery, and humor are the things Julie loves when she's reading. She loves them even more when she's writing!

Sign up for Julie's newsletter at juliemulhernauthor.com.

RAISING READERS
Books Build Bright Futures

Thank you for reading this book and for being a reader of books in general. We are so grateful to share being part of a community of readers with you, and we hope you will join us in passing our love of books on to the next generation of readers.

Did you know that reading for enjoyment is the single biggest predictor of a child's future happiness and success?

More than family circumstances, parents' educational background, or income, reading impacts a child's future academic performance, emotional well-being, communication skills, economic security, ambition, and happiness.

Studies show that kids reading for enjoyment in the US is in rapid decline:

- In 2012, 53% of 9-year-olds read almost every day. Just 10 years later, in 2022, the number had fallen to 39%.
- In 2012, 27% of 13-year-olds read for fun daily. By 2023, that number was just 14%.

Together, we can commit to **Raising Readers** and change this trend. How?

- Read to children in your life daily.
- Model reading as a fun activity.
- Reduce screen time.
- Start a family, school, or community book club.
- Visit bookstores and libraries regularly.
- Listen to audiobooks.
- Read the book before you see the movie.
- Encourage your child to read aloud to a pet or stuffed animal.
- Give books as gifts.
- Donate books to families and communities in need.

BOB1217

Books build bright futures, and **Raising Readers** is our shared responsibility.

For more information, visit **JoinRaisingReaders.com**

Sources: National Endowment for the Arts, National Assessment of Educational Progress, WorldBookDay.com, Nielsen BookData's 2023 "Understanding the Children's Book Consumer"